The
Studio
Murder
Mystery

The Studio Murder Mystery

By

A. C. and Carmen Edington

COACHWHIP PUBLICATIONS

GREENVILLE, OHIO

AUTHOR'S NOTE

The characters in this book are fictitious. All data, however, having to do with the making of Motion Pictures may be considered authentic.

The Studio Murder Mystery, by A. C. and Carmen Edington
© 2025 Coachwhip Publications edition
Cover image: © paseven

First published 1929
Arlo Edington (1890-1953)
Carmen Ballen Edington (1894-1972)
CoachwhipBooks.com

ISBN 1-61646-598-0
ISBN-13 978-1-61646-598-8

1

Sibilant whisperings around the sides of the great stages! The slithering splash of drainage from the roofs! Strange, weird shapes, forming themselves out of the billows of dripping fog, huddling in Behemothan groups in corners of the studio lot.

The skeletons of "dead" sets clothed in flowing veils of grey; dim hulks holding mystery, changing form with the ever-eddying mists enveloping them.

Dank expectancy in the night of deeds too dark for day-light doing! Cold, wet fingers of mist, creeping down the spine . . .

Lannigan, night watchman of Superior Films, clumped suddenly out of the void and shivered in his great coat as he pulled off his hat to slap away the moisture accumulated there.

"Sure, 'tis a foine night for a murther! Ye can't see thru' it no more than the divil's heart, Mac!"

"There's certain to be many a man killed to-night, that's a fact, Lannigan!" agreed the gateman. "Take a look out there! Wet . . . slippery as a greased slide, but they keep on breaking the limit as they always do around midnight!"

The two men gazed somberly out upon the boulevard. The street light across from the studio entrance made but a sullen and short illumination. Below it gleamed the black wetness of the road, and upon the road was the constant singing hum of wet tires. Cars, filled with midnight rois-terers from the beach clubs, speeded by.

"Domn fools!" said the Irishman.

"Aye!" agreed MacDougal quietly. Then, "Seibert's working late to-night," he added.

"Yep. Cursing and bellowing to beat the Dutch, same as usual, at that heavy of his, whin I come by just now. I tell ye Mac, if I was that young Hardell—rotten as he is, the dirty bum—I'd see Seibert in Hell before I'd take his dirty talk!"

The Scotchman shrugged indifferently. What he thought about motion picture directors and their actors, he did not express.

A car slipped up with its nose almost against the iron gates. A girl, startlingly fresh and lovely, leaned out.

"Oh, Meestair Mac! Eef you please!" she called.

"Right, Miss," and the gateman stepped quickly to his duty.

"I would like so much to drive into the lot, tonight, Meestair Mac. Me, I am the fraid to go out alone to the car, so late."

"Certainly, Miss Beaumont. You'll find lots of park-ing room. There's no one but Seibert working to-night," smiled the gateman, but underneath his courteous answer was a questioning tone that brought a quick explanation.

"You wondair why Yvonne comes so late, eh?" She laughed up into his eyes, forcing the man to meet her careless mood. "Well, I will tell you a secret. I am veree naughty! I say I will have that new script for that next picture I make, all read by to-morrow for Meestair Rosey! What you think I do? I go home and go to bed, and go straight to sleep . . . like this . . ." She squeezed her eye-lids tightly together so that their heavily mascaraed lashes pricked into the soft skin of her cheek. Opening her eyes swiftly, in mock dismay, she continued:

"I wake up! I remember! Quick I jump into the car, and come out here. I know the nice beeg Meestair Mac is here, and I am not afraid! Now I go up to my dressing room and get that picture script. . . ."

"Just a minute Miss Beaumont. I will turn on the corridor lights."

"Non! The gate you must watch. Anyway, me, I have the cat's eyes in the dark."

She waved her hand to him as she ran lightly up the stairs of the nearby building which housed the dressing rooms—the men's on the first floor, the women's above. The gateman looked after her a moment, his brow thoughtful. Then he went into his little office beside the gate and bent over his time sheet.

Yvonne Beaumont. In at 11:23 p.m., he wrote there. When he looked again in the direction of the dressing rooms, a light had been put on in the room he knew to be the pretty little French leading woman's. He liked the cheery friendliness of her chatter, but just now he wondered if it was absolutely truthful. He knew that motion picture folk have queer ways; that night and day are the same to them; that impulses are usually obeyed, no matter what conventions they seem to break. And yet—

"Hey, Mac! Open up!"

The gateman recognized the voice of Billy West, Seibert's assistant director, and he hastened to the gate.

The young man he let in slipped into the gateman's office and immediately set about lighting a cigarette.

"Beastly fog, Mac. Didn't dare take a hand off the wheel to light up, and couldn't have got a smoke going anyway with all the wet blowing in the window." He began puffing vigorously. "Seibert still working?" he asked. It was significant of the director of whom he spoke, that his assistant did not give him the familiar "chief", in referring to him. People did not drop into these little comradely ways with Franz Seibert.

"I expect so. I haven't marked him out yet," the gateman answered.

"Damn!" said the young man heartily. "I left my script book on the set, and I've got to have it tonight. We're finishing to-morrow, and that means the devil to pay, and sixteen new props and ideas he'll get at the eleventh hour! I've got to out-figure that bozo some way, and I sure need that book!"

"Tough luck," sympathized the gateman dryly. It was a well-known fact that there were times when the famous director preferred to work alone, and at such times no member of his crew, even his assistant, dared venture on his set. This was one of these times, for West had not been called by Seibert that night.

"Well, I'll hang around until he gets through," said West, and turning up his coat collar, went out of the little office and disappeared in the fog.

MacDougal's keen eyes had not missed West's seemingly idle glance at the time sheet, nor had his intelligence accepted the cigarette story. Yet, in a way, the arrival of the young assistant director eased his mind. West was known to be head-over-heels in love with Yvonne Beaumont.

"Some silly love business, despite all the talk about scripts, and he's followed her out here," MacDougal told himself, and marked Billy West in at 11:40 p.m.

Twenty-five minutes later Lannigan appeared again out of the mist.

"Sure, Mac, this do be the divil's own night, and no mistake! I could swear by the Holy Saints that there be spooks about! I saw one the now, skittherin' across the lawn—"

"Nonsense, man!" exclaimed MacDougal impatiently, adding, "You've sharp eyes to see anything on a night like this, Lannigan!"

The little Irishman did not like his tone, and he showed immediate resentment.

"And if it wasn't a night like this, Scot MacDougal," he said significantly, pushing his face up close to the other and peering sharply at him, "I'd swear by the Holy Saints 'twas a woman's figger I seen just now! A leetle lady, she was, and runnin' in the direction of Hardell's dressing room! Now phwat d'ye think of that, Scot MacDougal?"

There was a double meaning in the words, calculated to come close to the heart of the gateman. Yet, peer sharply as he might, Lannigan could detect no flicker of uneasiness in the steady gaze of the level eyes above him. After a moment MacDougal slowly removed his pipe, and replied calmly:

"There's no woman come on the lot the night, except Miss Beaumont, who's up in her room reading her new script. Furthermore, there's no other woman on the lot at all, save the nurse in the hospital yonder. And I don't hold with your idea about spooks, Lannigan! The wind and the fog make queer shapes sometimes, and a man's imagination puts life in them. That's all there is to that."

"All right, MacDougal, have it your way. But maybe now you'll be explainin' this to me. As I was crossin' the lawn to Stage Six, that same where Seibert is workin', the lights wint out! Not only thim on the stage, which same Seibert might have put out himself, but the big arc standin' between the stage and the dressin' rooms, which same has to be shut off in the dynamo room. Simultaneous, out of the bushes in the garden on the west side, come a black figger, and makes a sneak for the side entrance of the stage. I keeps on goin' towards the stage, thinkin' to find out what ails the lights, and meet the intruder likewise, but whin me foot strikes the gravel on the path alongside, that divil of a Seibert hears me and yells out like a roarin' bull fer me not to step foot on the stage! I yells back the same polite way that the lights are out. He howls that he ain't blind, and that he don't need thim anymore, and to let him alone! The domn fool acts like another man was the plague whin he's got his mind on his directin'. So, here am I, waitin' his highness' pleasure to fix thim lights. Also, meanwhilst this black figger I seen is most likely denudin' the stage!"

MacDougal laughed heartily and slapped the little Irishman on the back.

"Ease your mind, Lannigan. That 'black figger' was Billy West, who has been waiting a chance to slip on the set and get his script book, which he forgot and returned for a while ago."

"And a foine director, I call it, that won't let his own assistant near him, so that he has to go snoopin' around like a domn sneak!" said Lannigan, disgustedly. Then he added, triumphantly; "Ye haven't explained the why that arc wint out, simultaneous with the lights on the stage!"

"The lamp probably burned out. They do, you know," said MacDougal dryly, "and it happened that Seibert finished at the same time, and turned off the stage lights. Nothing supernatural in that, man!"

"Just the same, I tell you I feel it in me bones that there's strange happenin's on foot to-night!" Lannigan muttered. "Sure, I've a mind to go on that stage, Seibert or no Seibert!"

"Bide a while, man. You know Seibert."

"Sure, I know him," the night watchman was forced to agree. "Sure, I know the likes o' him," and he spat noisily into the gravel drive. Just then a car loomed silently out of the murk. The gateman jumped to the heavy iron barriers and swung them open.

"Good night, men," said the man at the wheel, and as the car slipped through the entrance, the other occupant of the front seat raised his hand towards his hat in a farewell gesture, and called:

"It's a great life—if you don't weaken! Eh fellows?"

Was there a sinister, chuckling undertone in the voice? There must have been something arresting, for both Lannigan and MacDougal found themselves staring intently after the car, and not answering. Then Lannigan shook himself shiveringly down into his collar.

"Sure, it's surprisin' he'd condescend to speak to the likes of us . . . 'men,'" he remarked sarcastically.

"Who?"

"Who? Who but Seibert himself! Did ye iver know him to bid a man good night afore? But he nivver gets anywheres with that high and mighty air with me. No sirree! I just look meek as Moses, and think murther in me heart! Domn his hide!" And again Lannigan spat.

The gateman stepped into his office and made two entries.

Franz Seibert and Dwight Hardell, out at 12:17 a.m.

Lannigan stuck his head in the door.

"Sure, Mac, 'twad be a hard master who'd deny a mon a cup o' coffee a night like this. Step across wid me now to the lunch room. Ye can eat a bite o' pie, and keep your eye on the gate, aisy!"

"Thought you were going to see to that light?"

"Domn the light. 'Twill keep till me next round."

There were ten of the mammoth white stages that marked Superior Films as one of the outstanding organizations in the picture world. Between these stages, and at other

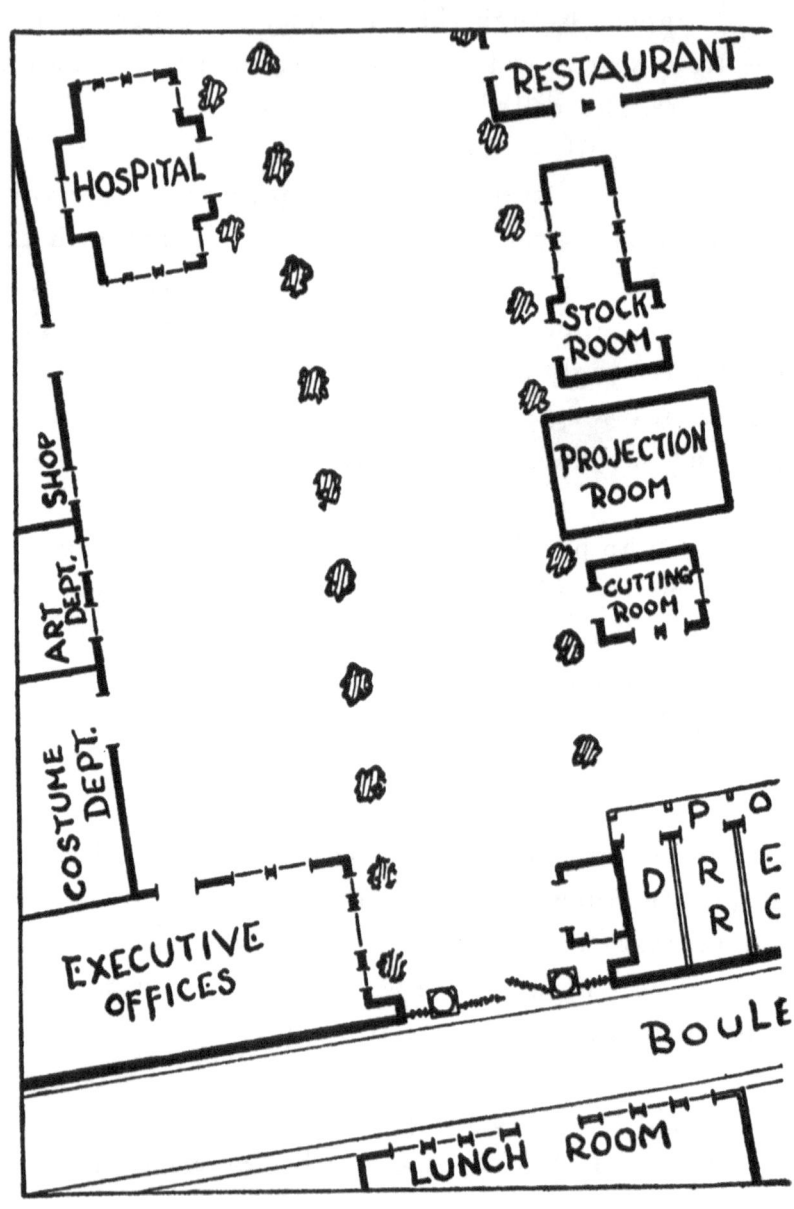

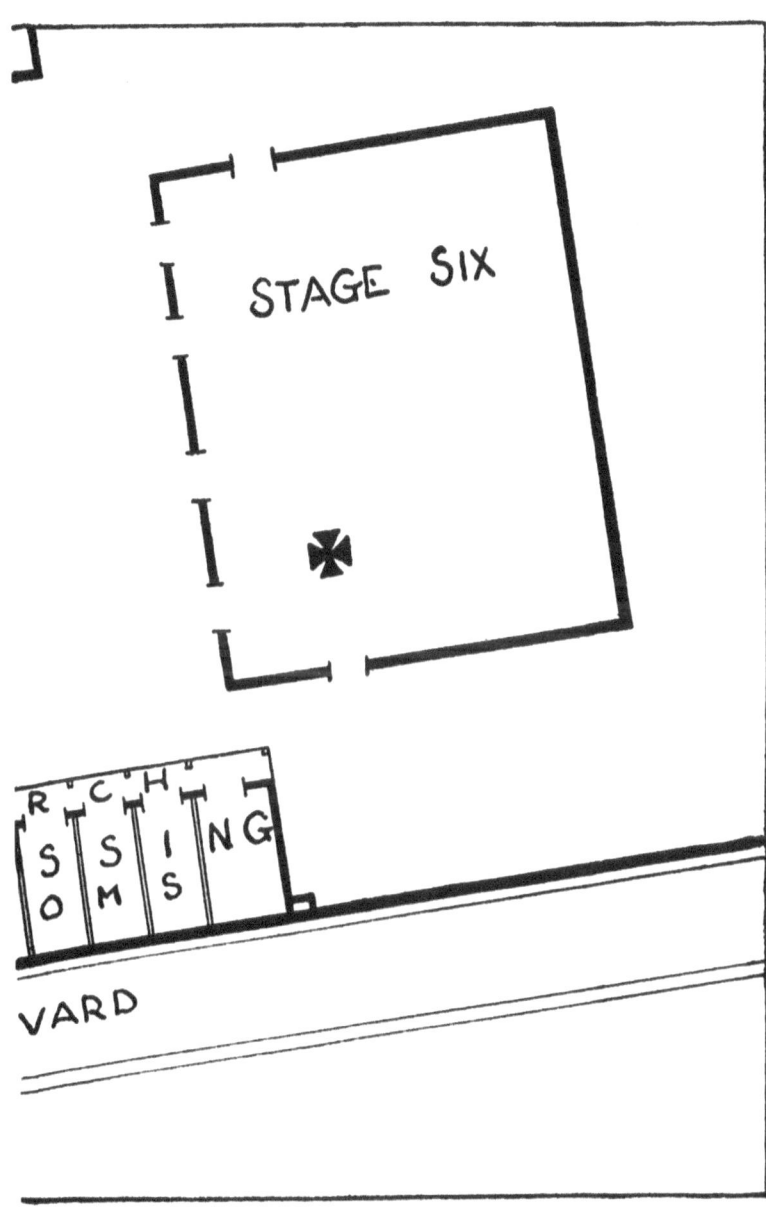

intervals throughout the vast property, powerful lights were kept burning all night, against possible thieves or intruders. Even so, there were spaces where the illumination did not reach and where the decorative shrubbery cast concealing shadows, for Superior Films was also noted for its beautifully landscaped grounds. On nights of the heavy fog that sometimes swept in from the ocean, these areas of shadow were enlarged. On this particular foggy night, Chance and a criminal became co-conspirators. The arc at the East end of Stage Six burned out, and remained out until Lannigan's next round. And thereby hangs this tale.

It was as Lannigan was going towards the storeroom for the new lamp that the superstitious Irish heart of him was made to leap convulsively in his thin chest. A high, thin scream split the air. It might have been a woman's terror-stricken cry. It might have been the miserable moan of a night prowling feline. It might have been, as Lannigan muttered as he crossed himself, "a banshee!" Very likely it might have been a banshee, for banshees are said to wail the passing of the dead!

2

The Southern California sun glowed down warmly upon the grounds of Superior Films. It was refracted brilliantly from the white gleaming sides of the great stages. It made the mist-soaked grass sparkle as with a million emeralds. It took thirstily back to itself the moisture that had drenched all things the night before.

The young lady from Kansas clutched her father's arm in ecstatic anticipation as they waited to see if the letter a friend had given them to one of the executives of the studio would be the magical "Open Sesame!" which would admit them to these exciting and enchanting realms. Finally, in charge of an utterly blase office boy, they went down the long graveled paths skirting the ten big stages.

Never in her wildest dreams had the flapper from Kansas visualized such beauty, for the extravagance of colors and materials used in motion picture sets is not conveyed to the audience from the screen.

She stood with hands clasped and eyes wide and entranced, before the exotic loveliness of a star's bedroom. Gauze curtains, embroidered in crystal and gold, swayed gently under her reverent little hand as she touched them to enter. Gold satin, of an undulant sheen, such as she had not dreamed could be put into human weaving, draped the bed and trailed off its end like a woman's gown, finally coming to rest in a swirled pool of crystal beads, on a floor that was paved with gold and set with jewels.

The beauty-worshipping little soul of her was hushed before the sparkling exquisiteness of the dressing table. Bottles, utterly ravishing bottles, holding precious and intoxicating fragrances. She put out a longing hand to the silver atomizer. Oh, to spray one's throat and hair, and turn one's lovely head to see one's lovely self! She sighed, and remembered that she was only a little girl from Kansas. . . .

"Well come on, Puss. You can't stand staring at these gewgaws all day," said her father.

"That's a very fine set. Everything is real. The perfume in those bottles cost $25.00 an ounce," said the office boy.

"Waste of money! Can't see it on the screen," said the man from Kansas.

"No, but it lends atmosphere. We try to make everything as real as possible. It helps our people get into the spirit of a picture," explained the office boy importantly.

The man from Kansas grunted. Then they both were made to wait while the girl stood spellbound at the sight of two wardrobe women passing by. Lace, rich and heavy, and creamy satin; chiffon underthings, of tints calculated to make the feminine heart swoon with desire; a great string of pearls hanging from one woman's arm, and tucked beside it the stately waving, scintillant feathers of a genuine peacock fan.

The little girl from Kansas clenched her thin hands unseen. Oh, that such things existed! That some women wore them! That she would go back to the beauty-starved days of her normal life, remembering and desiring these things! The woman soul of her was drawn up to a quivering worship of all the exotic beauty about her . . . it cried out, terribly, for possession.

"Come on, Puss. He's going to show us a dummy."

"Oh . . . a dummy," she repeated tonelessly.

"Sure! Looks just like the actor, and they use it in scenes where it's dangerous for the real man to work. I've always wondered about that. Never did take much stock in that 'double' stuff, either. Why, I've seen some things on the screen I just know couldn't be done by any living human." The man from Kansas became enthusiastic. "Why, I told 'em, I said, 'That fellow ain't alive! No sir! That's a fake figure!' I said. I had it all figured out, didn' I, Puss?"

"Yes, Daddy," answered his daughter dutifully. She hoped he was not going to tell the office boy how it was done. It never made any difference to her father, when he was revealing his wisdom, whether or not he was talking to the originator of the idea. It made his daughter very nervous at times. But the office boy knew the type. He quickened his steps, and the man from Kansas was put to it to keep up with him. He stopped talking and kept his breath for walking.

"Now don't yell when you see him. He's supposed to be dead, you know," said the office boy as he parted the black velvet curtains which enveloped the set on Stage Six.

But the visitors instinctively shrank away from the sprawling, stiffened figure on the floor.

"But . . . there's blood all over him! He looks so . . . so . . . queer!" The girl shuddered against her father.

"Catsup. Photographs like blood," explained the office boy laconically.

"Oh! . . ."

Daughter and father remained staring silently.

The figure was truly frightening. Grotesquely twisted in an uncommon death agony, the face a tortured, horror-stricken grimace of . . . what was it? Fear of death? But no, fear of something even more startling than death! A terrible amaze, an unbelieving surprise, was frozen forever in the dead staring eyes and on the set, cold features. This man had undoubtedly come to a monstrous end, if the evidences of the figure could be taken as indicative of facts. A short distance from his prone body lay a dueling rapier, stained with red. In one of the rigid hands, out-flung on the floor, was clutched a second rapier. From the satin-covered heart a small dark stream had welled, and made a narrow river on the floor.

"Can't tell the difference, can you?" asked the office boy with pride.

"Are you sure . . . it's not a real man?" whispered the girl.

"Say, do you think we have dead men lying around on our sets? I'll tell the world we don't! 'Course it's not real! But when we make a fake, we make a good one! If you don't believe me go over and feel of him. He's only wax and make-up and sawdust."

Trembling, but determined to be able to tell them back home how she did it, the girl crept toward the sorry fig-ure. Her father did not stop her. He was standing in dumb wonder at the mystifying cleverness of the simulation.

"Go on! Get down and touch him!"

Slowly she went down on her knees, stretched out her hand to lay it on the pale face. Simultaneously the office boy delivered a well-aimed kick at the dumb figure. There was an instant of arrested movement from them both. Their eyes flew to each other, widened in fright. Then the girl screamed in a wildly mounting hysteria.

"Daddy! Daddy! It's a man! It's a man! Oh . . . let's get out of here! I want to go home! I want to go home!" She threw her skinny little figure across her father's chest, her hands tearing convulsively at him. The boy remained staring silently. Then he suddenly cupped his hand about his mouth.

"I—I think I'm going to be sick," he gulped, and rushed headlong for the door and the blessed sunlight. In blind fear he hurtled down the stage steps and into the pompous paunch of the President of the Superior Films Studio.

"Whoosh!" went the air from Abraham Rosenthal's lungs, and with it the day-dreams of forthcoming record-breaking Superior Films features.

"Hey, boy! Vat you think dis iss, a race course?" he demanded furiously when he recognized the human catapult as one of his own office boys. But the lad had struck something living and warm, and he clung. The President attempted vainly to shove him off his midriff.

"Stop butting me, vill you?" he roared sternly.

"He's dead! Oh, Mr. Rosenthal, he's dead! I—I kicked him, and he's dead . . . really dead!"

"You kicked him, and he's dead? Vell, I don't doubt it. You haff only butted me, and I'm half dead already," snapped the head executive with characteristic sarcasm. "Stop it, vill you . . . GOAT!" He clamped his powerful, fat hands down on the boy's quivering shoulders and shook him soundly. "Vill you stop that blubbering, and tell me vat iss the matter?"

"He's dead—the dummy!"

The clasp on his shoulders was released as the President stood back and surveyed him with withering scorn.

"And you should be on my lot for two years, and then tell me the dummy iss dead! Dummy you! Iss it you haff no brains at all, to come bouncing off one of my stages and butt me in the stomach and tell me the dummy iss dead? Go to the office and get what money's coming to you, and get off my lot!"

"No, no, Mr. Rosenthal! You don't understand. I mean I thought it was the dummy, and I kicked it—him—and she thought it was a dummy. I told her it was, and she got down and put her hand on its—his—face, and . . . she's in there—"

"She! She! Who are you talking about?" interrupted Rosenthal impatiently.

"That girl from Kansas I was showing around. They had a letter to Mr. Cohen—"

"Are they in there yet?"

"I guess so."

"All right. Now do I understand that there's a dead man on that stage?"

"Yes—sir," shivered the boy.

"All right. Stop shimmying, and look natural. It's not your fault," said the President kindly, and then, snapping back to his executive sternness, "You go back to the office, and don't you open your head about this—not to anybody! Understand me? I fire you off my lot forever. I blacklist you in all the studios. Not a vord—*not a vord!* Understand?"

"Yes . . . sure, Mr. Rosenthal."

A few moments later a very much disturbed head of the Superior Films Studio came bursting, in not so very different a manner from the expeditious exit made by his office boy, from the side door of Stage Six. He disappeared rapidly in the direction of the executive building and entered his private office. On the way he stopped but once, and then to speak to two men on their way to work on one of the sets.

"Hey, you! I vant you should go right avay offer to Stage Six. Don't stop for nodding. I vill send a couple more men right avay, also—vid guns. I vant you should not let anybody, anybody, you understand? on that stage. I, myself, order it. I fire you. I blacklist you in all the studios if you let anybody set foot on that stage! Also, not a vord of this, not a vord to anybody! Understand?"

They nodded mutely, their eyes quickened with excited curiosity. The President looked at them intently for a moment, and then added earnestly:

"I am depending on you. I am trusting you. Something terrible has happened! You vill do as I say?"

"Sure. Sure." They agreed, responding to the note of confidence. The President sighed heavily, and clapped a fat, ringed hand on the shoulder of the man nearest him.

"Go qvick now!"

Then he went with unaccustomed swiftness to his office and closed the door behind him.

3

His fat bulk slumped heavily in his mahogany chair, the President of Superior Films stared unseeing at the ornate walls of his office. For the first time in his experience, the producer of countless screen murder mysteries was face to face with the real thing, and for the time it utterly unmanned him. He felt sick, even as his office boy had felt sick.

Abraham Rosenthal, in his search for filmable material, had studied all sorts of stories dealing with all sorts of situations. He had calmly scanned the pages of "The Murders of the Rue Morgue", and tales equally chill-producing. Yet, until now, it had never occurred to him that the actions of the people involved in such crimes were anything but what they should be. Now, sitting alone at his desk, the horror-stricken, dead face of the man out on Stage Six stared at him from every corner of his luxurious office. It was inked into his mind's eye, so that even when he shut his eyes until his fat cheeks pressed against, and cemented his lids, he could not shut out that awful picture!

Nothing in all the experiences of his emotional Jewish nature, or his fertile imagination, or his countless viewing of the death struggles of men murdered for his screen productions, had prepared him for the reality of a man struck stark and cold by another's hand.

He sat and thought of the books he had read. He thought how the people in them, after the first gasp of horror, went about their business as usual. He thought about women, especially. Women in houses where murders had been committed. He told himself that the author lied who did not state that they were paralyzed with fright on the spot, and never recovered. He felt that he would never recover. The busy, cheerful, productive days of Superior Films were over, and he, the head executive, was sitting like a quaking craven in his chair . . . afraid . . . afraid . . . to his very soul! He felt that it only remained to write "Finis" on the studio gate—and he mourned!

Sitting there alone, with so many things of the flesh, the warm, living flesh, about him; so many creature comforts that were now useless to that poor dead thing out on the set, his great body shook as with a palsy. The realization of death as an irrevocable end came to him! He saw his own body, stark in the grip of *rigor mortis*. He had never until that hour viewed a corpse before the undertaker's hands had worked upon it. He had looked down at his fellow beings in their coffins and observed their peacefully folded hands; had breathed the mingled heavy odors of many flowers; had listened, in a sort of soul-quiet, to the burial services; and at last, when the dead had been lowered reverently into their blossom-covered graves, he had thought of death as rest . . . rest. . . . But there was no sign of rest in that tortured body out there on the set! There was only retching fear; only an utterly hopeless horror and despair, as though the man had seen the coming plunge of the rapier, and had no recourse but to receive it, the while his soul sent out a terrible scream for mercy!

For a long time the President of Superior Films just sat, shaken to the fibers of his being. Slowly his first fear, the fear of body-starkness, passed from him, and a second came to take its place. The personal menace of the unknown murderer seemed to leap at him. An insidious, invisible menace that did not confine itself to an imagined personal form, but emanated mysteriously from the atmosphere surrounding him. When the curtain of the window at his back, moving inward with a passing breeze, touched his shoulder, he cowered away from it, trembling.

How long he would have remained in this craven state, or to what extent it would have metamorphosed the natural staunchness of his character, is not known, for at this moment Isadore Cohen, Production Manager of Superior Films, burst into the room. A thin, nervous, dark individual, he now had the appearance of a leaping and jibbering monkey.

"Mine Gott, Abie! They's a murder on Stage Six!" His voice was high and shrill with excitement. His eyes were unnaturally distended, and he flayed the air foolishly with his long arms.

The man at the desk continued to stare out from the trance of his own morbid thoughts. Then with a mighty breath, and a slight shake of his head, he turned his eyes seeingly upon the other.

"Sure," he said. There was no excitement in his tone. It was heavy, with a dull sound. The Production Manager could not believe his ears.

"Murder! Abie! I tell you they's a murder on Stage Six! On our lot . . . a murder! Mine Gott, vat vill happen to the business?"

This last word penetrated. The President was on his feet, waving a hand at the open door back of Cohen.

"Come in and shut the door! Vas you born in a barn, brainless!" he yelled, the fires of withering scorn in his big brown eyes.

When they were safe from listening ears, the two looked (for a long moment) silently at each other. A series of recent events reviewed themselves in their minds. They thought of tragedies in the film world that had left ruin, financial ruin, in their wake. A probable murder in a San Francisco hotel, and the public end of a popular comedy star. A man, well-known, and well-liked in the picture industry, who had been shot down in his home, and the consequent fall in public favor of persons involved in the crime. The irrevocable "thumbs down" on a lovely female actor, because certain shady pages in her past had been turned to the light. Last but not least, the predicted end of an internationally famous figure of the screen, because of things, scandalous things, sworn to by his wife.

Years before, when motion pictures were only the promising embryo of the gigantic industry they now are, Abraham Rosenthal had been wise enough to see that scandal could be the danger and ruin of the industry. Deeds of excess and license were always waving their dark wings over the people in the studios. Luxury and adulation, the wealth of Croesus, the ensorceling effect of public favor, "The King can do no wrong" attitude, the dwelling in a world apart, of their own making, where physical beauty and attendant material beauty bewitched—all these things had brought an inflaming, unbalancing sense of personal power and the unloosing of passions into the lives of some of the stars. They developed an entirely false sense of values and carried into their personal lives the sex lures of the people they characterized for the screen.

Yes, he had known the menace, and knowing the great temptation also, had understood and forgiven much. But one law he had always maintained in regard to his own studio. It was known by every one within its confines, from the garbage man who gathered up the cans filled with remains of midnight lunches on the sets, to the highest paid actor driving a specially made sport model through its gates.

"Vat you do avay from here, I cannot help. But vat you do on my lot, on *my* lot . . . that iss my business! I vill haff no scandal—no dirt! Right avay I hear about anything here, here in *my* studio, and out you go!"

For years this had been the unwritten law, scrupulously obeyed. And now . . . MURDER! Murder, creeping in at night, had trailed its black garments over the unsullied record of Superior Films; had thumbed its nose at the unwritten law, and with a mocking sinister laugh had flitted away. Away? Would it return? Ah, that was the question! Once in, when would it not come again, and with it, how many companion evils?

Murder is murder, even in a place where make-believe reigns, and regardless of where it occurs it has an unpleasant way of bringing in its train a host of unpleasant aftermaths. It was this last fact that Abraham Rosenthal was considering. He forgot the presence of his Production Manager. Fat lower lip outthrust, his pudgy hands tensely balled on his desk, he stared off at the opposite wall, covered with autographed photographs of stars who owed their worldwide fame, their fabulous salaries, to his inherent genius for picking winners. He stared at them unseeingly. Yet subconsciously they inserted themselves into the rapid shuttlecock processes of his brain.

For now he was conjuring up the direct consequences to himself, to his lot; to this child of his imagination that he loved beyond all else. He could visualize the screaming headlines in the Los Angeles newspapers; the telegraphed press dispatches to the New York dailies, and on, like an endless chain, to the smallest hamlets where Superior Films would be shown . . . where for years the cleverest publicity he could buy had gone, blazoning, with others, the fame of this Superior Films actor who now lay cold in his own blood—on a Superior Films set! The financial losses bit into him, and yet it was the artist that groaned, again and again:

"God of Abraham! My pictures! My pictures!"

He knew he must not sit there, doing nothing. He must put more guards on that set. He must at once take every step possible to keep the terrible news from leaking out, from upsetting the half hundred temperamental geniuses now in production on his various stages, artists whose every second cost him dollars. At last he remembered Cohen.

"Vot a terrible business!" he sighed, in all sincerity, to his Production Manager.

Cohen, who saw thankfully that his employer was with him once more, retorted:

"Business! Ve haff no business! I tell you, Abie, the business iss ruined! Oi, the papers! All over the front pages it vill be!" He was yelling again.

"All over the vorld it vill be, if you don't shut up!" responded Rosenthal bitterly. "Vill you please to calm yourself down, vonce?"

"Vill I please to calm myself down vonce? And you should say such things to me, ven I come to tell you they iss a murder . . . a MURDER on our lot!"

"*My* lot," interrupted Rosenthal. Some of his bland and immovable complacence was returning to him, and so, back to the old, and never entirely consumed bone of contention between them.

"*My* lot, Izzie!" he said firmly, and reached for a cigar.

Cohen grabbed his hair and tried to yank it out.

"All right! All right! *Your* lot. Mebbe it iss your murder, too?"

"How iss it, Izzie, that you should know about this murder, anyvays?" asked Rosenthal, suddenly remembering his immediate caution against spreading of the news.

"How iss it I should know about it?" retorted Cohen indignantly. "How iss it I *shouldn't* know about it, I ask you! Ain't I Production Manager of this studio? Ain't I? Ain't it my business to know vat goes on on my stages . . ."

"MY stages," came the imperturbable voice of the President.

"Mine Gott! All right, YOUR stages! Anybody's stages, I don't care! But I ask you, iss it not my business, as Production Manager of this studio, to know about vat goes on on those stages, Abie?"

"Sure. But vat I vant to know iss vy do you vish to make it efferbody's business? Vy do you come in here yelling like a hyena? Better you should go up on the roof vid a megaphone!"

Cutting sarcasm. Cohen looked his reproach.

"Vell, anyvays, Abie, vat are ve going to do vid it?"

"First, ve vill keep it under our hats!"

"But Abie! The police . . . the coroner . . . ve got to do something vid it? Ve got to tell the authorities already!"

"Better first I should talk to Julius."

"Sure. Talk to him. That smart alec lawyer ought to earn his salary vonce a year, anyvays!"

There was a silence while Rosenthal put in a call for Julius Stern, and was told the lawyer would not be in his office for half an hour.

The highly-strung Cohen put his hand to his head and shivered violently, at the same time breaking out anew in a voice high with near hysteria.

"Mine Gott, Abie! Such a thing to happen! Such a vay for a man to die!"

"Shut up!" roared the President, smashing his heavy fist down on his desk with a crash that cruelly tortured Izzie's already tortured nerves.

"Abie!" he pleaded, hugging his head with his hands. "Don't to do that again! I ask it off you! I vill keep still!"

"You bet you vill keep still! And you vill listen, vonce to me, and get this through your dumb head! Ve haff got to keep qviet about this! If you haven't got brains to know vy yourself, I haven't got time to tell you! But you haff got to stop yowling like a vild man about it! You haff got to shut up! Not a vord, not a vord to anybody! Do you hear me?"

"Sure, sure I hear you! How could I help it, ven you are yelling like a hyena yourself now? Vould you like it I should get you a megaphone vile you climb yourself up on the roof?"

Thus Cohen evened the score. The President started to retort in kind, and then realized the justice of the taunt. He sat down heavily, and for a moment preserved a dignified silence. Then, leaning across his desk, his finger pointed sternly at the other, he spoke slowly, and earnestly.

"Izzie, you go right avay now out to that set. You tell those fellows out there if they let anybody—*anybody*, mind you—on that stage, I fire them! Already I haff told them that, and they haff disobeyed me. They haff let you—"

"Let me? Vy not? Ain't I got as much authority to go on that stage as you, I ask you, Abie?"

"Sure, sure," responded Rosenthal wearily. "Sure you got authority, Izzie, but not now! Not now! You stay off. You vant they should find your finger prints all over, and arrest you for murder?" Seeing the instantly chastened eye of his Production Manager, he continued, "Izzie, I vouldn't to let anybody on that stage until the police get here. Not anybody! Not Mr. Hays himself. Now vill you shut up about it?"

He reached over to his precious cigar box and offered one of his more precious cigars to Cohen. Emotion choked him, and something suspiciously like tears of beseechment dimmed his sharp gaze.

"And for Gott sakes, Izzie, try to look at everybody like maybe nothing happened . . . like you don't know nothing . . . can you? Just look natural. Ve got to keep things out of the papers, or ve are ruined!"

"Maybe ve are ruined anyvay," said Izzie dolefully. "Haff you thought mebbe they tie up Seibert's picture in the evidence, or something? Ve got already five hundred t'ousand dollars in that picture. Perhaps already ve kiss that money goodbye!"

"I haff been thinking about that," said the other heavily. Then, after a moment: "Izzie, for Gott sakes get out of here, and let me vonce alone! I haff enough misery vidout you hunting up some more."

When Cohen had gone, Rosenthal wiped his head wearily with a great silk handkerchief.

"Oi, that fellow! He alvays makes me lose my temper, he iss such a dumb head. Mebbe it iss a good thing."

It was a good thing, for now the President of Superior Films was completely and finally jarred into his natural executive self. He had no time to indulge in morbidity. When he looked at his ornate walls, he saw other things than the white, dead face of Hardell. Cohen's effect on Rosenthal was always the same. It had been so for years. Up from the gutter they had come together, and previously it had been Cohen who was the employer, and Rosenthal the employed. Rosenthal sold gloves for Cohen. Whenever he had a hard sale to tackle, he always started the fight in Cohen's private office. Cohen's never failing stupidity invariably roused his fighting blood, and subsequently he went out and sold his customer! Rosenthal's quicker brain had soon won the ascendency, and thereafter he always kept Cohen by his side, first in this merger, then in that. Had he been accused of gratitude, he would have said, dryly:

"A Jew knows no gratitude ven it iss a matter of business."

Be that as it may, the two were always associated together, and perhaps Rosenthal knew exactly the value of the impetus he received from Cohen. At least Rosenthal knew that "picture sense" is a subtle thing, innately possessed, and not learned. He knew that he himself possessed it, despite his ignorance in many lines. He knew that Cohen could never possess it.

Rosenthal had that unbeatable combination—the born salesman's instincts, (and the world was now his prospect) and an innate appreciation of the artistic. Superior Films, with its splendid working organization, its mammoth stages, its bee-hive productivity, was answer to the first, and the sometimes rare beauty and absolute genius of the motion pictures he released was answer to the second.

Now he reached for his phone again.

"Find if Mr. Stern is in his office yet."

Julius would handle the police—the stupid flatfeet! They would walk all over his nice lawns (for he had a loving pride in the beauty of his grounds) and they would snoop around, bothering everybody with foolish questions. But Julius would see that official wheels functioned smoothly.

The bell rang, and his secretary said, "I have Mr. Stern on the wire." He merely grunted and thrust his fat lips closer to the receiver.

"Julius? Abie. Listen, Julius, drop everything right avay and come offer. You couldn't? Vell, iss there anybody near the phone? All right. Something terrible has happened, Julius. There iss a dead man on my lot! Yes . . . dead . . . murdered! Vat? His name? Hardell . . . Huh? Stabbed vid a sword. No, right avay I find it out, and put guards on the stage. No, I fire the whole bunch if they do. I vant you should get in touch vid the Police Commissioner himself, and send him out here. He vouldn't? Vell, send some good man—somebody ve can trust. Ve can't have this blabbed all over the place. I don't vant a lot of snoopers, you know. Vat? How should I know, Julius! All I know iss ve find him this morning dead as a mackerel. Mine Gott, Julius, you should to see him! I haff been all upset. . . . Vat? Aw, listen

Julius." His tone became wheedling. "Sure you can do it fine. I vant no scandal! Sure, sure, I understand all about that . . . sure ve got to spend money to keep it qviet, that's all right. . . . Vat? Sure I know he vas a rotter! Didn't I myself vant to sell him to International Artists, and who vas it vouldn't let me, I ask you? It vas you! Oi, to think I kept that low-lifer, vat gets himself killed by a voman . . . no, I don't know, I am just *saying* he gets himself killed by a voman. And now look at the fix I am in! Just because you vouldn't let me sell him . . . Oh, all right, all right! Have it your vay, Julius . . . 'bye," and Rosenthal hung up.

He leaned back and surveyed the beautiful women pictured on his walls. Just now he had no pleasure in the seductive lines of their lovely bodies. It was at their naughty, wayward feet that he laid the blame for this thing that had come to upset his studio. Mentally he went over the list of Hardell's affairs. The man was a true *enamorado*. Rosenthal admitted it.

"Sure, the dirty low-lifer needed killing—but on my lot it should happen!"

He sighed, but not long did he sit lost in regrets. There was an unpleasant task to be tackled. Again he took up his desk phone.

"I vould talk to Mr. Seibert."

"He is not on the lot yet, Mr. Rosenthal."

"Vell, soon as he comes, get him."

He would not have been human, had he not been relieved. There were still a few moments of grace left to him. Naturally a peace-loving man, Rosenthal dreaded the impending interview with his highest-salaried, and most temperamental director. He knew by experience that anything that halted or hindered Seibert when in production was invariably construed by that director as an intended and personal insult to himself. That this affair should happen while Seibert was on this picture, of all others, was in itself a tragedy. Already he had been ten months in production; part of that time in Europe. Already a fortune had been spent on the film, and a great sum in salaries not yet paid. The picture, aside from its production, had cost a small fortune, coming from the hand of one of America's foremost writers. It had been heavily advertised in all leading film-news periodicals. It was the first to bear the title, "Franz Seibert Productions." It was the director's special baby, his hope, the fulfillment of his directorial dreams. There was but one more day's shooting to complete it, incorporating scenes the director had written himself, and which were therefore the most important in his eyes.

"Vell, this vill be a fight to the finish, and for vonce I am going to high-brow that fellow," muttered Rosenthal as he waited.

4

Some people have the faculty of making myths of themselves. Such was Franz Seibert, the most outstanding figure in motion pictures when this affair of the murder of
Dwight Hardell occurred.

People who had never seen him, and who had never set
foot on a studio lot, said with bated breath that he was a
demon of a man who drove his actors unmercifully, swore
foully at women, for whom he had no respect, and spent
the producers' money like water . . . but that they would
walk ten miles to see one of his pictures! Ah yes, the public said these things, and flocked like honey bees about the
pot, to gloat over the sex intrigue, the subtle, insidious,
suggested emotional orgies, conveyed by the Seibert touch
to a film!

There were certain motion picture publicity writers
who said that Franz Seibert "knew his onions," that he was
wise to the fact that wickedness is irresistible, and that the
man deliberately created this famous aura about himself
to assist in the filling of his pockets. They were for him,
because to link his name with a news story automatically
threw into it all the atmosphere of excesses with which the
outsider invariably clothes motion picture happenings. In
short, it put the story over for the press folk, and they
were properly grateful.

And the man himself. Was he truly all the things that
gossip said of him? Certainly he drove his actors to the
point of collapse, but one was never known to refuse to
work for him. The President of Superior Films groaned
miserably, both before and after an interview with him,
because, as has been said, Rosenthal was naturally a
peace-loving man, but he knew that the doors of every
studio in filmdom were waiting to receive this erratic
director. Women whispered shocking things of Seibert,
but boasted openly if he gave them his favor. Underlings
in the studio thumbed their noses at his back, but quaked
visibly before the stare of his cold blue eyes.

This morning, because of a mob scene to be shot, a
crowd of people was surging through the main gates when
the royal purple of Seibert's great car bore swiftly and
silently down upon the entrance. Perforce, the director
was made to wait, the while his chauffeur blew his horn
uselessly. The day gateman stepped out quickly into the
elbowing mass.

"Get a move on, there! Can't you see Mr. Seibert's waiting?"

He shoved the fat backs of Russian mothers, who stol-
idly refused to be hurried. He swore under his breath at
insolent-eyed Czecho-Slovaks, Jews, Romanians, Arme-
nians, Japanese and Italians—all ragged and dirty from
habit, the scum of the foreign quarters—secure in their
possession of type. They did not need to worry. They had
no competition, and they knew it. Perhaps it would be
that same haughty director who would shortly yell at them
to make them surge forward or backward, and make angry,
mob-scene gestures with their arms and lips. What mattered
if they annoyed him now? If he needed them for his picture,
he would have to use them. What was the difference?

After slowly satisfying their curiosity, and displaying
their peculiar pride, they finally shuffled through the

gate. Seibert's car eased to a halt inside the entrance, and the gateman, catching Seibert's eye, stepped quickly to its side.

"I'm sorry, sir," he said instantly apologetic, "but we weren't expecting you so early."

The man in the car looked him over coldly. He said, his icy eyes a bit narrowed, his lips taut:

"You are to expect me when I arrive. Not sooner. Not later! There shall be a different entrance hereafter for these . . . animals!"

"Yes, sir. Very good idea, sir," replied the gateman.

Seibert's chauffeur slid the car softly to its habitual parking place in the drive, jumped out, and stood at military attention while his master alighted. Then he handed him a long white box, touched his cap, and closed the car door. Seibert, the box under his left arm, a slender, polished cane swinging in his right hand, proceeded to his private office. Anyone witnessing the little scene might have thought himself in Europe in pre-war days, and even Seibert himself, though dressed in the latest fashion of civilian attire, carried always with him the impression of the military. There was a white gardenia in his lapel, though one looked instead for a red ribbon across his breast and for the medals and decorations of the high military executive.

Seibert went directly to his office, and he did not exchange greetings with a soul on his way. Any other director, coming into the studio of a morning, would have been greeted in that bantering fashion popularly known as "kidding", and which is an outstanding and charming characteristic of motion picture fraternization. But not Seibert. He neither gave, nor received, pleasantries. Most of those he passed pretended to be concerned elsewhere, for people do not like to show themselves snubbed. A few new employes, daring to look at him smilingly, felt themselves left strangely chilled, and oddly reduced to thirty cents in their own opinion.

"Mr. Seibert has arrived, Mr. Rosenthal. Will you talk to him?"

"Ach Gott, yes!" replied the President reluctantly.

From the other end of the wire came Seibert's terse announcement, "I shall finish the picture to-day."

Like an Oracle of Irrevocability came the statement, without preliminary greeting, without culminating modification. With nine other directors nearing completion of their works, he did not give to the head executive the courtesy of identifying himself. But Rosenthal had not expected him to do so. He pulled the receiver closer.

"Ah, yes. Good morning, Mr. Seibert. Vill you please to come offer to my office right avay?"

A silence. Then Seibert said, "I am in *my* office."

Five words, terse, imperious. But they told Rosenthal a chapter. They said, "You know where I am. If you wish to talk with me, come here. I do not go to anybody's office, not even the president of the studio, unless it is my special wish."

This morning the chapter failed to register. Pushing his fat lips closer to the mouthpiece, the President of Superior Films bombarded the director's ear.

"Don't I know it you are in your office? Vell, also I am in *my* office! I shall be in it right along. Also *you* shall be in it, right avay. In *my* office . . . right avay! I would see you *here*. It iss very important, and I vill *not* go offer there to see you! Understand, Mr. Seibert?"

Without waiting a reply Rosenthal pushed away the phone and sank back into his chair.

"Now, go ahead. Blow up and bust! For vonce I don't care. I haff other troubles," the President said complacently.

For a long moment Seibert remained unmoving. He was staring down at his hands, clad, as usual, in their immaculate white gloves—a habit attire of his

known throughout the picture world. It was said that during the filming of difficult scenes he had been known to ruin five dozen pairs of brand new, made to order, imported, white kid gloves. Now he spread his fingers slowly, and every seam in the well-made kid parted with a spitting noise like the tearing of silk. Deliberately he opened the white box and got out another pair. This pair he also destroyed in the same manner. He ruined them with calculated, methodical movements, and there was something uncannily menacing in the way he did it. When but one pair of gloves remained—and on the floor lay a heap of tattered, snowy-white hand coverings—he rose to his feet. Going to a full-length mirror he smoothed on the last pair with fastidious nicety, adjusted his coat in a similar manner, straightened the gardenia, and put on his hat. For a moment he stood stiffly at parade, then picked up his cane and went out.

Ignoring all, except a woman star, to whom he bowed stiffly, he walked calmly past the executive building, past the open window of the president's office, and thence on, across the spacious green lawns, to the side door of Stage Six. Here he was accosted by one of his property boys.

"I'm sorry, Mr. Seibert, but we've been given orders not to let anyone on this stage."

The director tensed instantly, blazing fury in his cold eyes. Whether subconsciously or otherwise, the cane was raised menacingly toward the young chap standing on the stage steps.

"I don't know why, sir, and I'm sorry, sir. But I'm obeying orders. You can't go in, Mr. Seibert."

The boy was all but incoherent in his nervousness. For answer Seibert came up the remaining steps, and when

the lad backed against the door, barring it against him, he
raised his cane and brought it down vindictively upon him.

"You have evidently lost your senses. Stand out of my
way!" he ordered furiously.

As he swung the door open, and his form darkened the
entrance, there was a movement in the dim interior. An
army automatic was pushed into his stomach and he found
himself looking into eyes as insolently ruthless as his own.

"Where did you think you was going, bo?" drawled
a voice that had the soft slipping quality of fine edged
steel. Without waiting for answer, the voice continued, in
quicker tone, "Beat it! The kid gave you the orders. They
go . . . and you *git!*"

There was a singing exultation in the words, and an
old and re-captured joy of battle in the eyes that so boldly
gleamed upon him. But the director did not move. Instead
he said, calmly:

"It seems you do not know me, my man. I am Franz
Seibert."

"Sure, I know you! But your name's sauerkraut for all of
me. And if you raise that cane an inch higher, 'my man',"
he mimicked, and paused. With a quick change of tone he
jabbed the Colt's into the director's ribs.

"Go on! Do it!" he snapped fiercely. "Smash *me* in the
face with that damned cane, and I'll make it a pair." He
nodded significantly to the interior of the set, where the
stark figure of Hardell still lay.

Seibert lowered the cane quietly as he lifted his monocle
and fitted it into place. Unblinkingly and thoroughly he
scrutinized the man before him.

"I shall remember you," he said, and turning went with
leisurely step back the way he had come.

"And I'll remember you with a slug in your belly, you
lousy kraut!" the guard yelled after him. To a companion
on the stage, he called:

"Hey, Bill! Come here. Take this poor kid over to the hospital. He's hurt bad." Then he turned to the youth, who was now sobbing with pain, rage and humiliation.

"Where'd he hit you, buddy?" he asked.

"Right in the face, damn his rotten hide!"

"Ne'mind kid. Some day somebody'll shove that stick clean down his filthy throat!"

"And I slaved my heart out for him—him and his rotten pictures. The dirty bum!"

"You said it all," agreed the ex-army man.

"There it is! My contract! I wash my hands of this place, and of you! Am I, Franz Seibert, to be insulted and ordered about like a common office boy?"

"Perhaps you think that I, who hire you, should come to your office ven I vish to see you?" inquired Rosenthal, quietly removing the pieces of torn paper which had clung to the hair over his ear.

"I am not referring to that," replied the director coldly.

"Vell then, I do not understand, myself, how anyone else should be ordering you about, Mr. Seibert," returned the President blandly, still calmly removing the remnants of the contract, which had adhered to him in various places. After he had made a little pile of the torn pieces on his desk in front of him, he added:

"Now that you have thrown your contract in my face, have vished to cancel it, it does not matter anyvays!"

"It matters enormously, to me, that I am ordered off my set, without—"

"*My* set," interjected Rosenthal. For an instant the other man stared at him in white fury, then decided to ignore the interruption.

—"without an explanation, and by an ignorant nincompoop with a gun, on the day I am to finish my picture! On the day that the final, artistic touch is to be put to my masterpiece—for it is a masterpiece. You have agreed with me that it is that. I know that it is. I know that Superior Films will make a fortune out of it. I know exactly what I am worth to your organization. And yet you dare to allow me to be insulted in this mysterious fashion! Insulted, like an *ordinary workingman!* I, Franz Seibert, to be ordered off a set! It is unthinkable!"

"Mr. Seibert," said the President, his big brown eyes holding the icy blue ones, "I asked that you should come directly to my office. I vished to explain to you. But did you do it? You did not. You valked deliberately past my office. You said to yourself, 'I vill show him that he cannot order me, Franz Seibert, around?' Vell, ven you vent right by my office, I saw you. I also saw you go offer to Stage Six, because I had an idea that iss just vat you vould do. I could have sent a boy after you, and stopped you. But I did not. No, I let you have your lesson. Also, I said to myself, 'Now he vill come back here and say to me he has been insulted!' Vell, Mr. Seibert, mebbe last veek that vould have made me very much upset. But not now. Not now. I haff other troubles, beside vich you become . . . a nothing!"

There was dignity in Rosenthal's speech, and justice. If Seibert had a moment of regret at his lack of courtesy to the head executive, he could not show it now. He must hold up his position.

"I am not concerned with your troubles, Mr. Rosenthal," he said, frigidly.

"But that iss vere you are very much wrong. You vill be very much concerned in this, Mr. Seibert. Very much."

Ignoring this also, the director continued:

"I demand that you explain to me the reason of this happening; the reason I am grossly insulted and ordered off my set. Why, without a word to me, my property boy . . . my *property boy* . . . is given authority over me?"

A vein on Seibert's temple had started to fill. It showed blue-black against the fair skin of his sandy complexion.

"I vas trying to tell you," said Rosenthal patiently, "that if you had come right avay offer here; you vould have found out for yourself vy you cannot go on that set. Vy should I vish to insult you, Mr. Seibert? I asked you to come here first, so that I could save you some unpleasantness . . . so that I should explain to you."

"Explain! Explain! Will you, then, kindly start explaining and not talk so much about it? Can you give me any adequate reason why I should be ordered off my own set?"

Being a peace-loving man Rosenthal might not have responded in the fashion in which he did, had he not found that there are times when violence is necessary. Jumping to his feet, and inclining his ponderous body over his desk, he brought his fat fist down upon it with his famous resounding crash. "Vy should you *not* be ordered off that set, if I see fit? Are you running this studio? Are you its president? Ordered off *your* set! Ach, not! *My set!*" Bang! went his fist again. "*Mine!* You say you are Franz Seibert, and you are insulted because you cannot go on that set. All right. I am Abraham Rosenthal, and I cannot go on that set, either, and I haff more sense than to go around yelping I haff been insulted! You are Franz Seibert, yes, but do you know what only that means to me? It means you are just one off my directors, and I am hiring you, and I am paying you more money than you haff ever earned in your life before!" Bang! "I, Abraham Rosenthal!" Bang! "The head of this studio! You throw my contract in my face! All right! I take it back." He grabbed wildly at the torn pieces. "Sure, I take it back! I am money ahead ven I do not haff to pay your salary, and that iss good business. You are through anyvays. You are through directing that picture for the reason vy I phoned you to come offer here. There iss a dead man on your set! Vat do you think of that? Now do you vant to go on that set?"

His fat arm swung out, interrupting Seibert's reply, and his brown eyes glared back ferociously into the other's frigid stare.

"So," he continued, "you shall not go on that set. You shall not do anything until ve see vat the police vill say. Meantime, also, you vill tell nobody! You vill not go howling all offer my lot that you haff been insulted! You vill keep this murder to yourself! I forbid you to talk about it. Not a vord. I, Abraham Rosenthal, forbid you on my lot to talk about it. Now get out. I am busy!"

Rosenthal fell back in his chair and drew out his handkerchief. It was voluminous, and bordered with purple. He mopped his head thoroughly. It had been, for him, a wearying interview. After a moment he looked up to find that Seibert still remained, and was looking at him with a slightly scornful expression. It was as though he said: "Quite a display of feeling, but you do not think for one moment that it has impressed ME, do you?"

Rosenthal, looking at him, caught some of this. He repeated, with an insistence into which he put his last ounce of ferocity:

"I haff told you to get out. Vell, I mean it! Get out!"

"Will you be good enough to put down that mop rag and talk a little less like a wild man?" Seibert retorted. "I can make no head or tail of your attempted explanations. What man has been found dead on my set, and who says it is a murder?"

"You vill learn all that later. I do not vish to vitness any more of your temperamental brain storms!" snapped the President, and he waved the director toward the door.

"I will not leave this room until I am given some reasonable, understandable excuse for this morning's affront,"

Seibert said with a cold finality which forced Rosenthal to
yield.

"All right," he said, and sighed resignedly. He was now
in for it. No escape. "It vas Dvight Hardell, your heavy!
Now don't go crazy. I don't suppose anybody murdered
him just to insult you. Don't start anything, or I vill haff
you thrown out! I haff enough troubles vidout . . ."

"A little self-control might make you feel better, Mr.
Rosenthal," said the director pointedly, and with a lack of
the wild outburst Rosenthal had fully expected. Instead,
Seibert added quietly:

"I now understand perfectly why I was not allowed on
the set. The guards were police orders, of course."

"No. I thought of that myself. The police haff not yet
arrived," returned Rosenthal quickly.

"Very right of you. Correct," and Seibert leaned back
in his chair, his strong fingers gripping his chin and pulling at it in a reflective manner.

"Hardell! Dwight Hardell!" he repeated. "And only one
more day's work to be done! My picture . . . my picture!
Oh, the fool! The utter, inconsiderate—"

"Seibert, I told you not to start anything!" yelled
Rosenthal, jumping to his feet. "Stop it! Vat a foolishness
you are saying! Do you think that poor fellow vanted to
get himself murdered? Anyvays, vat iss all the fuss about
your picture? You ain't got no picture anymore." Rosenthal
indicated the scraps of the torn contract. Seibert gave him
a melancholy smile.

"That is all forgotten," he said. "I retract my action.
But this . . . this is terrible! My God, man, do you realize
that I've *got* to have Hardell for these last scenes? I've *got*
to have him! The picture is ruined . . . ruined . . . and I've
put my heart, my brain, my very life-blood into making
it the greatest screen play of the age." He rose and commenced to pace the floor.

"And now, because of the removal of one actor—one puppet—all is ruined! All my hopes, all my dreams, all my labor, gone!" He groaned, and split the last of his day's supply of white gloves.

"Now, now, Seibert! Sit down and ve vill talk this offer. First off, I neffer did agree vid you that those last scenes are necessary—" he held up his hand to silence the director's intended protest. "No, and the head of my editorial department said to me only the other day, 'I think Seibert iss going just a step too far vid that last sequence. Better finish it as ve first wrote it. Then it vill be a perfect thing—an artistic triumph!' That iss vat my editorial head said to me. Now, about Dvight Hardell. Billy Vest told me only last night he thought two of the scenes you shot yesterday vere all right—"

"All right! *All right!* They must be better than 'all right.' They must be perfect! It is the key situation of the story! The entire structure rests on it! That scene must be transcendental! It must clutch the very souls of people, and raise them to—" he shook his clenched fist over his head, the other hand gripping his hair.

"Now, now, Seibert, that iss only one vay of looking at it. Another vay iss, if that picture you haff made cannot go offer vidout this scene being like you say, then it iss a bum picture. No, don't interrupt me. I know vat I am talking about. If that picture has to haff such a scene, played vid such a transcendentalness, to be a success, better ve throw the whole thing in the ash can! Vell, you see, ve do not agree vid you. I do not. My editorial head does not. That iss a good story, and it vill make a good picture, vidout all this extra stuff you are talking about. Anyvays, I vas telling you. Billy Vest tells me that two of those scenes are all right. *All right!* That means *all right;* that means they vill go offer. Now, that leaves only the extra scenes you wrote yourself, and vich nobody else thinks are necessary. So you see, Seibert, you haff all this misery for nothing."

The director had been listening with but half his ears, evidently, for now he whirled on the President feverishly.

"Very well. I will use the scenes shot yesterday. I cannot bring the dead back to life. Perhaps, after all, he could not be made to do it any better than the last time he did it. That is probably true. But, I will not yield an inch on the scenes I was to finish to-day with my other people. I yield only to the inevitable! Because one of the puppets has been removed from the stage, does it follow that the show is over? Never! Because one of the pawns in the game lies dead on that set, am I to wait until the inspiration has died out of me; wait until the stupid police have made up their minds, and this whole stupid affair has dragged to a finish? No! I shall go on as I intended. I shall work on that set to-day, and I shall finish my picture. What is a murder to a picture? The murder of a man who was nothing but filthy vermin polluting the earth? I wanted to shoot his death scene over to-day. Well, I am forced to give that up. But because he has been killed, I will not give up everything else in connection with finishing my picture. I will work on that set."

"Seibert, you vould do that? You vould actually do such a thing?" He probed the other's cold features with the look of a shocked child.

"Why not? Because I do not throw up my hands and bewail the passing of a man reviled in life; because I do not tread softly, and whisper in the presence of his body, which, through some peculiar circumstance of its having become inanimate, has also become a revered object—"

"Stop it! Ain't you got no feelings, Seibert?"

"Sentiment in this case is merely a matter of habit and tradition . . . and fear of society. I have never bowed to such things," said Seibert coolly.

Rosenthal scrambled to his feet and pounded his desk, but his action was purely involuntary. He did not reckon its effect. He was beyond that.

"You are nothing but a director's brain, Seibert! You have no heart in your body! And I tell you I don't care how many times you say you vill vork on that set, I say that you vill not! I vill not allow it!"

"Nor will I," said a quiet voice, and a stranger walked into the room.

5

The President of Superior Films had his own hauteur when occasion demanded. It was only in inter-office squabbles, such as his daily skirmishes with Cohen, and his rarer, but no less combustive engagements with artists suffering from an overdose of temperament, that he resorted to shouting and desk pounding.

Now he swung about with slow dignity and eyed his unannounced visitor in the manner of aloofness he always maintained toward outsiders.

"Vell?" he said, with rising inflection. It was a leading remark, but the stranger did not produce the apology it should have invited. Rosenthal raised his eyebrows at Seibert, who adjusted his monocle and examined the newcomer from head to toe. Considering that he, the newcomer, had seated himself, stretched his lean length comfortably and was now leisurely filling a pipe, in short, making himself quite at home and settling down for a long winter, as it were, Seibert was excusable in his action. Rosenthal leaned over his desk and shot these questions at the man:

"Vill you be kind enough to tell me vat gives you permission to come into my private office and interrupt a conference? Vat iss your name, and vat iss it you vant?"

The visitor looked up and a whimsical smile broke the thin lines of his mouth. Men were men to him. Nothing less, nothing more. In each was a possible law-breaker. In each a possible quarry for his chase. Banker and beggar were alike when he was on the hunt. He said, in a drawling voice:

"My name is Smith. Ordinary enough, eh? Nothing startling in it. And what I want, ah, that is another matter. What I want, and what I do, sometimes do not agree. I wanted to go fishing today. In fact I was a member of a very nice little party, and we had chartered a boat to take us to Catalina. I have been thinking of getting into The Tuna Club for years, and now the chance is lost again. Not because I wanted to come out here instead, but because you wanted me to, Mr. Rosenthal. By the same token, Mr. Hardell probably did not want to be found dead this morning . . . but he was."

The President came around his desk with outstretched hand.

"You are from the Police Commissioner? That iss good. I haff been vaiting for you, Mr. Smith. I am very glad to see you. Ve haff had a terrible thing happen out here."

Hospitably he took up his box of cigars and pressed them on the detective.

"Thank you," said the latter briefly. His eyes were trained intently on the back of the director, who had turned from the room and was idly watching the passersby through Rosenthal's window. There was an atmosphere of extreme indifference about the back presented to him, and the detective had prolonged his little opening speech in order to set his professional mind at work on the two men before him. He had a habit of talking, seemingly at random, the while his brain caught and analyzed the conditions and people about him. But Seibert had turned away in the middle of his speech. Smith was now wondering if it had been a pose, or direct evasion on the part of the picture man.

Rosenthal nodded and made violent gestures at Seibert's back, getting over that he supposed his visitor would wish to talk to him alone. Captain of Detectives Smith, for he was that, raised his voice a bit, as he answered:

"No, no. I think Seibert will be able to help us."

Would the director turn around now? Would he resent the deliberately careless tone Smith had used in speaking of him, as though he were one of the office boys, instead of the man he was? After a moment Rosenthal, not too pleased, stepped over and took his arm.

"I vish to make you acqvainted with Mr. Smith," he said, somewhat sternly.

"Captain Smith," said Seibert, bending frigidly from the hips.

"Mr. Seibert," responded Smith, equally formal, and chuckling secretly at his own unaccustomed punctiliousness.

"Sit down, Seibert. Perhaps you can throw a bit of light on this thing," he said, motioning to a chair.

"I am at your service," responded the director stiffly.

Smith nodded. "Getting right to the known facts, our office was informed that you had a man, Dwight Hardell by name, dead on one of your stages. You say, murdered. The case was turned over to me, and with two of my men, Clancy and Ryan, I came right out. They and the Coroner are on the stage now. That is, I expect they are. I had a little difficulty with Mr. Cohen, your Production Manager—"

"That Izzie!" groaned the President.

Smith smiled. "I gathered he had been told in a pretty strong manner not to let anyone on the stage, but I finally convinced him."

The detective's long body lost some of its lazy indolence, and his voice some of its deliberate drawl, as he continued: "First, I want to locate the person who last saw Hardell alive."

"That is the customary procedure," put in Seibert dryly. It was apparent he did not think much of it.

"Quite so. Nothing original in my method here," returned Smith, undisturbed. "However, what often commends the customary to my mind is the indubitable fact that it *customarily* brings results! I presume that is why the customary has become customary, Mr. Seibert. Do you agree with me?"

The director shrugged. It was apparent he thought the question a superfluous one and beside the point. Smith, seeming not to notice, continued:

"First, Mr. Rosenthal, I wish you would tell me all you know about it."

"Not so much," said Rosenthal. "I am sorry, but I can only tell you vat has happened this morning after my office boy found him. I haff not a ghost of an idea vat—"

"That's all right. Just tell me your part in it," Smith broke in.

"Vell, I vas valking around by Stage Six this morning, first thing I come on the lot, ven my office boy, he comes out very much excited. He has been showing some visitors around, and seeing that Mr. Seibert iss not vorking yet, he takes them to his set to see the dummy. Mr. Seibert vas using a dummy of Mr. Hardell the last thing yesterday, and the office boy thinks it mebbe iss there yet, and he thinks to get a kick out of seeing the visitors ven they look at it. Ve make dummies so real you cannot tell the difference, only close up, from the live man. Vell, this dummy was supposed to be a dead man, you see, and the young lady in the party, she iss scared right avay she sees it. My office boy, he goes over and kicks it, thinking, of course, it iss only the dummy. Mine Gott! He finds out it iss really Mr. Hardell, and he iss dead!"

"What is the reason for the dummy in this picture?" Smith asked.

"Vell, it iss a long story, but I vill explain. Mr. Hardell, who played the villain in the picture—ve call it the 'heavy'—iss killed in a duel vid the hero, who stabs him in the heart. Ve take a close-up of him as he iss dying from the wound. Then a third man, an enemy of the villain, comes in and sees him dead. He vould haff liked to kill him himself. He goes offer and runs his sword through his heart, several times, because he iss such a devil, you understand? Ve did not vant this scene should look tricked, so ve make a dummy," Rosenthal said naively. Smith chuckled. The President's eyes twinkled a moment, and then he continued:

"So, to make the scene look real ve make a dummy, and then the other man can stick his sword into his heart, in a close-up, as much as he vishes, and the audience vill not say, 'Ha! He only stuck it between his arm and his body!' Understand? That vould spoil the whole picture. It vould make the whole thing look exaggerated . . . unreal. Ve put a little container of catsup under the dummy's vest, and ven he iss stabbed it runs out. That iss the blood."

"Humm! Still, I think it very strange your office boy did not know the difference between a dummy and an actual dead man," Smith mused.

"Strange? No, not at all, Mr. Smith. Perhaps you haff never seen the kind of dummy I mean. Mebbe though you haff seen the statue of Lindbergh they haff just put up in the court of the Chinese Theatre in Hollywood? No? Vell, if you had, you vould understand. I am told many people try to talk to him. Ve can do anything in pictures, Mr. Smith. Ve can do really remarkable things, and effery day ve are discovering new—"

"Ways to fool the public, eh?" broke in the detective.

"I vould not say it that vay," replied the President with dignity. "Making motion pictures iss an art. Vone of the big arts! Ven I say that effery day ve are discovering new things, I mean that effery day ve are perfecting that art."

Smith nodded, appreciating the other's sincerity.

"Has it occurred to you, Mr. Rosenthal, that it is a very peculiar thing that this man Hardell should be found in the same position in which his dummy was arranged on the stage yesterday?"

"Yes, yes. That iss right. The dummy was lying just vere they put it yesterday. That iss, I mean to say, Hardell vas lying in that position."

"Very peculiar."

Rosenthal's brown eyes opened with this thought, and its mysterious significance.

"I haff been so upset over finding him dead that I haff not thought about that. Now you speak of it, I see that it iss very strange . . . very queer. Vat do you say, Seibert, eh?" He turned sharply to the director.

"A mysterious murder usually has many strange aspects, gentlemen," replied Seibert indifferently. He was leaning back in his chair, his hands resting quietly on the head of his cane, his eyes pursuing some plan of his own.

Smith determined to force the man to take an active interest in the affair.

"Mr. Seibert, when did you last see Hardell alive?"

Seibert turned to him and made an obvious effort at drawing his attention from elsewhere. Then he said slowly:

"Of course I am not prepared to state exactly, as time was a matter out of my consideration last night, but I believe it was about 12:40."

"What makes you believe that?"

"Because I left the stage with Hardell about 12:15 a.m. I can state that from the fact that the night watchman, Lannigan, made his round just previous to my leaving; and a short time before, Hardell had looked at his watch and reminded me that it was growing late. It was then 11:35."

"Very good. Now, Mr. Seibert, if you will be kind enough to tell me what took place between the time you dismissed your company yesterday afternoon, and the time you last saw Mr. Hardell. You do not need to cut your story down to its shortest length. I would like a full tale."

Seibert took out his monocle and polished it a few minutes before he replied:

"I expect you have heard, Mr. Smith, that motion picture directors, like most artists, are extremely erratic at times? Well, I am no exception. In fact, I believe I enjoy the reputation of being about the worst-tempered director in the business. I abuse my people. I swear at the women. I am unrelenting as a slave-driver."

The President of Superior Films found difficulty in concealing his amazement at this open-hearted confession.

"I had had a very difficult time with Hardell yesterday," Seibert continued. "We worked most of the day on one scene—his death scene. I despaired of getting what I wanted. The man was not an actor. I have always known that, but he was physically the ideal type for the part and I thought that I could force him, through my own will power, to put over the scene as I have dreamed it . . . as it is necessary for the highest art of the picture. Well, finding Hardell was not answering my direction as I had hoped, I asked him to return last night. I wanted to put him through that scene until he got into it what I needed, even if it took me all night."

"Wouldn't a man be pretty well worn out, after working at high emotional pitch all day?" Smith asked. "I mean, wouldn't he be pretty nearly incapable of acting at all?"

The director smiled indulgently. "Ah, that is where you are ignorant. No. The contrary is true. More often than not, the nearer to exhaustion an actor becomes, the more superb he is in his characterization. Why? Because, at last, *at last,* he has forgotten self, forgotten the ego! He has become steeped, to the exclusion of all other realization, in the part he is playing. Also, in a scene of this sort, when an expression of physical agony is needed, the very appearance of exhaustion on the actor's face helps him to put over his action and—"

Smith raised his hand. "Thank you. I understand. Now please go on with the facts."

"We dined together in Hollywood, and returned to the lot at nine o'clock. Hardell went to his room to make up and change, and I went directly to Stage Six, where my set is."

"A question, Mr. Seibert. You say, 'your set.' Is there usually more than one set on a stage?"

"I see you are not familiar with picture-making, nor the demands of the business end of the industry," replied the director with an amiability that secretly astounded his long-suffering employer.

"The stages here, as you no doubt have noticed, are unusually large. Stage Six is 150 by 600 feet. That means about two acres of floor space. So, except in the case of unusually large sets, there are always a number of them on a stage at a time. Each set is cut off from its neighbor by a wall of canvas, and the company enters a set through a gate, or door, in this canvas wall."

"Thank you. Very specific. How many sets were in use on Stage Six last night? I mean, about how many people were around there when you were rehearsing?"

"The stage was dark."

"Dark?"

"I mean that, otherwise than my own set, it was not in use. That is the term we use when we mean idle. The stage was of course not literally dark."

"Give me an idea of how it was lighted?'

"On my own set I was rehearsing a close-up. For this, in addition to the overhead banks of Cooper-Hewitts, we had, I think, three Kliegs, and two 120 Amp. spots."

"On your own set. Was the rest of the stage dark?"

"Oh, ve alvays keep a row of overhead incandescents burning all night," Rosenthal interrupted. "Not much light, very dim, but enough to keep a person from falling over objects on the stage."

"Were these burning all right last night?"

"Yes."

"You had an electrician to work your lights, as is usual, I think, Mr. Seibert?"

"No, I prefer to be absolutely alone on the set when I am rehearsing for a difficult scene. For this reason I have had my electricians hook up the lights on one switch, so that I can control them myself."

Smith looked quickly at Rosenthal, who nodded his head.

"That iss right. Often Mr. Seibert vorks that vay."

"Then I am to understand that you and Hardell were absolutely alone in a building of, we will say, two acres in area, which was, with the exception of the space immediately surrounding you, in semidarkness?"

"That is correct," returned Seibert calmly. "We finished about twelve o'clock, for as I have told you, I heard Lannigan coming along the gravel path. I had just turned off the lights on my set and I called out to him not to come in."

"Why did you do that?"

Seibert smiled apologetically. "Temperamental idiosyncrasy, if you will," he admitted. "Lannigan would be garrulous if I would allow it. I was tired, and I did not feel like putting forth the effort to keep him in his place. There are times, when one is working all day with people, that the mere sight of another one of them is just a bit more than bearable."

Smith nodded, understandingly. "Excusable," he said. "Now, after putting out the lights, what did you do?"

"Went out to my car, which I had driven to the West side entrance of the stage. Hardell did not return to his room. He was very tired. He left the lot in his costume and make-up. I believe he even left the light burning in his room. We drove immediately to the gate, and out. It must have been about 12:15 when we passed through."

"Did you have any conversation with the man at the gate? I presume there is one, at night?"

"Yes. Always. MacDougal, I believe, is the gateman's name. I think I said good night. Perhaps not. I am not in the habit of speaking to the common employes. Hardell waved his hand, and said something about it's being a hard life. It was a very nasty night last night—foggy and chilly."

"And then?" prompted the detective.

"As I had asked him to dine, and we had driven to the studio in my car, I naturally took him home," replied Seibert. "That is," he qualified, "I dropped him a short way from his hotel on Hollywood Boulevard."

"At what corner did you drop him? What cross street?"

"A short distance from Highland. Not at the corner, because of traffic signals. I should say the time was about 12:35, judging from the time it usually takes me to drive that distance. However, it might have been a bit later, as I drove carefully on account of wet roads."

"Mr. Seibert, do you know of anybody who could verify your statement? Did you meet, or pass anyone?"

"Not anyone who knew me."

"Do you usually drive yourself?"

"Frequently. It is a change. Gets my mind off my work. Customarily, however, my chauffeur drives me.

"Where was he last night?"

"It was his night off."

"Was there anyone in your house when you returned?"

"My houseman had gone to bed. My chauffeur, however, had returned before me, and was wiping off some dirt on my other car. I allow him to use it on occasions."

"You spoke to him?"

"Yes."

"What time was it then?"

"As I had gone directly to my home, I imagine it must have been about 12:45."

"Hm . . . Seibert, do you realize, unless other evidence is found, that you were the last man to see Hardell alive?"

"It may be that that will be proven the fact. However, no doubt the hotel clerk will clear me there."

"What is his hotel?"

"The Alta Vista."

"Supposing the hotel clerk does not clear you?"

"That puts me in the position of a suspect, according to customary procedure . . . which, you say, customarily brings results," returned Seibert calmly, looking the other in the eyes.

"Correct," Smith replied tersely.

Seibert shrugged his shoulders. "It is evident I shall have to produce another witness," he said with light indifference, under which the insolence of the normal Seibert was faintly apparent.

Smith shot a sharp look at him. "That is my business. I will attend to that," he said.

Seibert did not reply, but bent to light his cigar with a steady hand. After a moment, he straightened and turned to Smith.

"If that is all you require of me, I shall ask you to excuse me. I have—I must re-adjust my plans for my picture."

"I understand. But just a few minutes more. I want you to help me on this. Forget you are a motion picture director. Take down the smoke screen. What kind of a man was Hardell?"

"What sentimental novelists love to call a 'cad'; what men call a low down skunk, and . . . worse," replied Seibert immediately.

Smith looked to Rosenthal for confirmation.

"That iss right. He vas a dirty bum," agreed the President regretfully.

"There are many types of dirty bums," Smith replied. "Of what particular brand was Hardell?"

"Vomen!" said Rosenthal succinctly.

"Ah! *Cherchez la femme!*" murmured the detective.

"That is your clue," agreed Seibert, and added, "however, while undoubtedly he was mixed up with a great many women, who *undoubtedly* harbored desires for revenge, I do not know of any one of them who could have killed him."

"Would have, you mean, Mr. Seibert, not 'could have'. Someone undoubtedly could, and did, kill him. Unless we entertain the idea of suicide, which from the description of the body given me by Mr. Cohen, I do not now think probable," Smith said.

Seibert bowed. "I stand corrected."

"We must face facts, you know," said Captain Smith, smiling. "I would like to have you tell me of anyone who might have had any reason whatsoever that would suggest a possible motive for this crime. Kindly put your minds on this—both of you."

Rosenthal drew in his head and thrust out his heavy lips. His brows came together tightly as he tried, ineffectually, to pick out a presentable fact from the things he knew about Hardell. Seibert screwed his monocle into place and stared off into space over Smith's head. Finally he spoke.

"Looking back over a period of ten months in a man's life—a man such as Dwight Hardell was—there are always things which have the possibility of leading to murder. But, outside of one or two incidents, I do not know of anything which definitely suggested such a thing."

"And those one or two incidents?"

"Women, of course. There was quite a scene with the daughter of the gateman, MacDougal, only last week. I gathered that he had been playing fast and loose with her, and that she had not understood the sort he was."

"Was MacDougal on the gate last night?" snapped Smith instantly.

"Yes," from Seibert, and from Rosenthal, protestingly:

"Mr. Seibert, you should not to suggest such a thing of that little girl! I know her. She iss under contract to my cousin of Killing Komedies. She iss a nice little girl. Vild, yes, but not a murderess!"

"Well, let's hear about her, anyway," Smith said soothingly. "No harm to her in that, Rosenthal."

"I happened to come upon them in a darkened corner of the set. The girl was reproaching him—accusing him of being untrue, I think. There were the usual recriminations. She is a fiery little thing. Got quite worked up. You know the sort of scene with that sort of man, and that sort of a girl." Seibert shrugged expressively.

"Mine Gott, if I had known it I vould have fired him off my lot, or made him marry her!" ejaculated Rosenthal at this point.,

"Hm . . . Any other women?" Smith asked the director.

"I believe there was one for every one of the ten months I directed him."

"As bad as that? A regular rotter, eh?"

"A dirty low-lifer," muttered the President.

"Lately," said Seibert slowly, "I believe he was interested in my leading woman, Yvonne Beaumont."

Rosenthal turned an immediate and indignant purple.

"Now, Mr. Seibert, that iss too much! Miss Beaumont iss vone of the loffliest little girls vat has effer been on my lot. I cannot sit here and haff you say such things about her!" His brown eyes glared angrily at the director.

"Anything serious between them?" snapped Smith. "What do you know of the affair?"

Seibert threw out a belittling hand.

"Do not misunderstand me. Miss Beaumont is a very different type from the other girl. There was no affair, but she is . . . French. Flirting is an unconscious thing, we might say, with her. She is mischievous, vivacious, entirely feminine. The world is made up simply of men, and romance, to her. I think Hardell attracted her because of his terrible reputation. She has been leading him on. Not, I think, with any idea of giving herself to him, but just— well, as a cat plays with a mouse."

"Hm . . ."

"Vell, I think really Mr. Seibert that you are on the wrong track. I know for a fact that Billy Vest iss head offer heels in love vid her, and that she iss—"

"Ha! Now we're getting somewhere! This West is probably jealous!" Smith exclaimed.

"No! NO!" exploded the President impatiently. "Now don't you go saying Billy Vest did it. I know him. He iss a fine, upstanding young fellow. He iss not a murderer."

"To your mind, nobody on your lot is a murderer," smiled Smith soothingly. "But undoubtedly somebody is!" Then, seeing the look on the President's fat face, he added: "We are only discussing possibilities, Mr. Rosenthal. We are not incriminating anybody. Sometimes the actual solving of a crime is done before the detective sees his people. A house is built to fit the foundation previously laid down for it. It happens that way, frequently, in solving crimes. The solution is often built to fit the structure erected by just such conversation as this. Personalities, sometimes the viewing of the body, even, influence the mind of the detective. For that reason I did not go on the set this morning before coming here. I like to get all the information I can while my mind is clear of the deed itself. Going back to yourself, Mr. Seibert, have you, personally, had any trouble with Hardell?"

"No, and yes. As man to man, none. As director to actor, a great deal. But nothing beyond the trouble I frequently have with my people until a picture is finished."

"Meaning just what?"

"Meaning that, as I said, few of them are able to forget the camera. They are all, instinctively, what we call 'camera hogs.' When they should be thinking picture, story, and characterization, they are thinking camera, audience, and the most presentable side of their faces. Sometimes I have to go through days, of what do you call it—brow-beating? before I reduce an actor to the malleable material which finally makes the perfect puppet whose strings I pull."

"Hm! Then you do not go much on individual interpretation? Freedom of the actor to play a part as he wills?"

"What kind of a general listens to his underofficers?" inquired Seibert. "Is that the way battles are won? How much suggestion do you, for instance, take from your men, Clancy and Ryan?"

Smith laughed. "You score," he admitted.

"Actors, as people, are nothing to me," Seibert continued. "It is known that I treat them frightfully. It is necessary to the perfection of the picture. When it is over I can put my arms around them, and tell them how splendidly they have cooperated with me."

"Hm . . ." said Smith dryly. "You had no personal motive for wishing Hardell removed from this life?"

"There are times when I am directing when I could cheerfully choke every member of my cast!"

"I am not to take that as a round-about confession of the murder?" asked Smith dryly.

"Ah, no. Not at all, not at all," returned the director in kind. "I was talking merely from the artistic standpoint. I should have said there are times when I could gladly throttle their ego, kill their vanity, if in so doing I could lower or exalt them to utterly forgetting self and thereby squeeze out of them some spark of genius."

Smith, listening to the man, knew that indeed he had done just that. It was not because of mediocre pictures that Seibert was the highest paid director in filmdom. The man was a master.

"Just one more question. Have you any idea why, or when, Mr. Hardell returned to the studio?"

"I am sorry, but I cannot help you there. The gateman undoubtedly will have a record. Now, if that is all—"

Smith got to his feet. "You have been very explicit, very thorough. I thank you."

"Not at all. I am at your command, at any time," returned the director, and bowing stiffly he took his departure.

Smith sat looking into space. Rosenthal, displaying a courteous tact, sat silent until the other man should be ready to talk. After a minute Smith said suddenly:

"Rosenthal, I've an idea Seibert behaved uncommonly well. I've an idea he is not usually so amiable."

"Amiable! Mine Gott, I should say not!" exclaimed the President fervently.

Smith took his cigar out of his mouth and his eyes probed deep into the other's.

"I have an idea that he is a very good actor," he said.

"Vell, certainly I half never seen him behave like this. I vas vaiting any moment for him to blow up."

"Rosenthal, what would Seibert have done if he had behaved about as usual?"

The President threw out his hands eloquently. "I tell you he iss a firecracker . . . a bomb! The least little thing, and pouff! off he goes! Vat he vould haff done vould haff been to say he vas being insulted, that he, Franz Seibert, vas being insulted, that you should ask him those things, that you should make out that he had anything to do vid Hardell being murdered."

Rosenthal did a very good imitation of Seibert's customary manner. Smith nodded his head.

"Uhuh! I thought so," he said quietly.

"Vell, ven you think of it, mebbe though he thought for vonce he should act decent," chuckled the President.

"Why?"

"Vell, mebbe ven his life depends on it, he can act like a gentleman. You haff told him he iss already a 'suspect.' Mebbe he thought better to talk nice to you!"

"Maybe," agreed Smith. "At any rate I'm going to strain his decency a little further. I'd like to have him on that set when I go over there. Will you ask him to come?"

"Sure, I ask him," but as he said it a reminiscent twinkle came into the President's eyes. "You haff heard me tell him he iss not to go on that set? Now you ask me to tell him to go. Vell, I tell my secretary to do it."

"And I'll write him a line for her to take over. That lets you out," laughed Smith.

6

The Unknown!

Men build ships to sail away to it. Women dream of romances to be lived in it. Children's eyes brighten, little hearts gladden, and pulses quicken, at tales of it!

To the greater portion of this earth's people, a motion picture studio is—unknown. Even to the people who work in it, it remains unknown to the end, for the surprises of its magical realms never cease and each day brings its own bewitchments. It is the Magician's box, out of which anything under heaven can be called by that Master Magician, the Producer. To-day its people may find themselves walking the streets of New York, in the year 1927. To-morrow they may be in the land of the Ancient Chaldees. The day after they walk entranced in the spell of Tibetan monasteries. Play-acting all, yes, but the most convincing play-acting in the world, for, even to the grains of sand on the ground, the minutest detail is true to the life it represents. Ay, verily, another land, another age, exists, and the spell of its spirit steeps itself into the actors. An American born extra, wearing a single garment and carrying the begging bowl of the East Indian holy man, goes about with lowered lids, even when the camera is not grinding. He is become the thing he represents.

The lure of Romance, and the love of Adventure! The never quite out-reasoned belief in the Genii of the Lamp! The eternal hope in the human heart of dreams come true! The palpitant intoxication of fabulous riches, and the fascination of black magic! The child-heart, that never loses its delight in fairy tales! These are the secrets back of the world-wide interest in the making of motion pictures; these are the things that make the call of the silver screen invincible.

Captain of Detectives Smith, and President of Superior Films Rosenthal, stood on the gravel walk just outside the latter's private office. Smith, like a big-eyed small boy, was watching a gay and motley throng that was now coming from all parts of the studio lot to gather on a space of green lawn just in front of Stage Six. Caps and bells, mummers, tightrope artists, jugglers, a gay parade that, in groups, or singly, streamed from the front entrance, the dressing rooms, and the wardrobe building. And, miraculously, the entire grounds took on a holiday spirit, so that the gay blowing of fete horns and the merry tune of a band seemed as natural to this place of business as the shining of the sun.

"You see," said Rosenthal, waving a fat arm at the laughing crowd. "Vat do you think those people vould do if somebody vent out there and told them a dead man vas lying on Stage Six? Mr. Bonet iss just finishing his picture. He has been vorking very hard. He has been out in the desert on location, and much of the time in Death Valley. You know vat that means? He iss vorn out. I haff promised him two veeks vacation, starting on Monday. Vell, then, he must finish to-day. Also, I haff two people from International Artists. The star of this picture I haff borrowed from them. It vas very hard to get her, but she vas the only voman for the role. My contract says that she vill be finished by Monday also, because International Artists are making a picture in London, and already her passage iss booked and right avay she finishes here she goes to New York to sail. So many other details I vill not take up your time to tell, but you see I am forced to keep my people in production—murder or no murder! There iss too much money involved in making a motion picture, Mr. Smith. Already, because of this, ve haff one production tied up. Ve cannot afford to shut down the studio."

"I understand. Those people out there—you would have to pay them, having engaged them, whether they worked to-day or not? Those professional entertainers?"

"Sure, sure! But that iss a comparatively small item. It iss my big people, my principals—"

"Yes, yes," agreed Smith absently. He was watching a carnival that had popped up before his eyes like a mushroom is said to pop out of the earth. Tents, umbrellas, banners flying, music playing, balloons soaring, and high above the crowd, swinging in a silver seat that flashed in the sun, an acrobat, waiting to catch a little figure in spangled tights thrown like a kite over the heads of the people. He could not believe that it was all only "make-believe".

Rosenthal continued: "Maybe Mr. Bonet does not shoot that scene for two hours. He vill spend all that time getting the people vorked up to the desired pitch."

"Looks to me like they were there right now. Look at those kids, begging for sweets, and those people playing those queer, lively games."

"Those are the extra people. They are not so hard to get vorked up. They respond to such things. They lift their parts. I haff a liking for the extra people. They are sincere. It iss the stars I vas speaking of. They often get, vat you call? . . . blasé. They vant to kid all the time! They are so sure of themselves, you see. They know they can snap into the action as soon as the camera starts." He put his fat, jeweled hand on Smith's arm. "Come, ve vill talk as ve go along. But I vould like to impress upon you that these people must not—they *must* not—get a hint that there iss a murderer loose on this lot and a dead man on that stage. I vant you should speak to your men about not saying a vord—"

Smith stopped in his tracks and turned to look into the President's eyes.

"That's three times you have made that statement," he ruminated thoughtfully.

"Vat statement?"

"That the murderer is loose on this lot. Rosenthal, are you keeping something from me?"

The President turned wondering eyes upon him.

"Vy, no. Certainly I haff not been keeping somedings from you. I haff told you all I know, about efferything! Myself, I do not know why I say that. It iss a . . . feeling."

"Uhuh!" Smith nodded, understandingly. "Intuition is another name for it. You have said that three times without conscious knowledge of meaning it. I've had the same feeling myself. And what's more, I know of more than one murder mystery that has been solved by following that little 'feeling', intuition."

"You mean—just by guessing?"

"Not consciously guessing, no, but by acting upon some thought that keeps thrusting itself into a person's brain, or speech, involuntarily. Just as you have demonstrated. You did not realize you were saying that, did you? No. I thought not. You could not have worked out such a theory?"

"I haff not tried to vork it out at all. That iss your job. Anyvays, I haff been so vorried over it, I haff just—vell, just vorried I guess," he finished naively. "Mine Gott, I tell you, Mr. Smith, I haff neffer felt so terrible offer anything in my life! To see that man lying there! I tell you it vas terrible! I tell you I vas afraid for my life for a long

time aftervords, and that iss the truth. Me, in my own studio, I should be afraid like a little boy in the dark!"

"I understand that, too," replied Smith seriously, not
displaying or feeling any derision of the other's professed
cowardice. "Instinctively we all fear death. That is why
one of the big tests of a suspect's innocence is bringing
him into contact with his supposed victim, or something
the victim has worn. It brings the idea of death to him.
He is afraid of that other dead human, because it reminds
him that he, also, must die. He shrinks from the thought,
and subsequently he shrinks physically from the contact."
He took out his watch and glanced at it. "Ten-thirty. I
presume the Coroner has completed his examination, and
Detective Clancy will be more likely to have the case all
solved by this time! In my note I asked Mr. Seibert to
meet us on the set at 11 o'clock. I would appreciate it if
you will conduct me on a little tour about the grounds in
the meantime. I want to ask questions, and I expect you'd
rather answer them yourself, under the circumstances."

"Mine Gott, yes," Rosenthal replied quickly.

On their way they walked through the crowd of holiday
makers.

"Bonet iss already shooting. Don't look at the cameras.
They are on the left. Ve vill valk along like ve vas just
sight-seeing vid the rest. Not too fast. Nothing iss chasing
us, you know."

Involuntarily Smith had quickened his pace. An instant
and new respect for the screen actor was born in his
bosom. He wanted to do a dozen things he would not
have thought about ordinarily. He wanted, desperately, to
scratch the back of his leg. He wanted to turn and stare
directly where he had been cautioned not to stare—into
the cameras. It seemed as though their clicking buzz was
drawing him to them like a magnet. He grinned stiffly and

self-consciously when Rosenthal made some comment, and halted him for a moment beside a side-show. Once halted his feet rooted and it was difficult to start up his limbs to go on. They seemed temporarily paralyzed. In other words, Captain of Detectives Smith, famous man-hunter, was having a bad case of stage-fright.

"Whew! That was running the gauntlet, all right!" he whistled. "Great stuff, the President of Superior Films, and the Captain of Detectives acting as extras! Hereafter I take off my hat to 'em!"

"I thought you vould get a kick out of it," chuckled the President slyly. "But don't get all excited. Mebbe you don't get on the screen after all. They vill probably not print the first shot," and Smith was surprised to find himself as disappointed as a small boy over this news.

"Well, to business," he said. "First, I want to go outside and walk in through the gate."

Once outside, his keen grey eyes took on the trained hunter's look. He glanced quickly at the concrete walls that were the dividing line between the boulevard and the studio grounds.

"The wall of China had nothing on you," he commented. "Of course it doesn't enclose the entire fifty acres of your property?"

"Vell, hardly," replied Rosenthal, smiling. "Ve haff a high wire fence, charged vid electricity, around all sides but the front. Now that iss not only a vall, or a fence, I mean. Ve haff all our dressing rooms, executive offices, and so forth, in buildings along the front. The vall iss only the backs of the buildings. Ve haff no vindows on this side, only, as you see, those places for ventilation. Ve haff perfect protection here. You vould be surprised, Mr. Smith, how crazy people are to get into a studio! They vould do anything!"

Captain Smith nodded. "I expect so. You have no arc light at your entrance," he said sharply. "Why is that?"

"As you see, ve are right opposite an inter-section, vich iss highly lighted. Ve haff lights immediately inside the gate, and ve haff never thought it necessary to put an entrance light outside."

"Hm! That makes it interesting," Smith murmured thoughtfully.

As they returned, the gateman stepped into his little office and marked them in.

"So you even keep tabs on yourself, Rosenthal?" said Smith, noticing this.

"Oh, yes! Efferbody iss marked in and out. Vid myself, you see, it assists in locating me in case I am vanted."

Inside there was a main drive leading to the back of the grounds where it curved around and skirted the big stages. On each side of this drive, set in from the build-ings along the front, were other buildings, each surround-ed by a space of green lawn and shrubs.

"Are those all stages?"

"No. On the left, here, iss the executive building, vich you vere in. Back of that iss the offices of the Production Department. The next vone iss the men's vardrobe, and the second to that the vomen's. Then iss the hospital. You can see the Red Cross offer the door. Then comes the store. Ve haff everything— hardvare, furniture, paint, silk, vall paper—efferything in there to be used in making pictures. Then, that long building back of that iss the lumber house and yards, then the garages—"

"Help! Is there any end?" laughed Smith.

"Vell, ve are a big concern. Now, coming offer across the back of the front lot, iss the plaster vorkers factory. Ve make most of our cement and plaster "props"—fountains, statues, fireplaces, you understand? Ve also copy the old

masters. Ve haff an artist, a German, in that place. I tell
you he iss a second Michael Angelo! Then come the offices
off the publicity writers, the readers, the art department,
vere our set designers vork, and further along, the property rooms. Ve haff efferything in those property rooms.
In our carpenter shop, vich I forgot to mention, ve make
anything! Ve make most off our antiques."

"So do the dealers in antiques," Smith replied.

"Now, this building to the right of us iss the commissary and restaurant, and offer there another building for
'props'. I tell you ve can furnish anything at a moment's
notice, Mr. Smith. Ve can turn a beggar maid into a
princess, and ve can turn a hovel into a palace! Ve haff
efferything, efferything, right here in this studio to do
anything vid! Ve can dress a set, or a whole building, in
any period you vant, sixteenth century or tventieth, vidout varning." There was loving pride in the President's
tone. Smith was genuinely impressed.

"A city within a city!" he exclaimed.

"Sure, sure! Whole countries vidin a city, ve haff here!"
Then he added, regretfully, "And now . . . ve haff got a
murder, too."

"And right here's where we start checking up on that,"
returned Smith quickly. He turned directly to the right,
along the walk leading to the dressing rooms. A narrow
porch ran the full length of them, both downstairs and
above. Leading to the upper floor were four flights of
stairs, at intervals. As Smith gazed upward, a girl, apparently undressed except for a wisp of chiffon gauze about
her, emerged from one of the rooms.

"Vone of the dancers for the carnival," said Rosenthal.

Another door opened and a second girl came out, wind-
ing a scarf around her as she came and calling to the matron to bring some whitening for her back. The dressing

rooms were over-crowded to-day, and they spilled their lovely overflow on the narrow verandah. A moment later Smith was treated to the unusual sight (for him) of a girl having her legs and back covered with white cream. As he gazed at the matron's swift, practiced hands, she gave the slim young thing an extra rub and a pat with a great powder puff she carried, and started her toward the stairs.

"Run now. You were called five minutes ago."

The girl, a flutter of pink and white flesh and sheer gauze, came lightly down the steps, under Smith's very nose, without so much as a glance at him, and off toward the carnival. The detective, after a brief lowering of his eyes to follow her course, turned them upwards again, to fill them with a bewildering vision of floating draperies, feminine curves, rosy bodies, carmined lips, great black-accentuated eyes, and beautiful legs! Rosenthal gave him a sly dig in the ribs.

"Ve don't allow men on the second floor. Also ve don't like to haff them stand out here and stare at our girls. Business iss business, and playing iss playing. Those girls are only thinking of their vork now."

"And how do you know I wasn't thinking of mine?" returned Smith, grinning. Then, soberly, "There's an idea, back in my mind somewhere, that a woman could walk along that narrow porch up there, to the end nearest Stage Six, drop down that last flight of stairs, and over to the Stage, and the night gateman, if he stayed at his post, would not be able to see her. However, I will check up on who was here last night when I talk to the gateman. No hurry." He did not say it, but just now he had a more important theory to explode—or prove!

"Vy make it the upper floor," chuckled Rosenthal, still slyly teasing him for his ill-concealed admiration of the feminine galaxy. "Vy don't you figure how a man could go along the lower veranda and do the same thing . . . eh?"

"Because I'm pretty sure that if anyone did do such a thing last night . . . it was a woman!"

"But I don't see how—"

"Sometimes I am not able to explain how myself, Rosenthal, but the idea occurs."

"So? A voman! Vell, I expect that vould be the vay of it, vid a man like Hardell. Still . . . a voman . . . vone of my girls. . . I don't like it."

Smith appreciated the innate gallantry of the President, who had shoved his fat hands into his pockets, and with lips puffed out, was staring off into the distance with a rueful expression. Finishing his observation, Smith took the other's arm and turned him off toward Stage Six. Once there he did not go in, but stopped at the door.

"Large doors for furniture, and wieldy objects; little door let in the middle for pedestrians," Smith said to Rosenthal. "Are they kept locked at night?"

"Ve seldom lock doors on the stages. Ve keep our grounds so closely vatched that there iss small danger off people getting on to the stages. A day and night vatchman both make the rounds. Shall ve go in?"

"Not yet. I want to wait for Seibert. Ah! that must be him now."

Smith's eyes narrowed as he watched the approach of the coming director. Seibert had gone back to his habitual insolence of manner. Eyes cold and looking straight ahead, cane swinging smartly with each step, there was something ruthless, even cruel, in his manner. The detective got the impression, as Seibert strode through the merrymakers, that human beings meant nothing to this man. He found himself wondering what the man would do if one got in his way or halted his progress. But no one did. One and all they were careful to keep clear of him, and the detective did not lose this small, but significant item.

And yet, when Seibert reached them, he bowed courteously with a punctiliousness far from displeasing, and again Smith found himself involuntarily aping his manner.

"Ah, I have kept you waiting. I apologize," said the director.

"Not at all. It is most generous of you to come," replied the detective.

They turned to enter. "Funny . . . why so many doors?" Smith said. Rosenthal shot him a surprised look, but kept his lips closed.

Seibert explained, most thoroughly and graciously.

As they opened the door a cool air rushed out. Going from the sunshine and laughter of the crowd outside, into the vast roofed space in semi-darkness even in mid-morning, Smith was conscious of an atmosphere of mystery and expectation. He did not know that it is always that way on motion picture stages. So many strange things are done there. So many strange things are yet to be done. Each entrance brings its own new acts in the countless dramas of life that are played on its boards. Even the studio familiar feels his curiosity and imagination stimulated as he steps through the door of a motion picture stage.

Seibert stepped back to allow Smith to enter.

"Looks black as the hinges to me in there, and I don't know the way," Smith said and motioned the director ahead. Bowing slightly, the other man acquiesced.

Hardly had they entered when the detective stumbled. Seibert instantly expressed his regret.

"Watch out for cables, switch boxes, and beams," he cautioned. "Sometimes construction on a set makes it necessary to bend double. I will go ahead and keep you posted."

"Do all the members of your company have to come in this tortuous way?" Smith inquired.

"Sometimes, if a set is put in the middle of the stage, and there are other sets being 'struck', or erected about it. However, we took the longest way in. My set can be reached easily from the side entrance."

They skirted the walls of a log cabin, walked stooping through a pirate's cave, skidded across the polished floor of a small cafe set, and came to a stop before the last canvas fence. Through cracks, Smith caught the gleam of a ghostly, bluish light. Again Seibert motioned him to enter first, and again he stepped back. When the director opened the canvas gate and stepped into the set, the detective was watching him keenly through lowered lids. Inside, the source of the peculiar light was seen—a bank of Cooper-Hewitts, swinging from the rafters, were throwing over all a sickly, greenish-blue glare. The dead face of Hardell, upturned on the floor, was ghastly, horrible, beneath it. Smith stopped in his tracks.

"That man's mortified!" he exclaimed in horror.

7

And indeed the flesh of the dead man's countenance appeared putrid. But Seibert's face showed no surprise. He replied indifferently:

"A mistake often made by outsiders. We all look the same way, including yourself. It is the lights."

Smith did not raise his eyes from their fixed stare at the murdered man. "Are you sure?" he asked. "Kindly come here and examine this body."

But Seibert did not move. "Certainly I am sure," he returned crisply, and at that the detective's eyes shot upward and transferred their probing look to the director's face. Seibert was not looking, as bidden, down at the murdered man. Instead he had fallen into one of his familiar attitudes—eyes straight ahead, face stony, throwing out an aura of haughty insolence.

"I wish you would examine that rapier, Seibert," Smith said. "Is it the one you used when rehearsing the death scene?" Again his eyes riveted sharply upon the other. There was a palpitant second, and then Seibert stepped forward, bent down towards the body and made to take the rapier in his hand.

"Don't touch it," said Smith sharply.

"Pardon. I was forgetting. You will want prints. However, I can say decisively that this is one of the pair of dueling rapiers we have been using in the picture."

They were interrupted by Detective Sergeant Clancy, who now stepped out from where he had been looking at the camera, trained exactly over the dead man. Clancy was a typical flat-foot who had been elevated from the pavements because of a lucky capture of a murderer, a strong political pull, and a long period of dog-like devotion to his uniform. What he failed in mentality he made up in energy. Brute force, and a dogged driving along one line of thought, usually the obvious, was his dominant trait. Compared to Captain Smith he was as a broadsword to a rapier; as a bulldog to a wolf-hound.

"Lord, chief, you'd think this was Washington Boulevard! Look at the tracks, bloody tracks, all over! And finger prints! The darn place's swarming with clues!"

"Have you photographed everything?" Smith asked tersely.

"Sure."

Smith turned to Seibert and Rosenthal. "I shall ask you gentlemen to excuse me for a while. I want to study the set, and the body, and discuss the case with the Coroner."

"Ve understand, ve understand. Ven you are through perhaps you come to have lunch vid me?" said Rosenthal.

"Thank you. If it works out that way. I must sacrifice pleasure for work just now," Smith answered. He liked the President, and his voice showed it.

As Smith watched Seibert's quick, though courteous bow to him, before he left, he realized that if he had thought to ruffle this man's equilibrium by playing the dumb bell and straining his short patience, he had not succeeded. He dismissed the director immediately from his mind, as he turned and saw the Coroner coming towards him from where he had been sitting in a corner of the set.

"Well, he's had his last close-up," said the little Doctor, gesturing down at the murdered man.

"Yes. Is it murder, Doc?"

"No doubt of it. And instant death. The weapon pierced the right ventricle, splitting it open."

"Hm. Did he move afterwards?"

"Little, if any." He hesitated, and then added, "Only to fall, of course, in case he was standing, but—"

"How long has he been dead?"

"I cannot give you the exact time, but undoubtedly for hours."

"My evidence puts him alive, in Hollywood, at 12.40 this morning. To return to this studio, from the point given, would take at least 20 minutes. Allowing him time to get on to the set and go through what preliminaries naturally must have taken place before he was murdered would take . . . well, I do not believe, take it all together, the man could have been killed earlier than 1:30 a.m."

"It is my opinion he has been dead for ten hours. Possibly twelve," the Coroner replied.

"Could you state the time to within an hour?"

"I might, on further examination. However, from a cursory one, I should say that putting the time at 1:30 is too late. I do not care to state so definitely without a more thorough examination."

Smith stood looking down at the corpse thoughtfully. Finally he said:

"Dr. Newcomb, you know that in murder cases time is one of the main clues. In this case it is particularly important. It may be the sole proof of the guilt or innocence of the party, or parties involved. I am going to ask you to call in a consultation of physicians to verify your opinion. Wait a minute, please. Don't be offended. I know that you and I have worked together many times, and I have always found your judgment right. But in this case—in this case

I am up against the most baffling combination of circumstances I have ever been faced with. I've simply got to get this question of the time settled as accurately as possible."

"Putting it that way, all right. I'll have in three other men when I get the body to the morgue."

"Thanks," said Smith briefly. He bent to look closely at the narrow blade clutched in one of the dead man's hands.

"There's its companion, the death instrument," said the Coroner, pointing to a dueling rapier, a slender, wicked length of shining steel that lay on the floor by the murdered man's side. The blood on it had dried, as had also the thin stream which had oozed from the dead man. Smith's eyes did not linger on the weapon. Its part in the grim drama was only too apparent. The detective gave an exclamation of surprise, however, at a line of footprints which was plainly discernible, and led directly from the body to one of the two canvas-backed chairs standing by the camera platform.

"And that's not all," put in the Coroner, watching him. "Those footprints start on the other side. Look." He pointed to the left side of the body. "Whoever made them stepped into the blood where it first reached the floor, flowing from the heart, and then *stepped over the body* and went on, towards the chair."

"Hm! That does make it interesting," Smith said softly, and bending down he examined the marks.

"Man's shoe. Bull-dog grip, rubber heels," he said as he started walking carefully in their path. "The blood that adhered, when he stepped in the flow, was heavy enough to mark him to—this chair," he finished, laying his hand on the one of the two marked, "Assistant Director." He turned quickly to the little doctor.

"How long would it have taken for the blood to flow out of so small a wound—enough blood to make those tracks?"

"That's a question with two answers, Captain," replied the Coroner. "Whoever made those prints could have stepped in blood a short time after the man was killed, *but* it seems to me it would have dried considerably, become considerably thickened and sticky, to adhere in sufficient quantity to make all those tracks."

"Looks that way to me. Shall we say . . . fifteen or twenty minutes?"

"That's as good an answer as any. Look, the man was conscious of blood on his foot, for it is very apparent that he tried to scuff it off."

"You're right!" The two men straightened and looked questioningly at each other. The little Coroner was the first to speak.

"And he didn't care whether he left those tracks or not! Never tried to remove them, evidently. My God, the thing looks as savage as a lion's kill!"

"It looks just that," agreed Smith slowly, his eyes busy on the set. "But all isn't evidence that's evident, Doc. I'm going to look for something not quite so—er—*planted!*"

He went softly about the set. Once he bent with a satisfied exclamation to a section of the canvas wall. After a moment's scrutiny he went on, stopping now here, now there, at various objects and places within the space enclosed. After a few moments he went back to the body.

"How was he killed? I mean, explain the blow to me, if you can."

"The rapier, undoubtedly, and thrust with nice precision between the ribs directly over the heart," said the Coroner, whose tone bespoke that he had been eagerly waiting to make this explanation, and to add some strange opinion of his own.

"The blow," he continued, "was driven with sufficient force to pierce the heart and penetrate the muscles of the back, but not to pass clear through the body. Now, the cut is straight—not on an angle. Whoever made the thrust must have been standing directly in front, and in full view of the murdered man, or—or *over* him!" he finished dramatically.

"Over him? You mean he was down on the floor?"

"Captain, if I were to tell you what I thought, you'd say I am crazy. It looks to me like that man was in the exact attitude in which we see him now, *before* he was killed! I do not believe his features would have had time to set in that exaggerated grimace of horror—more marked than the expression Nature puts on a man when he dies in this way—*after* he was struck. It looks to me very much like he was lying here, in this position, waiting for the blow."

"And yet I sense a surprise," Smith said. "Ah, I have it! He knew that death was inescapable, because of something he had done. He saw it coming, and yet, the horror of it could not fail to startle him. And the expression . . . was the revelation of a guilty conscience! There is fear there. Fear—probably because of sins committed in the past— and fear of something, as you say, that he saw was coming and could not evade. Evidently he knew it was no use to try, for the rapier in his hand is not blood-stained."

"He didn't have a chance to use it. The position of the hand—the grip—shows that."

"Could a woman have made that wound?" Smith asked.

"Certainly. Any normal woman, or any frail woman, under emotional excitement, could have supplied the explosive nerve force necessary to drive her muscles."

"I thought so," said Smith. Then he knelt by the dead man's side and a low chuckle escaped him. "Doc, we're on the wrong track. He wasn't on the floor waiting for that thrust. He fell to the floor afterwards."

"What tells you that?" asked the little Coroner argumentatively.

"If I hadn't had my mind on so many other angles at once, I'd have told you that, first glance. Why . . . this . . . and this." He pointed to the wig which the dead man wore, and which was pushed slightly awry, as though shoved up from the back, and at two faint, sliding marks in the dust on the floor where, in falling, Hardell had skidded an inch or so on his heels.

"Well, that explodes that theory," said the little Coroner ruefully. It was evident that he did not like giving up the strangest angle on one of the strangest cases in his experience. After a moment he said:

"It's my first experience with a murdered motion picture actor. Maybe he automatically assumed that frightful expression when he saw the blow coming—force of habit, as it were. Ordinary people aren't so handy with their faces."

"There's more in that than mere humorous supposition, Doc," returned Smith quickly. "How do we know but the man took this way to tell the world he was foully done in? Made use of his profession to the end?"

But their surmises in this questionable direction were interrupted just then by the entrance of Clancy, who was breathing heavily, and evidently, triumphantly.

"Nothing to it, Chief!" he said exultantly. "What d'you think? I walked right off this stage and smack into a guy lifting this off the dead man's bureau! I was going over there to take a look around, like you told me, and I caught him at it. You've got the whole dope right there in writing." He handed his superior a piece of paper, which had been folded and torn across. The heading and the signature were gone, but the text remained. It read:

I have decided I am the fool to come out here to meet you, just for those letters. I am here, yes, but those letters, they are mine! I shall have

*them! 1 shall end everything between us to-
night.*

Smith's mind leaped back to the conversation in Rosen-
thal's room, and the French girl Seibert had mentioned.
"Here's where Yvonne Beaumont comes in, Rosenthal or no
Rosenthal to the contrary," he told himself. To Clancy he said:

"Find Miss Beaumont's room. She'll probably have a
box of this paper there. If not, at her home. It's expensive
paper, and most likely monogrammed. Anyway, wherever
it is, get it. I want to match it up. Also, get all the details
as to her actions last night. And, on your way out, tell
those guards I want to be alone. Don't come back here and
disturb me, you or Ryan, no matter what else turns up.
Understand?"

The little Coroner and Clancy gone, Smith gave his
whole attention to examining every portion of the set, and
every possible inanimate hint leading to a clue. He had
been at this for about five minutes when Clancy thrust his
red face through the little door.

"Say, Chief!"

Smith turned a stern face in his direction. He did not
answer, and his grey eyes began to flicker ominously.

"Wait a minute," Clancy said. "You fired me off so
quick I didn't get a chance to finish. That guy I took the
paper from is Billy West. He's Assistant Director to Seibert, and the dame's his sweetie! She came out here last
night, and he followed her out."

"Clancy, did you know that five minutes ago, or did
you just find it out?" questioned his superior severely.

"Well—ah, now chief, what's the diff? I knew part of
it, anyway. I told you there's nothin' to it! I matched up
that stationery first thing. Got a stack of it in her desk up
in her room. I found out this dame's been playing around
with this guy Hardell, the first thing I came on the lot. It's

common gossip, and so's the fact that West's crazy about her! After I got the paper identified I slipped down to the gateman, and he let me take a peep at the time sheets when I showed him my badge."

"Clancy! I told you to keep under cover. If a word of this leaks out—"

"Say, ain't they goin' to know it when they take the stiff off this stage? Anyway, the gateman's wise to keep his mouth shut. I didn't tell him what it was all about. What I'm trying to get over is that this Beaumont woman and West were both on this lot last night around the time the little Doc says Hardell was murdered. I tell you 'sall over, Chief! All we got to do is third degree them birds."

"So ''sall over', eh, Clancy?" returned Smith, with a twinkle chasing the displeasure from his eyes. "Well, I grant you this much. It looks . . . that way, anyway."

"Sure. The dame did it, and all you've got to do is tell her her sweetie's going to hang for it, and she'll come through with the goods!"

"All right, boy. We may try out your theory, anyway. Did you arrange to have last night's gateman and watchman over here for me right after lunch?"

"Ah, shucks, boss! I got so excited over bumping into this guy, I forgot it. Anyway, you don't need to hurry about those fellows. We've got the straight dope. It's a cinch either this French dame, or her sweetie, did the dirty deed."

Immediately Smith's expression changed. From a halfsmile of tolerance, it became a thin-lipped scrutiny of questioning annoyance. Under it Clancy's generous bulk diminished perceptibly.

"I'll 'tend to it right away, sure, chief," he said hurriedly, and turned to beat a shamed retreat.

"Clancy!" called the Captain of Detectives with soft sharpness.

"Yes, chief."

"Somebody mistook Hardell for a dummy, and kicked him! Watch out I don't make the same mistake about you!"

8

"Well, did you find out anything?"

The President of Superior Films leaned forward eagerly as the Captain of Detectives lounged into his private office. Smith laughed, and thought the fat Jewish gentleman looked very much like an impatient small boy.

"This isn't a motion picture, you know, and you can't get the whole story at one sitting," he answered good-naturedly. Rosenthal threw out his hands apologetically.

"Sure, sure. I must remember that," he admitted. "But surely you haff found out something?"

"Quite a lot. Too much, in fact," remarked the other dryly. He went over to Rosenthal's desk and chose a cigar.

"Mighty good cigars. They help a fellow to think," he murmured, lighting it. Rosenthal instantly reached into his desk and took out an unopened box, which he pushed toward the detective. Smith laughed.

"Just a gentle hint, eh? Well, don't you fear, Rosenthal. I'm going to do more thinking on this case than I've ever had to do before. I can tell you that much right now!"

Rosenthal's brown liquid eyes sparkled. "Vell, I really did not mean it that vay. Howeffer, I just got my last order and I haff plenty. So don't let yourself be vidout a stimulant to your brain at any time." He took up one of the rare weeds and lit it. "Perhaps ve should think together," he

89

smiled. For a few moments there was silence. Smith leaned
back in his chair. It was a good chair. A better chair than
he had in his living room at home. His feet rested in the
soothing softness of the silken pile of genuine Chinese
rugs. He looked at the silk velvet that hung in rich folds
to the floor, at the windows, and at the various *objets
d'art* that decorated the room. A little gaudy, but beautiful
withal, this business man's office!

"No wonder everybody goes crazy over pictures," Smith
said. "It's getting me—and I'm not easily swept off my
feet."

Rosenthal shrugged his shoulders. "Ve haff our troubles, too. Look at me now! Not a night shall I rest until ve
get this thing cleared up! Vat iss going to happen ven it iss
known? I vill tell you! The public vill jump on me, on pictures, on actors, vid vone grand leap! Ve vill be accused of
efferything . . . all kinds of vickedness! A murder happens
in any other business, and the only thing that the public
vonders iss—vell, how did it happen? A murder happens in
a picture studio, and just like that, ve are all sinners! All
mixed up in it . . . the whole picture business! Ve are like
vone big family. If vone of us gets murdered, efferybody in
the business comes into it!"

"A murder can happen anywhere. Even in a church. But
I see your angle, and it's true to a great extent. We'll hope
to keep this as quiet as we can. I'd like to use your office
this afternoon to question those men."

"Sure. Maybe you vant I should go out?"

"No. I want you should stay right here," returned Smith,
smiling. "You know your people better than I do. You can
help me get at the truth . . . spot an evasion quicker than
I might, perhaps."

"Sure. I understand. That iss right!" agreed Rosenthal,
and he pushed a button on his desk. When his secretary
came in he said, "I shall be in conference all afternoon.

I do not vant anybody—not anybody—to interrupt me. Only the people I tell you to let in."

"Mr. Cohen has been waiting to see you," she said.

Rosenthal made a grimace. He did not want to see his Production Manager just then. However, it was not best to injure Izzie's pride too deeply.

"All right, all right," he agreed after a moment.

Cohen made one of his jibbering entrances. Naturally nervous, in fact, afflicted with a disorder that caused him to jerk and twist the muscles of his face spasmodically on occasions of undue excitement, the poor fellow was now in an almost pathetic state. Rosenthal gave him one look, then said:

"Izzie, you should to go home."

"Go home! I should to go home! Vell, you should to go out and see vat iss going on at Stage Six! Then perhaps ve all should to go home, and stay there!"

"Vat iss the matter?" asked the President sharply.

"Vat iss the matter? Mine Gott, everything iss the matter! Right avay somebody finds out there iss guards on that set, efferybody comes to stand around and look! Those extras Bonet used this morning, they are thick as flies!"

"Iss Bonet through with them?"

"Sure. He got his stuff right avay. He vants to get through."

"All right. You go right avay and order those people off the lot! Vy do you come to me about it?"

"Mine Gott, ain't I got a right to come here to you? Ain't I got a right to talk about this thing at all, Abie?"

"Sure, sure, but—" for once Rosenthal realized resentfully how much of Cohen's work he had always done. He sighed. "Vat else iss wrong, Izzie?"

"Only this. They got to get that fellow off that set, ain't they? Vat you going to do? Put a makeup on the dead wagon? Haff you thought of that, Abie?"

Rosenthal turned to Smith. "Vell, that iss right. Just so soon they start carrying Hardell's body off, efferbody comes to look! I can do a lot vid my people, but they are not like prisoners! Sometimes they got a right to make a move by themselves!"

"Won't they think it's just some ordinary stage business? Might be moving out anything, you know," said Smith.

"Maybe they think that yesterday, but not to-day! Not after vone person gets thrown off that stage by those guards!" Cohen said convincingly. For a moment the three men sat silent. Then the Production Manager had a thought.

"Say, Abie, vy don't ve camouflage him? Roll him in a carpet, like they did vid Cleopatra in that Roman scene last veek! Then ve take him out, and put him in the 'prop' delivery vagon and nobody iss the viser."

"Mine Gott, Izzie, you and Seibert make me sick to my stomach! You ain't got no feelings, no feelings at all!" exclaimed the President, his voice rising vehemently towards a yell, as it usually did when talking with Cohen. Smith repressed a chuckle and settled himself to enjoy the scene.

"Vell, maybe you got more brains as vell as more feelings. You figure it out yourself!" sulked Cohen.

"Ve could leaff him on that set until to-night, ven efferbody iss off the lot," mused the President thoughtfully, but shook his head in the midst of his planning. "No. Ve cannot do that. Ve cannot be disrespectful to the dead. That iss not right. Izzie, ve got to stand it. Ve got to let them take him avay the usual vay." He turned to Smith. "You haff made all your investigations? You haff finished vid the body? You and the Coroner? All right. Now Izzie, you tell me that Bonet iss all finished? All right. How many people ve got vorking yet?"

"Ve got Von Richten on Stage Three. He has three peo-ple only this afternoon. They vas vaiting for lights ven I vas out there just now. Then ve got that vestern stuff in the back lot. Ve got two out on location, so they don't count. Vell, I tell you Abie, ve ain't got so many. Bonet vas the only big set to-day, and he's through."

"All right. Now I tell you vat you do. You send a boy to effery stage and set. I send a message to them all." He rang for his stenographer, and when she had come in, he said, "I vant you to make a dozen copies of this, and give them to Mr. Cohen. Are you ready? All right. I vant you should say this: To Members of This Studio: Because of the unfor-tunate death of Mr. Dwight Hardell on this lot to-day—" he broke off to look at Smith. "Ve don't know just ven it happened, so it's all right I say to-day?"

"Surely. Nothing is established exactly."

"All right, go on to-day, there vill be no more further production. Efferbody iss hereby dismissed until to-mor-row. Sign my name to that, and get it right out."

And when Cohen had gone out with the secretary, Rosenthal again turned to the detective.

"I tell you, Mr. Smith, I vill feel a lot better ven that poor fellow iss buried. He vas a rotter, sure, but he vas punished. He vas punished! I tell you, Gott attends to those things, Mr. Smith."

"I think that, too," answered the other quietly. Then, after a moment: "Perhaps you would like to know some of the things I discovered?"

"Sure."

"To begin with, there were four people on that set, the scene of the murder, last night."

For a moment the President sat looking back unblink-ingly into the detective's grey eyes. Then he said, thought-fully:

"Four people you say? Vell, there vould be Seibert, and Hardell, and maybe Billy Vest, but I do not think so. Seibert sometimes vorks absolutely alone. Vell, then there vould be Seibert and Hardell. That iss two. You mean two more besides them, then?"

"I mean four besides Hardell, the murdered man."

"You mean four people vere mixed up in that murder? You mean you got four suspects?"

"That's more like it, when I identify the fourth, who at this point is just 'another woman'," returned Smith.

"Another voman! You haff then vone voman already?"

"Proof positive that Miss Beaumont came out here last night to see Hardell, and evidence tending to show that she—"

He was interrupted by Rosenthal's low moan of protest.

"I could not to belieff it! You do not know her! No, there iss something the matter vid your evidence!" he stuttered. "And already ve are going to star her! Already ve haff bought a story, just for her, and Bonet iss to direct it! Ve haff the news stories in all the papers, last veek, and in all the fan magazines. Ve haff our releases all set. I tell you, Mr. Smith, this iss terrible! I do not belieff it!"

"Sergeant Clancy has the case all cut and dried," said Smith, grinning reminiscently. "To his mind Miss Beaumont is the guilty person. But so far she is really just a possibility." Then he told Rosenthal of the note taken from Billy West, and written by Yvonne.

"Vell, and because she writes a silly letter, you make of her a murderess! That man Clancy iss a dumb-bell . . . a fool!" exclaimed Rosenthal angrily.

"Ah, but there were finger prints on the set—a woman's fingers marked in blood on the canvas door—and plenty of other finger marks. When these are matched up with the ones on the letter, I am afraid . . . but, we will go to

the third party, a man who wore rubber-soled shoes, bull-
dog grip. Does your night watchman wear such shoes?"

Rosenthal held out his fat hands protestingly. "Mr.
Smith, how should I know vat my night vatchman vears?
I do not look at the feet of my people. It iss their faces I
should look at!"

"Forget the question. I was only thinking of identifying the man. But, such shoes were most certainly on that
set!" He described the trail left by them, adding, "If the
wearer of these shoes is the murderer, we know that he was
on the set for several minutes after he killed Hardell; or,
he left, and returned a few minutes later. If this is the man
I think, and if the evidence of the gateman shows him to
have been here in the studio at that time, he will have to
have a mighty good alibi. Now, as to the fourth person.
We will call her the 'unknown woman'. I say fourth, but
this person may turn out to be the same as the writer of
the note—Miss Beaumont. Our unknown woman was also
on the set at the time of the murder. She either committed
it, or witnessed it. How do I know? I shall have to keep
some of these tale-telling clues to myself, but you shall
know them all in time. She was frightened and forced to
hide, at one time. Later she must have gone to the body of
Hardell and, in an attempt to find if he were dead or not,
leaned down and touched him. She got blood on her hand,
which evidently terrified her, for she fled the set. I know
that she was terrified, and that she fled, because she left
her finger marks, in blood, on the canvas door. A person
in a normal state of mind would not have done that. If the
finger prints on the door, and the ones on the letter paper
are identical, you see what we have? Miss Beaumont. Also,
other things carry out the theory. She was angry at him.
Perhaps afraid of him. In any case, she was furious because
he persisted in his attentions. A furious woman sometimes

acts—and thinks afterwards. That the murder was unpre-
meditated, if committed by this woman, is probable . . .
most likely. She killed him, and then became horrified
and hysterical. In short, she rushed away. Now, as I said,
we have four suspects; Seibert, who was undoubtedly the
last man to be with Hardell the night he was murdered;
the wearer of the rubber-soled shoes, who has left his
blood-stained evidence for all to see; Miss Beaumont, who
wrote Hardell that 'to-night' she would end all between
them! Rather a significant remark, don't you agree? And
then, this fourth party—a woman, from the small finger
prints—who dipped her hand in Hardell's life blood!"

Abraham Rosenthal sat in stunned silence. Accustomed
to visualizing a scene presented to him, trained by his profession to put life and movement into mere names of persons, he was now looking at this dim set, through which
dark and sinister figures flitted, and in which a man had
been stabbed to death. It was all frightfully real to him.

"Gott of Abraham!" he finally groaned. "Iss it that all
my people are murderers?"

"Yes, all men are murderers, Mr. Rosenthal," said Smith
soberly. "There is a time in every human's life when the
veneer of custom is thrown aside, at least in the mind,
and in such times the taking of another human's life becomes a probability—at least in thought. I believe that
a great many people have felt an irresistible impulse towards murder. To some it may come through a desire to
strangle, with the hands. To some it may be an over-pow-
ering impulse to pull the trigger. I fully believe that some
men who have become murderers have only yielded to this
momentary impulse—and then the thing is done! They
may never have had another such impulse in their lives.
Might never again. And yet, for the brief lack of that control—"

The President of Superior Films groaned audibly. "No, no! That I do not think. I, myself, haff never felt like murdering anybody."

"Think carefully. Back in those difficult days when you were climbing up from the gutter—oh yes, I know your history—when life seemed a hard and bitter struggle, when other humans with money and power seemed cold and selfish beasts—"

"Vell, mebbe a couple of times they vas low-lifers I vished vould die," admitted Rosenthal naively.

Smith smiled. "And if you had had those 'low-lifers' at your mercy, at a time when you resented their power, their existence, most . . . what then? My theory is not improbable. Men and women, as they exist to-day, are but the sum total of the genesis of their ancestors, plus the variations and inhibitions which civilization has instilled in them. Take away the inhibitions. Man killed in the beginning, and the only code he had was whether it was right or wrong to himself. To-day we are living under mass determinations of right and wrong, which have laid down a code barring killings, except as a safeguard for the masses. Yet, to-day as in the leopard skin days, man thinks, and acts, individually. Instinctively, he is a killer. He may go through life without being aware of it. He may not. He may be aware of it, and draw away in horror from the idea. That is because of his culture, up through the ages. I have studied human nature, especially that human nature which has yielded to the killing impulse, and I am convinced that all humanity contains in itself the impulse to take life, should occasion arise that makes it necessary. Wars prove that. Murders prove that humanity contains this impulse, also, when occasions arise that create the killing thought even when it is not necessary."

Rosenthal shivered and shrugged his shoulders as if to shake off the weight of a very unpleasant philosophy.

"Vell, you haff had more experience in that line than myself, certainly, but I am very glad, Mr. Smith, that I do not belieff such things! It vould make me very miserable. I should look at efferbody like they vas already murderers!"

Smith smiled, and said, "Well, maybe it's a good thing a lot of us who have decided ideas about things don't go around preaching them or thinking of them all the time. I assure you I do not go around looking at people as though they were murderers. Only when I'm on a case like this . . . and . . ." he pulled out his watch. "Clancy ought to be along pretty soon with your watchman."

Rosenthal did not answer. Smith reached over and took a cigar, and for a little while each man sat with his own thoughts.

There was a knock on the door. Smith opened it to admit Clancy, who was propelling before him a dried up wisp of a man in rough clothing. Over the latter's shoulder, suspended on a heavy strap, hung a circular machine which identified the man immediately as the night watchman. Lannigan, for it was he, stood with his sharp little eyes shifting monkey-wise from Rosenthal to Smith. The President motioned him to a chair and he sat down, plainly overcome at being admitted, and seated, in the holy of holies. At Captain Smith's words, however, his eyes came to rest steadily upon his questioner.

"You are Lannigan?"

"Yis sorr. Patrick Lannigan."

"You are the night watchman of this studio?"

Lannigan straightened his bony shoulders and there was an air of truculency in his manner as he replied:

"I am thot!"

"Is that the time clock you used last night, on your back?"

"Sure, it's the wan I always use. Yis, it's me time clock."

"Can you open it and take out the tape?"

"That I cannot. 'Tis the head fireman who does that."

"All right. Clancy, take that clock over and have it opened. Bring back the record."

As Clancy reached for the clock, Lannigan swung himself away. His face instantly took on that expression so typical of his sort, a sullen, closed look. Smith saw he was to have trouble prying anything out of this man. Neither would it do any good to tell him "police business". That would only seal his lips the tighter. His kind had an instinctive and instant resentment of the law.

"Lannigan!" spoke the President of Superior Films sharply, "I vish you to give your clock to that officer!"

"Oh! And an officer, is it now?" said Lannigan, with drawling sarcasm.

"I vish, also, that you answer vat questions Mr. Smith vill ask you. He iss Captain of Detectives," Rosenthal added sternly.

But this announcement made no apparent impression on the little Irishman. He only darted one of his swift, bright glances at Smith, and his long upper lip tucked down tighter over his nether one.

"I'll be answering no questions till yez tells me why the likes of him is after taking me clock away, and what for I am hauled out of me bed to come here this time o' day!"

Rosenthal started to speak, but Smith held up his hand, silencing him. It would take tact, not bulldozing, to handle this belligerent little Irishman.

"Lannigan, get this straight. I don't believe you have anything to do with this matter—with the reason why I am out here. But I do believe you can help me a great deal. A detective, Lannigan, is at the mercy of the people he questions. You could tell me a long string of things that didn't happen at all, and it would cause me a lot of time and trouble to get the truth of it. I'd get it. Never fear that. But it would considerably inconvenience me. I don't think you want to do that, do you?"

Lannigan did not answer. It was evident it made no difference to him how much he inconvenienced the detective. Smith continued to look pleasantly at the man, tapping his chair arm thoughtfully with his pencil, his little red note book open on his knee. Musingly, his eyes went down to it. Then, when he looked up there was a quickened expression in them.

"Lannigan, I've always wanted to hear a banshee. Did you ever hear one?"

The watchman looked at him searchingly, quick to detect if the other was poking fun at him. He found only serious and sincere curiosity in Smith's face. For a moment he struggled with the resolution to keep silence, then, as if it burst involuntarily from him, came the statement, in a lowered voice:

"Well, sor, and what would you think if I was to tell you I've heard one meself?"

"I'd believe you, Lannigan. Where was it you heard it?"

"On this very lot, sor. So late as last night, sor!"

"Hm . . . I thought so," mused Smith. "I've heard that sound described many times, Lannigan, but never by a person who'd heard one so recently as you say you have. I'd appreciate your telling me what it was like."

"There's nothing like it, sor, except maybe the scream of a woman scared half out o' her wits, or a domn cat. It fair raises the hair on yer head, sor!"

"I thought so," murmured the detective again. "Lannigan, what time did you hear the banshee?"

"Well, it must have been around 12:30 this mornin'. I had just started on me 12:30 round. I usually ends me round at Stage Six on the hour, sor, but this time I struck straight across the lawn, and over to Stage Six first, to see what ailed the light at the East entrance, which had wint out the round before. I found 'twas a burnt out globe. So I straightway turns back to the storeroom to get a new one. Just as I reached the end of Stage Six, I heard the banshee."

"And you're sure it was 12:30?"

"Yis sor, but more likely it was 12:40. Anyways, it was not beyont that time, fer I had just come back from me lunch across from the studio, which same I wint over to eat right after Seibert and Hardell left the lot, which same time was at 12:17."

"How do you know that?"

"By me clock, sor. I laid it by whin I wint to eat, it bein' heavy and in the way. When I laid it down I glanced at it like I always do, sor."

"Lannigan, how are your rounds scheduled?"

"I leaves the gate, where I starts, on the half-hour. I goes straight around, and makes it back to Stage Six by the hour. Then I cuts straight back to the gate, and chats a bit with MacDougal. Usually, though, me time between is taken up doin' odd jobs about, so that me time at the different stages isn't always the same. Sometimes I makes it right on schedule, and sometimes I don't."

"What kind of odd jobs, Lannigan?"

"Oh, pickin' up after them domn spalpeens." He stopped to shoot a defiant look at Rosenthal. "Begging yer pardon, sor, but they do be domned careless. Some of thim leaves lights in their dressing rooms and offices. Electric fans goin' in the summer, and electric heaters in the winter. And, would yez believe it or not, many's the time I have to shut off the faucets in the lavatories—"

"Yes, yes, I understand, Lannigan. Some people are very careless. Now, I want you to tell me exactly what happened on this lot last night, from the time you came on until you left."

"May I ask, sor, what it's all about?"

"I'll tell you later. It was a nasty night out here, and plenty of opportunity for things to happen."

"It was a grand night for a murther, sor, as I told Mac-Dougal."

"You said that, did you Lannigan?"

"I did sor, and I meant it!"

Smith checked a desire to banter further with the little man. He sat back and composed himself to listen. Lannigan related faithfully, as follows:

"Well, I come on duty as usual at sivin. I made me rounds, and near froze to death with the dirty fog creepin' down me back. Nothin' happened up to me 9:30 round, whin I heard Seibert carryin' on as usual on Stage Six. Thin later Miss Beaumont comes on, so MacDougal tells me, and Billy West. About that time things begin to happen."

"What things?"

"Well, sor, nothin' you can put yer finger on, and Mac-Dougal he tells me I'm a domned liar. Not in so many words, you understand, but that's his manein', all right! Anyways, whin I starts on me 11:30 round I sees a woman's figger runnin' down the women's dressin' rooms in the direction of Hardell's room. I see it sneakin' down the steps, sor! Thin, later, I see a dark figure stealin' out of the bushes on the west side of Stage Six, and makin' for the Stage door."

"That was about midnight?"

"Just at, sor. I was just fetchin' up at Stage Six, which same would be near twelve o'clock. Whin I gets up to the Stage, the figger has disappeared. I thinks to meself it's inside, and makes to go on the stage. Then Seibert bellows out for me to stay off."

"Does he often do that?"

"Sure, it's second nature to him, sor. Bad cess to him!" with another quick glance of defiance at Rosenthal.

"You're right, Lannigan," Rosenthal said. "Mr. Seibert has too much temperament."

"Timper, plain and simple, I'd call it, sor. Well, thin I goes back to the gate, and talks a bit. Pretty soon Seibert and Hardell come out in Seibert's car. Seibert, to me amazement, because it was unusual, sor, speaks to us! He says, 'Good night, men,' and Hardell, who's always been in the habit of exchangin' a word whin he comes and goes, sings out, 'It's a great life if you don't weaken!' I'm tellin' this, sor, because whilst I nivver had much use fer a dirty bum like Hardell, he knows how to treat a man decent whin he meets him."

"You could swear that Seibert and Hardell went out of this studio, together, at that time, Lannigan?" Smith's voice took on a sharpness.

"And why couldn't I swear it? Ain't it the truth?"

"And what time did they go?"

"Just before I wint over to have me lunch, as I said. It was 12:17 by me clock, sor, and that was the time Mac-Dougal marked thim out."

"All right. Now, did you see any more dark figures?"

"Right after I hears the banshee, I sees wan skeedaddlin' across the lawn from Stage Six."

"You're night watchman of this studio, aren't you?"

"I am thot!"

"Then wouldn't it have been your duty to investigate these queer happenings?"

"Sure, and didn't I want to do that very thing, sor? Didn't I tell Mac me suspicions? And what does he say to me? He says I nivver seen that first figger at all . . . that the only woman on the lot is Miss Beaumont, and I can see by her light she's up in her room, and the other wan he says is Billy West makin' a sneak fer the stage as soon as he can to get his script. And the third, which same I sees after I hears the banshee, Mac won't hear to at all. He tells me it's me ignorant Irish superstition, and if I thinks I hears a banshee, which same I couldn't have heard at all, there not bein' any such creatures, why thin of course I couldn't have seen any other dark figger," and Lannigan spat disgustedly on his hands and rubbed them.

"And so he wouldn't encourage you to make a search of the lot?"

"Encourage me? Not him. I was goin' to ask him to come along, but I sees he thinks I'm a domn fool."

"But you heard that banshee, don't forget that!" said Smith insistently.

"I ain't likely to forgit it, nor would ye be yerself, sor!" snapped Lannigan impatiently.

Smith smiled. "That's right. Now, Lannigan, who do you really think that last dark figure was?"

"Judgin' by what's been goin' on on this lot fer some time past, I'd say it was MacDougal's daughter, which same inference is what made Mac so mad the first time I told him."

"The first time?"

"Well, you see, sor, not knowin' Miss Beaumont was on the lot whin I sees the first dark figger goin' in the direction of Hardell's room, I thinks to meself it must be Mac's daughter. Which same I would not have mintioned to him only he made me mad whin he pokes fun at me fer me Irish superstition."

"Did you tell him you thought it was his daughter?"

"Not in so many words, sor, but he knew what I meant."

"Hm. I understand his daughter has been mixed up with Hardell. Perhaps you know about that?"

"I could tell you things would open yer eyes, sor— which same I finds out whin I makes me rounds of the stages at night."

A groan came from Rosenthal. He banged his fist down on his desk. Not with a crash, but hopelessly.

"On my lot! On my stages! The dirty low-lifer!" he muttered. He was overcome with an overwhelming sense of his impotency. He had made the unwritten law, and they had broken it—broken it to the end that murder had been committed in his studio. Murder, of all crimes! The realization that he had not, after all, controlled the behavior of the people who worked for him, in such things, sobered and saddened him.

"So it made MacDougal mad, did it? Then, I take it, he doesn't like this affair between his daughter and Hardell?" Smith asked.

"Like it? He turns cold as an icicle, and mutters he'll kill the man if he catches 'em."

"You've heard him say that?"

"Didn't I just say I had? I ain't the only wan. Others have heard him, too. The day watchman, fer wan."

"And what time did you suggest to him that you might have seen his daughter? Was it before, or after, you went across for your lunch?"

"Before. Shortly after midnight it was, sor."

"That's all for the present, Lannigan, thank you," Smith then said.

"If it's not askin' too much, sor, will you tell me what happened last night?" burst from the little man.

"Dwight Hardell was murdered on Stage Six."

"Holy Mither o' God!" breathed Lannigan, and crossed himself piously.

"Lannigan, could MacDougal go to Stage Six while you were out on your round, and you not see that he was missing from the gate?"

"Sure, and he could—" started the Irishman, and then checked himself. "You're nivver thinkin' old Mac did the deed, mister?"

"It appears he had a desire to see Hardell dead."

"Saints presairve us!"

"I vish to know vat made you tink Lannigan heard a scream—a banshee," inquired Rosenthal.

"Two and two make four," Smith answered. "The woman who fled the set was so frightened she left her finger marks in blood on the canvas door. More likely than not, she screamed."

"But," Rosenthal leaned forward quickly, and Smith was surprised at the evidence of real probing into the matter in his statement, "but you say she screamed and left blood marks at the same time. Vell, Mr. Smith, maybe she pricks her own finger. Mr. Seibert tells us he and Hardell are not on the lot at the time Lannigan tells us he heard the banshee, yet you tell me the banshee vas the voman who dipped her hand in Hardell's life blood. If ve are to belieff Seibert, and MacDougal and Lannigan, Hardell vas in Hollyvood at the time you make out he vas on my lot— murdered!"

"Bravo!" applauded the detective. "Keep this up and we'll want you on our force." Then, soberly, "You've thrown the monkey wrench in the machinery, all right. There's a hitch somewhere. Maybe Lannigan's clock was an hour out of the way. We'll have to check up. Anyway, there's something rotten in Denmark about it! Well, we'll talk to MacDougal. That daughter of his, now—"

"That iss foolishness! I know that little girl. She iss vid my cousin offer at Killing Komedies! She iss vild, yes, but she iss not a murderess! Neffer vill I belieff that!"

"MacDougal, then?"

Rosenthal shrugged, "Of course I should not vant to think that of him, either, but he iss a qveer fellow, qviet, and . . . vell, you see him yourself."

9

"While Clancy is getting MacDougal over, I'll step in to your restaurant and have a bite," Smith said, unfolding his long length from Abraham Rosenthal's all too comfortable chair. The President of Superior Films drew a sucking breath of regret.

"Tsk! So! You haff not yet had your lunch? Ve vill go right avay."

"I want to go alone." The detective could be abruptly truthful at times. "I want time to mill over this testimony, and I want to study your people. Also, I have taken a lot of your time to-day," he amended.

Even the news of the murder could not quite quell that irrepressible spirit of— Smith stopped a moment in his tracks to analyze it. What was it? On every hand he caught the tag-end of a bantering remark, the last chuckle of a burst of laughter! These people about him seemed to be playing, always playing. He had sensed it that morning, when the director Bonet was roaring orders through his megaphone, and there was the apparent nerve-tension of catching a mob at the psychological moment, of gathering and holding together the many ends that went to make up the successful photograph of the scene by three variously angled cameras trained on a constantly shifting group of humanity, taking in with each turn the action of individuals and stars alike. Smith thought of certain 'snapshots' he had taken, and how everything always seemed to get in the way and to worry him. Even in that period of high tension, when certainly those picture folk were working, and working hard, there was the undercurrent of, as Rosenthal had said, "kidding." Earlier in the day, wandering about the lot by himself, after his study of Stage Six and its grim figure, Smith had peeked into a set where an old man sat thumbing over some faded, yellow letters, and weeping weakly all over his long beard. Up until the instant the camera started, this man was jazzing his body in his chair, snapping his thumbs, and entertaining the rest of the company with a running fire of ludicrous comment. Then, the "snapping" into the scene . . . the tears, welling up as easily as tho from a faucet turned on . . . the "Cut" shouted by the director, and the old man jumping up with alacrity as he said:

"Me for a coke, fellows! Never too old to drink. Gimme a bottle . . ." then slapping his own wrist as he spilled a drop on the long false beard. "Naughty! Naughty! Papa spank!" he chided himself.

It wasn't what they said, so much as the way they said it. The laughter, bubbling all the time underneath; the happy-go-lucky, comradely joy of life, effervescing below the surface. The doing seriously of serious scenes, but never taking themselves seriously. Smith felt the charm of it. He had a moment's wistful hunger to be one of them, to love life and live it to the full, as these people loved it and lived it! Like the little girl from Kansas, he thought longingly of the beauty that money could buy, and how these people were surrounded with it on every side. Even the most ordinary and lowly object of furnishing was made a work of art. He wanted to climb on the band wagon and join the gay throng, to go laughing and shouting merrily down the road of life. He thought of these people as holding their lips to a brimming cup, a cup in which all the desires that life brought to one were jammed and packed!

Then he went into the commissary and had his first contact with the caste system of the studios. Rosenthal had told him to take a table at the end of the room farthest from the door. He had wondered why. Now he caught it all in a glance. Near the door were extras, eating belated luncheons like his own, or having tea, or cold drinks. Then came people who seemed to him to have more importance. Up near where Rosenthal had told him to sit he recognized two famous motion picture stars. He laughed to himself as he sat down. There were no marked divisions of the room, but the divisions were there. He felt that it would surely follow out that way throughout the industry. The extras to the extras, and the stars to the stars. He realized what a hard won fight it must be to reach the brimming cup! As he was finishing his coffee, a waitress came to him.

"You are Mr. Smith? Mr. Rosenthal said you would be at his table. You are wanted on the phone."

"That you chief?" he heard Clancy's voice in the receiver. "I've got that guy MacDougal."

"Has he learned what has happened?"

"Nope. He was reading his paper in his kitchen, but you know there wasn't nothin' in it."

"Well, don't tell him. I'm going right over to Rosenthal's office.

The difference in Clancy's attitude towards this man, compared to that he used towards Lannigan, was in itself sufficient evidence of the difference in the two witnesses. As tall as Smith, yet stockier, and with an upright, military bearing not so different from Seibert's. Level, blue eyes, staring out calmly, almost bleakly, from under beetling bushy sandy eyebrows. A massive face, without rounded contours. High cheek bones, a long straight nose, full but firmly moulded lips, the whole dominated by a strong, square jaw. A sandy mustache, clipped squarely, added to the grim look of efficiency.

"A hard man, and a set one," said Smith to himself as Clancy brought him into Rosenthal's office. Then he rose and held out his hand. "Royal Northwest Mounted Police, I understand, MacDougal?"

"Eight years, sir." Then to Rosenthal, "You wished to see me?"

"Captain Smith vishes to ask you some qvestions," answered the President of Superior Films, waving him to a chair with his fat hand, in which one of his choice cigars smoked fragrantly.

Ignoring Rosenthal's frown and outthrust lower lip, Smith tendered the gateman a cigar from the open box on the desk. MacDougal put out his hand in refusal.

"Thank you. I smoke a pipe," he said courteously.

Smith sensed the pride in the tone. The man would not accept one of the President's cigars, offered by another! It was one of those straws which show the way the wind blows. Smith knew the unbending nature of this man's make-up on the instant.

"MacDougal," he said without preamble, "there was a murder committed on this lot last night!" He said it with his eyes narrowed, and every intuitive help he possessed trained on the gateman. He saw a sudden tightening of the other man's attitude.

"Who was it?" MacDougal asked quietly.

"Hardell."

"Hardell? But he left the lot with Seibert, and he did not come back!"

"That's what I wanted to know. He didn't come back you say, and yet . . . he was found murdered this morning on Stage Six." Smith looked searchingly at the other. "So you see, he *must* have come back."

"Not through the gate, Captain," asserted MacDougal quickly.

"Could he have gotten in any other way?"

"I do not see how he could."

Smith pondered this.

"Are you in the habit of going across with Lannigan to eat lunch?" he asked.

"Not in the habit of it, sir, but I did step across last night. It was a mean night. Cold and foggy."

"Hm. Much fog?"

"Thick as pea soup."

"When you went across, did you lock the gate?"

"If I do go over, I usually lock the gate. Last night, however, we had people on the lot. Thinking they might be wanting to leave, I left the little door open."

"What people were on the lot?"

"Miss Beaumont, and Mr. West."

"No one else? No other . . . woman?"

MacDougal met his eyes squarely. "The nurse in the hospital. That's all."

"Your time sheet shows that Miss Beaumont did not leave until 1:30 a.m., and that Billy West left fifteen minutes later," said Smith, glancing at the record which had been sent over from the Production Office earlier in the day.

"That is right, Captain."

"Then, MacDougal, you did not see them leave while you were in the lunch room?"

"No, sir."

"Were you sitting with your back to the street, depending on your sixth sense to make you turn when anyone approached the gate?"

"Hardly, sir! The counter runs, also, along the side. By sitting on the end seat, I can easily keep my face turned towards the boulevard. I did not take my eyes off the gate for the short time Lannigan and I were there."

"But no one left the lot, during that time?"

"No, sir."

"Then, MacDougal, if you did not see anyone leave, how can you be sure someone did not enter? In short, you do not know, for certain, whether you *could* see a person going through the gate, from that distance, in that fog, do you?"

"Putting it that way, I do not, sir," admitted the man without hedging.

"Putting it that way, MacDougal, we have, as yet, only the word of Seibert that he drove Hardell to Hollywood. What was to prevent his dropping Hardell a short distance from the studio, and Hardell coming back to . . . meet your daughter?" asked the detective significantly.

For an instant the Scotchman's face took on a hard look. He opened and shut his well-knit, strong hands, on his knee. When he spoke, however, his voice was quiet and direct.

"You've no right, Captain, to bring my daughter into this. I will grant you this much: Seibert could most certainly have dropped Hardell a short distance, and Hardell might have slipped through the gate when I was across the street. Why he came back I cannot say."

The detective sat for a moment holding the other's eyes with his own. Failing to force the Scotchman to evade his gaze, he said directly:

"MacDougal, if you had gone over to Stage Six on your return, could Lannigan have seen you?

"Lannigan went immediately to the Stage himself, to see about a light. Then he went to the storeroom, to get a new globe. I could have gone to the Stage and entered from this end, while he was leaving by the other, or walking away from the Stage at the other end, with his back to me. It would have been easy," said MacDougal, unhesitatingly.

"I thought so. MacDougal, are those the shoes you wore last night?"

"No. I have to be on my feet, as you know, and I wear rubber heels when on duty."

A noise came from Rosenthal, and Smith shot him a warning glance for silence.

"MacDougal, a man wearing rubber-heeled shoes stood at the side of the dead body of Hardell, stepped over it, and walked across the Stage! He left a trail of bloody footprints!"

An inscrutable look came into the ex-Redcoat's face.

"That could be a clue . . . or a plant," he said quickly.

"Correct. Before we assume it to be a plant, we will assume it to be a clue. I shall have to see the shoes you wore last night, MacDougal."

"Certainly."

"Why did you refuse to accompany Lannigan on a search of the lot to investigate the figures he saw?"

MacDougal smiled with a certain scorn. "You do not know Lannigan like I do. However, I did not refuse to accompany him. He did not ask me. If I humored all his hallucinations, I'd spend my time touring the lot."

"Hm. You accounted for one of the figures as being West. You did not explain the other two. MacDougal, I believe that the figure Lannigan saw, following the scream of 'the banshee', was your daughter!"

"My daughter was not on the lot!" came the retort, cold and crisp.

"You did not mark her in, no," agreed Smith significantly.

"Do you think, sir, that I would abet my daughter in meeting a man like that? Do you think I would admit her to the lot, and try to conceal it? I have forbidden her the lot after dark." MacDougal's eyes held dignity and pain. Smith sensed the depth of his love for this wayward girl.

"I think that there are angles of this case which, so far, are baffling," returned Smith impatiently.

"I appreciate your position, Captain," said the gateman quietly.

"Then you appreciate the fact that, regardless of your feelings, I must get at the bottom of this!" snapped Smith. "Where was your daughter last night? Do you know?"

After a moment's hesitation, MacDougal said, "I do not know."

"Where was she when you returned home this morning?"

"She sometimes has to be on the lot—she works at Killing Komedies—early. She had gone."

"Do you know she had gone to Killing Komedies?"

"I have no reason to think otherwise."

"We will check that up right now," returned the detective, looking at Rosenthal.

"I vill haff my secretary find out," said the President.

When Smith again looked at MacDougal the man's face had whitened about the mouth.

"You have Miss Beaumont marked out at 1:30 a.m. and West fifteen minutes later. What reason can you give for them to be on the lot so late?"

"Miss Beaumont came out to read a new script, which she had promised to have finished by to-day. I expect she was reading it. There was a light in her room. I cannot account for West remaining so late. He came to get his script book which he had left on the set. He was forced to wait until Seibert finished, as Seibert sometimes allows no one on the set—not even his assistant. Why he remained after that I cannot tell you."

"Did you notice anything unusual in the manner of either one of them, when leaving?"

"Miss Beaumont is very often in a state of excitement. That is her nature. She becomes enthusiastic over things, and is friendly to everyone. She seemed nervous and what we might say 'flighty', last night. Whether it was anything unusual, or just the nervous reaction from reading a highly dramatic story, so late at night, I cannot say. She feels her roles intensely."

Smith realized that MacDougal was a keen observer of human nature, and also an intelligent one.

"How about West?"

"Nothing unusual, beyond the fact that he looked a bit hollow-eyed. However, that is customary after a long grind with Seibert."

"Are you sure?"

"The position of Assistant Director is that of a buffer between the Production Office and the Director. He is between the devil and the deep blue sea, or, to be more specific, between the efficiency of the Production Office, which balks at recognizing temperament, and the artistic abandon of the director, who cannot comprehend the position of the Production Office. With a man such as Seibert, the assistant's job is a doubly nerve-racking one."

"Thanks," said Smith. He sat a moment, looking down at the little red book on his knee. Then he said, "MacDougal, you cannot swear that Miss Beaumont was in her room all the time her light was on? You cannot swear that Lannigan did not see her running down the corridor, and the stairs, towards Hardell's room?"

"No, sir. I cannot swear that."

"You cannot swear that Billy West was in his office, as you suppose, during all the time he was on the lot?"

"No, sir. I cannot swear to that."

"You cannot swear that Hardell could not have reentered while you were across at lunch?"

"No, sir. I cannot swear to that."

"Lannigan cannot swear that you did not leave your post after returning to the lot, and go over to Stage Six?"

"Unless he made it a point of watching me, which I am sure he did not, he cannot swear to that."

"Why are you sure he did not?" was Smith's quick follow-up.

"I modify that. I assume that he did not."

"Where were you when a scream came from the direction of Stage Six?"

"I did not hear such a scream."

At this point Rosenthal's secretary knocked at the door and was bidden to enter.

"Beth MacDougal left Killing Komedies yesterday afternoon, because she was feeling ill, and did not go to work this morning," the secretary reported.

10

Billy West swallowed the last scraps of that part of the note he had been able to conceal when he wrestled for its possession with Clancy. The silhouette of Yvonne against the light, laying it on Hardell's dressing table, had leaped into his mind the minute he had come on the lot, and Jimmy, the office boy had—but we are getting ahead of our scene. Now he smiled wryly to himself, and thought that he would never again deride the foolish actions of people under stress of emotion, for no sooner had he laboriously gotten down the last morsel when he realized that so long as the police had a fraction of the mauve note paper, even minus the signature and monogram, they would trace it down! Had anyone told him yesterday that he would be doing such a stupid thing, he would have snorted contemptuously, "You're cockeyed and crazy!"

He wondered angrily if he had completely lost his wits over this affair. It made him more furious at himself because he knew this was a time in which every sense he possessed must be used to the utmost.

He looked, even as the President of Superior Films had looked, at the autographed photographs on his walls. Yesterday they had been pictured faces of people he liked, and who liked him. Now they seemed to withdraw from him, and became a part of another existence—his past!

They became dream people, in a dream existence. What was nightmarishly real to him was the fact that he was sitting locked in his own office, with the broad back of a sergeant of police patrolling his window, and the suspicion of murder darkening his future. Yet not a twinge of regret for the man lying in his blood out on Stage Six agitated him. In fact, he did not think of him at all. His thoughts were milling in a desperate circle about himself and Yvonne. Yvonne, her grey eyes swept by heavy lashes, looking at him pleadingly. Her quick, pretty little movements re-visioning themselves in his brain. Her small pale hands, thrown out in a gesture of appeal, and her dainty body stiffening furiously as she stood with the telephone in her hand, talking to Hardell in her apartment the night before! What had happened after that? He remembered the night as a long dwelling in Gethsemane. He had been betrayed. His love of Yvonne had been betrayed by Hardell. He knew he had been in a condition when any extreme act might have been possible. He knew he had even thought murder, in his heart.

Coming as something comforting was the thought of the office boy, who had found Hardell. Because he must keep his mind busy, or go crazy, he went over the little scene as it had happened that morning.

The office boy's name was Jimmy, as is the name of many an office boy. He hated Seibert and he worshipped Billy West. Billy was a war ace, and had killed the enemy from the air. He was a being set apart, even in a world knowing the common aftermath of war.

When West came on the Superior Films lot the morning Hardell was discovered murdered, he had seen Jimmy hunched strangely in a chair behind the rail which divided the privileged from the unprivileged in Rosenthal's outer office.

"What's matter, old pal?"

Jimmy looked up, greenly, at the hand on his shoulder. "Nothin'."

"You look sick. Hospital for you, kid, and castor oil."

"I'm all right. Honest, Billy!"

"Honest, Jimmy?"

How could he lie to his hero? He evaded the frank brown eyes looking down at him, waiting for the truth. He wriggled uncomfortably.

"Jimmy, have you been smoking again?"

"No. Honest I haven't," but still the evasive eyes that could not meet the brown ones. Silence. Billy did not believe him. Without another word he was turning away. Jimmy caught at his arm.

"I—it isn't my fault, Billy, honest. I do feel sick, but—I promised not to tell anyone."

"Then don't," said Billy, briefly.

There was a moment in which Jimmy pondered.

He'd given his word of honor to Billy not to smoke until he was eighteen years old. He had not given his word of honor to Rosenthal. At the worst Rosenthal would only fire him. If Billy thought he'd lied to him, he'd lose him for a friend. He couldn't do that. He gulped, and cast a swift look at the door of Rosenthal's inner office. He clutched Billy somewhere about the middle.

"Hardell's murdered on Stage Six. I—kicked him!" he breathed in a rush of partly remembered terror at that gruesome figure. He felt Billy's body go taut in his encircling arms. Billy did not speak. He looked up at his face. It was white. Then, without a word, and with a wild look in those frank brown eyes, his hero put him firmly from him and strode out the way he had come.

Frantically Jimmy's vivid young imagination, which had lapsed into coma under the startling reality of what he had seen, leaped into action. With the sophistication of the modern youngster, he began putting two and two together. Billy and Yvonne. Yvonne and Hardell. It made four! He recoiled from the thought of Billy having so brutally killed a man. Then he remembered war. Of course. Human lives were nothing to an ace who had snuffed out the existences of many of the enemy. And then Jimmy listened with a sickened heart to a strange sound about him. It was the shattering of the cymbals of the Glory of War!

Rosenthal's desk phone rang. Captain of Detectives Smith was treated to a family portrait of the Head Executive of Superior Films.

"Yes, yes, sure it iss me, Mama! Vat? Didn't I have Miss Dunham phone you I vas busy, Mama? Vell, I am busy! Now, Mama, vat a thing to say! I am all alone, except for—" and Rosenthal rolled his liquid brown eyes over to Smith, and hesitated. His statement was an unfortunate one. There was quite a lengthy return from the other end of the wire, under which the generous body of the Head Executive wriggled apologetically for Smith's benefit. With one fat hand waving in the air, he put his lips closer to the phone.

"Vell, since you vill say such foolishness, Mama, I vill tell you. It iss a man. A detective . . . now, Mama, don't get excited. Calm yourself down vonce! You hear me? I vill tell you ven I get home. Vill you please to tell little Izzie to shut up, so's I can hear vat you say? Vell, all right, let him talk to me." A pause, and then:

"Now Izzie you be a good boy and go to bed. Papa iss not coming home yet avile. Izzie, I tell you papa iss busy! Vill you please to behafe yourself? All right . . . all right . . . I vill get it to-morrow. Now go to bed right avay, and don't bother your Mama!"

When he had hung up the phone he turned to Smith with a helpless gesture.

"Everything that boy vants! He thinks his papa iss made of money!" A complaint with pride in it!

"Well, aren't you?" drawled Smith.

"I am made of vorry right now," returned Rosenthal lugubriously, adding, "Vell, if ve are to haff our dinner and get through vid this mess to-night, ve had better go offer to the commissary right avay."

"You succeeded in locating Miss Beaumont?"

"Yes. Her maid tells my secretary she has gone to Newport Beach. Right avay I send a message to her friends' yacht, and she says she vill be here at 8:30. Vell, it iss now 8 o'clock. Ve got to hurry."

"Hm. I want to question West first. Can we have a sandwich and a bottle of something to drink sent over?"

"Sure. I get it right avay."

Smith thought it must be the first time Rosenthal's shining mahogany desk had been utilized as a lunch counter, and then was a little surprised to see the door open and a table brought in. The sandwich and bottle of something to drink materialized into fried chicken and a bottle of something very choice to drink, and salad, dessert and coffee.

"Vat you think about MacDougal?" asked Rosenthal, looking up from a crisp chicken wing.

"That he is the damndest liar in the bunch, so far," returned Smith promptly.

"Tsk!" exclaimed Rosenthal, his eyes widening.

"Absolutely. He knows something he's not telling. The minute I pin that murder on his daughter, he's going to throw a monkey wrench into the machinery that will make it impossible for me to get a conviction."

"Vell, maybe his daughter didn't do it."

"Maybe. I tell you, Rosenthal, all my evidence is up in the air. There are too many clues and too many suspects."

"MacDougal iss not a murderer," returned the other thoughtfully.

"No. He's only a killer," exclaimed Smith dryly.

"Vat iss the difference?"

"Just this. I'm not a murderer, but I'm a killer if necessity demands. There are men who would step around a rattlesnake, and others would stop to kill it. If MacDougal killed Hardell, he did it in the same way he would kill a rattlesnake—and as deliberately. He's hard, and he's clever. He knows just how he's going to handle this thing, and he's got it all planned out. His training as a Redcoat gives him the advantage. He knows the law."

The detective drained his glass with appreciative eyes looking over its rim. Then he said:

"If you don't mind, I'll have Clancy bring West in now. I want to get him out of the way before Miss Beaumont comes."

"Sure, I am through, myself," returned the President courteously. He rang and had the table removed. The two men leaned back and puffed luxuriously.

Captain Smith saw a good looking young man, in whose brown eyes lay a baffled look. He was cornered, and he knew it, and while his face showed a certain desperation—a hunted expression—it also showed a hesitancy at making a sudden break for freedom.

"There's something more in this than he's going to tell me," Smith told himself, and immediately took on an entirely different attitude than the ones in which he had questioned Lannigan and MacDougal. Rosenthal felt a mounting resentment and surprise, in which he regretted his quick intimacy with the man. It was all he could do to keep from throwing him out of his office when Smith shut him up tersely because of a protest at the detective's ruthless methods with the young Assistant Director.

Perhaps, if Rosenthal had not been honestly fond of Billy—

"And so, you say you only went to the set for your script? Would that take you two hours?" Rosenthal heard Smith pursuing the questioning.

"What I did after getting my script is my own affair, sir!" West answered.

"You're wrong, my boy. Perhaps you'll feel more like explaining your actions when you've spent a night in jail."

"You have no evidence upon which to give you a right to arrest me."

"You are already arrested! Sergeant Clancy arrested you. What you mean is, that you have given me no evidence upon which to release you."

"You will have to prove what you say!"

"I expect to! Where was Miss Beaumont, after Seibert and Hardell left the lot?"

Billy West shut his lips.

"All right, if you won't answer that, perhaps you will this: Who was the woman you talked to while on the set, after Seibert had left?"

"I did not talk to any woman!"

"I found a woman's finger marks, in blood, on the canvas door," snapped Smith significantly.

Billy started perceptibly, and Smith could see he was holding his breath in a manner that told the detective his heart had leaped, startled.

"When we match up those prints with the ones on the note you so obligingly tried to secret, which was written by Miss Beaumont, we will know the identity of the woman who made those prints," Smith stated with finality in his voice, as though it were already a settled question, and adding, as if by an afterthought, "Miss Beaumont was the only woman who came on the lot last night, according to the gateman's testimony and time sheet."

Billy West steadied himself against a sudden whirling of things around him. His already haggard young face grew more so. Smith pursued his advantage.

"Miss Beaumont, your sweetheart, has all but confessed to the deed in her letter. Did you have time to read it? No. Just saw her name and handwriting and thought you'd better get it out of the way, eh? Well, perhaps if you had read it you would know—"

"Stop! I'll make a clean breast of it. I did it!"

Smith relaxed back in his chair, a slight smile of satisfaction on his face. Rosenthal groaned.

"Mine Gott, Billy! Vy did you? Vy did you? The dirty low-lifer! And you should ruin yourself for him!"

"Don't worry, Mr. Rosenthal. It doesn't matter; it's all right," and the pale-faced young man smiled bitterly.

"Billee! Why have you the handcuffs on?"

Every man in the room turned to look at her. She stood leaning against the door, one pale little hand at her heart, her grey, dusky-lashed eyes wide with horror, her sweet red mouth quivering. Rosenthal was immediately at her side, with one huge, comforting arm about her.

"Shu! Shu! Yvonne," he was saying, patting her soothingly, and yet finding no words with which to lie to her. She put him gently but firmly from her.

"I'm all right, Rosey, but I must know the truth! Billee! Talk to me! I have heard when I come on the lot that Dwight is murdered! Tell me! You . . . didn't . . ." she stopped, and her great eyes, now tear-filled, questioned him.

"He says he did, Miss Beaumont," said Smith quietly.

The girl wheeled on him, her tremulous grief all consumed in the instant flash of her temper.

"Says he did! And you—a detective—you believe him! You put on the handcuffs just for that! Bah! That is American . . . stupeed! In Paris—"

"I am aware that in Paris you have some master criminologists," interrupted Smith smoothly, "but even in your native city, I imagine a confession is given some credence until proven untrue."

"Ah, you agree it must be proven! I ask you, what proof have you now that Billee did this so terrible thing? What proof beside his silly word?"

"We arrested him because he was found in Hardell's room, taking a note from his dressing table—a note written by you!"

She laughed scornfully. "And because of that, you try to make him theenk *I* did it! Then, natural, he tells you he did it himself. Is it not what any man would do, M'sieur? I ask you? And you believe him? Non! Non! He did not! Billee, foolish one, tell him the truth!"

"Yvonne—" He looked up miserably, and stopped. What could he say? There was nothing to say. He could not tell the truth!

"Veree well. I tell it myself, then! It was I—I, M'sieur, who came out here last night to meet Mistair Hardell! Because he have some letters of mine—"

"Yvonne! Stop!"

"No, Billee! I will not stop! I—"

West turned to Smith, crying, "She's only trying to save me! Don't listen to her! Go on; ask me questions. Try to prove it! I went on that set last night, and you'll find my finger prints to prove it!"

"Which reminds me. You have on rubber-heeled shoes. Just what I am looking for. Did you wear those shoes last night?"

"Yes."

Smith walked over to Rosenthal's desk. From the pile of papers—the time sheet, the tape from Lannigan's clock, and a few miscellaneous articles he pulled a folded paper.

Opening it, he revealed that it was smeared with a rusty-red stain.

"Take off your shoe, West," he said then.

Awkwardly, flushing miserably because of his bound wrists, the prisoner bent to obey him. Yvonne went to him swiftly.

"No, dear—" She stood back, and the sound of a sob came from her. Smith watched them both with cool indifference. When the shoe was off, he took it, and with his penknife dug out a deposit in the nail holes in the heel. This he smeared beside the other stain on the paper, and held it out for them to see.

"Matches up, eh? A laboratory test will prove it. You must have stood by Hardell's body quite some time, West, to let his blood get into your shoes like that, and to leave the remarkably clear trail across the floor," he said quietly. "I was going to question you carefully as to your actions on the lot last night, but you have saved me the trouble for the present, or rather, your confession and this—" and he pointed to the paper.

Yvonne put her hands to her face, and moaned. "Billee! Billee!"

Rosenthal stared at West in horror.

"Have you anything to add to your confession?" said Smith, addressing West.

He drew the back of his hand across his forehead in a dazed way, before he answered. Once he opened his lips, as though to ask a question. But he did not. Finally he said:

"No. That . . . is . . . all."

Yvonne was pounding the back of a chair with tight clenched fists.

"Oh, you are crazee! Crazee, all of you!" she sobbed furiously.

Clancy, coming in, stood a moment, his cheeks puffed out in surprise at this exhibition. Smith brought him sharply to attention.

"Did you check up on Seibert's story?" he asked.

"Sure, Chief. His chauffeur says he came in all right like he said, and spoke to him. Says when he went up to bed, Seibert had his light on, and was sittin' by his window readin'. That was about an hour and a half, maybe two hours, later." Clancy stopped and looked at West, and at the handcuffs.

"Didn't take you long, did it Chief?" he asked significantly, a grin spreading over his face.

"He has confessed," said Smith tersely.

"Huh!" grunted Clancy. Even in his most sanguine moment, he had not hoped for such an easy capture. He stood, slowly sizing up the man in handcuffs. The victorious insolence in his face made West long to get up and punch him. He made no effort to hide his desire, and Clancy, well trained in the meaning of such looks, deliberately fanned it into an outburst.

"Huh! A boob amateur tryin' to put one over on a guy that stole his sweetie!" he sneered.

West lurched at him, his hand-cuffed hands raised. If he thought Clancy was to be taken unawares, he was mistaken. The sergeant of police had turned his back squarely upon him, but now he wheeled on the instant, his fist swinging out unerringly. West was slammed into a chair back of him.

"None of that stuff!" he hissed. "You're goin' with me, and you're goin' quiet!" Wrapping a hand hardened to such practice in the back of West's collar, he hauled him upright.

"Listen, you damn murderer! Try that again and I'll smash your chin back so far you can use it for a collar button!"

"Clancy!" The Captain of Detectives looked meaningly at his sergeant.

"No little squirt of a crook can act up with me, and get away with it!" retorted Clancy belligerently. He turned

back to West, and thrust his big paw down his collar.
"Come on, you—"

There was a flash of steel, and the boy's hands swung
up and down. His eyes, suddenly a black blaze, leaped to
Smith's.

"Take these damn things off me, or I'll wreck the place!"
he roared. "Pretty soft of you! Out here one day, and the
best you can do is pick on a girl! Somebody tells you a lot
of rot, and you start right in throwing dirt on her name!
That's a hell of a way to catch a murderer! You knew damn
well I'd confess to it! All right. I did. But that doesn't give
you the right to put a filthy bum like this over me! You
take off these handcuffs, and you do it quick! I'll go to
jail, but I'll go like a gentleman! I'll go when you send a
man with a decent tongue in his head."

"Clancy, you can step over to the hospital and get the
nurse to fix you up," said Captain of Detectives Smith at
this point. Astonishingly speedy had been his seizure of his
sergeant of police when West's manacled hands had swung
down on his head. Astonishingly steely was the grip that
kept the frothing Clancy from leaping at West's throat.
There was an instant in which Clancy hesitated, his hands
curled and quivering with the intent, and then he touched
his cap and stepped into the hall.

"Tell Ryan to come in," Smith called after him.

"Ryan, this is Mr. West. Take him down and lock him
up. There's no need to call attention to yourselves. Perhaps Mr. West will drive you in."

"Right, sir." Then to West, "Are you ready?"

Yvonne, shrinking back in her chair, looked at Smith with
eyes in which contempt and loathing burned.

"You know he did not do eet!" she said in a low, tense
voice. "You are a weecked, a bad, a terrible man! God will
puneesh you one day! I say eet!"

She looked, and spoke words, like a child, but her voice was charged with passion. Her eyes accused him in a way that threatened to break through his composure.

"I do not *know* anything about this case—yet," said the detective.

"Vell, I should tink it vould be all offer, vid poor Vest's confession! Ach, that boy! I cannot belieff it," Rosenthal sighed. Surreptitiously he took out his handkerchief and wiped his eyes.

It was when Lannigan was well out of the way that the night gateman, with a grim look to left and right, turned down the driveway of the Superior Films lot and made for the studio emergency hospital. The door opened almost immediately to his knock, for Mona Brown, the nurse, had been expecting him.

"Why didn't you let me know Beth was here?" asked MacDougal sternly.

"Because the child's in mortal terror of you, and she asked me not to," the nurse retorted sharply.

"Did she leave the hospital last night?"

"I put her to bed, and when I went in to her this morning, she was raving . . . out of her head. That's all I can tell you."

"I'll talk to her."

"Your daughter's sick, and mighty close to brain fever. I've watched it coming on for a month. You go easy with her, or you'll have the doctor to answer!" she told him, tight-lipped.

For answer he strode by her, opened the door to the left of the hall, and closed it after him.

Mona Brown stood with clenched hands, staring at it. She drew a long, audible breath, and muttered to herself:

"What else could I do? They'd find it out anyway, and . . . maybe . . . he'll protect her! There's nobody else." She turned away and went up the stairs to her own room.

MacDougal, looking down at the white, tear-stained face of his only daughter, his motherless girl, clenched his teeth so that the muscles knotted and quivered. He thought of her mother, that simple Scotch woman, who would have died by now of a broken heart had she not died earlier of a second child-birth. How like her mother the girl looked. How like—and yet, how unlike! Where the mother's cheeks were roses from the airs that blew over Scotch moors, the daughter's were white beneath the rouge, and deep black shadows marked the eyes. Her mouth, a piteous thing, drooped like a hurt child's. A child she was—and hurt!

His eyes went to her clothes, lying over a chair. They told him more than the nurse had said. Beth had the Scotch tidiness. Only in an hour of distraught mind would she so fling her things about. He bent to straighten the scarlet shift she called a dress. Scarlet, he thought—scarlet. Well might she wear scarlet! A sound, half sigh and half groan, wrenched itself out of him. He stood with the bit of soft silk in his hands, turning it, starting to fold it. His hands encountered a change in the texture and he bent quickly.

Blood, dried stiff along the hem—

Swiftly he folded the garment into a flat packet and thrust it into his shirt front.

11

The Coroner's inquest over the body of Dwight Hardell has gone down in newspaperdom as the tenth wonder of the world. The sob sisters who handled it were reduced to a state of mental intoxication from sheer excitement. They found themselves beggared of adjectives in the first round. Such a thing, as you probably know, seldom happens to sob sisters. The newsies for once did not have time to scream their extras. The papers were snatched away from them faster than they could hand them out. Black headlines vied with exclamatory columns on the front pages. We herewith reprint as follows:

THREE CONFESS TO SLAYING OF ACTOR! ALL PICTUREDOM PREDICTED TO BE INVOLVED IN MYSTERIOUS CRIME. WAS FIENDISH DEED MOB ATTACK OR SMOKE SCREEN THROWN UP BY MOTION PICTURE MAGNATE OF SUPERIOR FILMS TO CONCEAL TRUTH WHICH IS TOO FRIGHTFUL TO REVEAL?

And more. Head writers let space and type go to the devil, and strung their lines half-way down the front page. Sob sisters wallowed in exaggerated expressions, as follows:

"What threatens to be the most sweeping exposé of pic-turedom was begun to-day with the Coroner's inquest over the body of Dwight Hardell. Startling enough in itself is the murder of the well-known actor—startling and fiend-ishly brutal!

"Lying stark and cold in the satin and laces of his period costume, his white wig not whiter than his dead face, his hand still grasping the glittering dueling weap-on with which he tried to defend himself, that is the way Dwight Hardell was found yesterday morning by an office boy on the Superior Films lot. Mysterious and uncanny is the fact that he was lying in the exact position in which a dummy of himself had been arranged the night before, for a dissolve shot. Mysterious and uncanny is the collection of clues discovered by Captain of Detectives Smith, not one of which bears out another!

"Startling, also, is the confession of William West, an assistant director of Superior Films, to the murder! His shoes were found to be the same which had made a bloody trail across the stage, but the finger prints which were found on the canvas door of the set were a woman's! A woman's voice, also, that sent out the scream in dead of night, which night watchman Lannigan took, and rightly, for a banshee wailing the passing of the dead! A woman's hand that wrote the 'death note', found in Hardell's room, that stated 'I shall end everything between us tonight!'

"This 'death note' was written by Yvonne Beaumont, a Superior Films star. The murder confession was made by William West, known to be madly in love with the beauti-ful French actress, and from these facts the answer seems simple enough. He confessed to shield her. But, despite all this, it is not so simple, after all, for an unknown woman enters into the case! The bloody finger prints were not made by Miss Beaumont. That is the rumor which leaked out from headquarters this morning. Who, then, is this second woman? The night gateman at Superior Films says he marked both Miss Beaumont and Mr. West in on the night of the murder, but he denies admitting any other person except the murdered man and his director, Franz Seibert.

"So many and so bewildering are the mysterious angles of this crime that it is difficult to know which thread in the tangled maze to follow. Here is a stiff one for amateur sleuths—Dwight Hardell was marked out by the gateman at 12:17. He did not return, yet he was found dead on Stage Six the next morning!

"Are Lannigan and MacDougal, the watchman and gateman respectively, in a conspiracy to shield someone, and is the time of Hardell's departure, as given by Mac-Dougal, erroneous? And where does Franz Seibert come into this, for he, also, states that he left the lot with Hardell at 12:17 a.m., and this statement is corroborated by the gateman and the watchman.

"Startling and bewildering enough are all these things, but it is predicted things more startling are yet to come, and that the history of some of the most famous people in pictures will be made public before the truth of this strange crime is uncovered."

"It is common gossip that Seibert is working with Abraham Rosenthal to cover up the actual truth of the case, and that every attempt is being made to mystify the police and the public, in order that their minds may be occupied with false trails. And now for the happenings in the Coroner's room this morning! Picture two young people, one a beautiful French girl, the other a handsome American lad, each sitting at opposite sides of the room. Dark, tragic eyes meeting dark tragic eyes; pale lips murmuring soundlessly to pale lips across the space.

"William West and Yvonne Beaumont.

"West under guard. Beaumont accompanied by her law-yer.

"The Coroner was completing his questioning, having taken the testimony of MacDougal, Lannigan, and Jimmy Cairns, the office boy. He had come to the confession of William West. The lovely actress leaned forward, her great eyes dilating. For what was being said? That the blood on the stage, flowing from Hardell's heart, and the blood found on the bottom of West's shoe, which he admits having worn the night before when he went to the stage to get his script book, were the same! A sob came from the lovely throat of Miss Beaumont, and her little white hands fluttered to her heart. Then, when it seemed she would swoon, she had suddenly risen from her seat and her clear voice broke through the stillness.

"'Ladies—gentleman! Will you hear me? I have some-seeng to tell you! Someseeng you will not, at first, believe. But I will make you see it. First, I tell you zat I have had ze—what you call—affair, wiz Mr. Hardell!' At this point the beautiful girl raised her head and looked bravely at her audience. 'I will tell you, also, it was only what you call ze . . . flirt, wiz me. Me, I did not loff heem. Non! I am French. I am ze flirt, *oui!* I play wiz heem. For why? Because when first I come to this countrai, two years ago, I learn zat he eez one veree bad man. He break all ze hearts of ze pretty ladies. Me, Yvonne, I say to myself, "I will do zat same to heem. Zat will be fun!" But I do not know how weeked he is. Pretty soon I am afraid! He follow me! He make me scare! He come to my apartment in ze night, and I will not open ze door, and he stand outside and say terrible sings to me. Zen,' she clasped her hands and her eyes went to William West, across the room, and her lovely little face flushed and softened. 'Zen, I find I am—in loff. For ze first time in my life, I am in loff! I tremble wiz fright that my Billee find out about zis what you call 'affair' wiz Hardell.' Everyone in the room turned to look at William West, who sat clenching his hands and gazing with all the pleading of his heart at the brave girl who was giving her secret to the world.

"'Zen, Hardell, he say he has kept some silly letters I have written heem. He say he will show them to Billee. I am wild! I cry, I beg, I get mad! He only laugh. I have tell Billee I have nevair before lolled a man. He have believe me. You comprehend, good people, what I feel? Zen, zat night I go out to ze studio to get ze letters. Hardell say he carry zem always wiz heem. I write ze note, and go down to pin it to his dressing table, zen to steal my letters, and to go away. But I cannot find zem. Zay are not zere. I wait for ze lights to go out on ze stage, and for him to come back to change his clothes. But—he does not come. I wait and wait. To-morrow he say he will show ze letters to Billee. Zen, I go to the stage. I am afraid for Mr. Seibert to see me. He is veree cross to be disturb. I hide in ze bushes until zay go away. And—Dwight Hardell does not go to his room. Non! He goes away wiz Mr. Seibert. I know, because I hear heem talking together. I am afraid to look, but I hear. Zen I am afraid to leave, because I see Billee coming. He goes on ze stage, and pretty soon he comes out and goes away. Zen, what do you sink? I see zat Hardell coming back. What for? Me, I do not know. I only see heem coming back. I get up and go quietly, *quietly,* after heem. I find heem on ze set, practicing to fall—but zat I weel explain. When we take ze dissolve from ze dummy to ze real actor, ze real actor and ze dummy must be in exactly ze same place. Comprehend? Mr. Hardell had to fall, when he is killed by ze duel, inside some lines made wiz chalk, where afterwards zay will put ze dummy. Ze day before he was—before I—before he was found murdered, Mr. Seibert take many, many times zat scene, but it does not suit heem! So, zay come back zat night to rehearse. Zay will take it over again ze next day. Hardell, he tell me he come back to practice zat fall by heemself. I find heem doing it. I say, "I have come for my letters!" He laugh! I tell heem, over and over, how much I loff Billee. He laugh! And zen—' for a moment her eyes dropped and she put both white hands to her cheeks, 'zen he forget heemself! He make ze bad loff to me. I run, but he is too strong. He catch me! I fight! I bite! I keeck! He tell me he—he tell me zat to-morrow I will be glad to say I will marry heem.' Once again the brave little head was flung up and the great dark eyes swept the room. There were murmurs of sympathy, and low-voiced expressions from the men in the audience.

"'Ah, good people, it ees zen zat Yvonne becomes . . . a murderess!' She swayed. Her lawyer put out a hand to steady her. Her voice, coming through sobs, cut into the hearts of her listeners.

"'I manage to get away for ze instant. I find ze other sword. I prepare to defend myself. I tell heem I will keel heem! But he only laugh! He theenks I cannot do eet . . . but see!' She held out her small white wrist. 'I have learned to fence in Paris. Feel, M'sieur,' and she bent to the man nearest her. 'Is my wrist not strong? Oui! You comprehend? Ah, always I have been so proud of ze fencing! But, no more, you comprehend, good people? I—I keel him!' She slipped unconscious into the arms of her lawyer.

"On the heels of this breath-taking confession, when people were still wiping their eyes, and solicitous hands were tending the lovely form, when analytical minds were expressing the opinion that Hardell must have subconsciously assumed the death position he had been practicing for so long, when others were asking, 'How did he get back on the lot?' a new voice was heard. A man's voice. MacDougal, the night gateman came to his feet, with a paper in his hand. A stern, hard man! A man with a grim mouth. A man who plainly is not afraid of God, man or devil! He made this startling announcement:

"'In order that the innocent may not suffer, I ask the Coroner to read this statement to the people gathered here.' Somebody took the paper up to the Coroner, and while every breath in the room was held, he read:

"'I killed Dwight Hardell on the night of December 15th. To this confession I set my hand and seal. Signed, Scot MacDougal.'

"To say pandemonium reigned would be putting it mildly. The mental confusion in the Coroner's room was beyond description. Up to the press time of this issue, nothing more definite has been divulged, but unappeased curiosity is running rife. Who, then, is the real murderer of Dwight Hardell? That is the question to which, while there appears to have been three answers, there is, as yet, no proven reply."

There was more of the sob sister's story, but this covers the main points.

Captain of Detectives Smith was perusing the lay of the sob sisters with a derisive smile, when Ryan came into his office.

"It's a sweet dish, eh, Cap?" he inquired, looking over his superior's shoulder. They read in silence for a moment, and then Ryan added:

"Which one of 'em do you think is guilty?"

"I think they're all liars!" exclaimed Smith angrily. The expression on Ryan's face brightened eagerly.

"Why? Anything new?"

"No. Merely common sense. *Two* of them have got to be, anyway! But which one does that leave us? Maybe all three are lying, but the devil of it is, the more I go into the case the more I can see that any one of them could have done it."

"Well, it's a cinch Beaumont's safe, the way she got everybody going yesterday! All she has to do is to look twice at a jury, and she's cleared—that and the self-defense plea."

"Huh! Her lawyer, Vlatcher, isn't the kind to take a chance."

"What ya mean?"

"Frame-up!"

Ryan considered this, a frown pulling at his brows.

"But Chief, that girl sure *must* have been telling the truth. Her face, and fainting, and all! And the fellow who felt her wrist says it's all she claimed it is. I tell you, she sure got *me* going, Chief!"

Smith looked up with a dry smile.

"The sooner you two boys get married, the sooner I'm going to get a heap more savvy out of you."

"Why?"

"You'll know more about women, that's all. Ryan, there isn't a woman on earth who isn't a born actress—on occasion! Added to that, with Beaumont we've got a professional. You don't suppose any canny Jew like Rosenthal is going to pay perfectly good money to a girl who can't act, do you? Not he. He's got too much sense. For two years that girl has been drawing down seven hundred dollars a week, to *put it over!* Starting next month she gets fifteen hundred, and a starring contract. Add that to the cleverest lawyer on the coast, and what have you?"

Ryan thought a moment. "Ha! I've got it! When West confessed, she went to get Vlatcher to defend him. And, being Vlatcher, he made use of what he had to the best advantage. It's a cinch West's confession isn't worth a darn if there's another in the offing."

"You said it, fellow. But here's another angle. If one of those two is guilty—and I'm not yet convinced this isn't the case—Vlatcher will pull them both scot free unless we can pin the dead wood on one or the other of 'em! That's going to be some job, and he knows it."

For a few moments they smoked in silence, then Smith laid down his pipe.

"Well, what did you find out on that Seibert stuff?"

"It checks up O.K. He said he stopped in the traffic hold at Santa Monica and Hyland, didn't he? Well, he did. There's a cigar shop there where he has his cigarettes made to order, or ordered, or something. Anyway, the guy knows him well. Hardell buys there, too. Seems the guy saw 'em both the night of the murder."

"Can he swear to it?"

"Yep. Recognized Hardell by the lace on his sleeve, and the way he has of waving his hand to him. Seems while they were waiting he called to have a box of cigars brought him, and the cigar store kid went out and slung it in the back seat, because by that time the traffic was moving. Hardell called out to 'charge 'em'."

"Well, that's that," said Smith. "All right, we'll mark that off. Now let's go over the whole thing before Clancy comes in. Added to the fact that any one of the self-confessed murderers could have done it, is the fact that each one of the three had a *motive!* Undoubtedly MacDougal has been keeping something up his sleeve. The daughter, of course. We could eliminate both Beaumont and West on the theory that one confessed to save the other. Let's prove it. Start with Beaumont, and the scream. She did not mention hearing any such scream while she was hiding by the stage. Answer to that is, she was lying. She never hid by the stage. She doesn't know anything about the condition in which—"

"Wait a minute, Chief!" Ryan interrupted triumphantly. "You, who know so much about women! The girl screamed herself! You don't think a girl's going to go through what she did with Hardell, and not yell, do you? Sure, it would be an unconscious cry, but she'd do it."

Smith looked over at the other, and the customary deep-lying twinkle appeared in his eyes.

"You're learning, my boy. To dodge an argument I'll grant you that she did it herself. But to continue, she spoke of a struggle. There was no evidence of a struggle—"

"A guy could get pretty rough with a girl and not wreck the scenery, even at that, couldn't he, Cap?"

"Maybe so. Anyway, this is the fly in the ointment: How did Hardell get back on the lot? She says he came back. The gateman says he didn't."

Ryan leaned forward. "Chief, I've worked with you a long time, and I know that sometimes you have queer ways of going at things. I've seen you pass up what appeared to be the key to the plot, and come out a winner at the end. But here's once when I think you're off on the wrong foot." He hesitated, but Smith was listening keenly.

"Go on."

"I'd drop everything, every blamed angle of this crazy mix-up, and find out HOW Hardell got back! He got back. That's a sure thing. But HOW? When you get that, you'll get the right dope."

"Think so?"

"I sure do!"

"Well, I think so myself. I've been sort of letting that slide and checking up on the things that time could wipe out, you understand? But it's come to where it can't slide any longer. It's the puzzler, and it's got to be solved. But now back to West. We've got the same set of circumstances as with Beaumont. He had a motive. Jealousy, or vengeance because the man was a rotter and annoying his girl. He knew, or suspected, that Beaumont went out to the studio to meet Hardell. He probably saw her go onto the set. Anyways, he up and confessed as soon as I sprung those bloody finger prints on him. Either he did it, and saw that, through the peculiar circumstance of Beaumont's finding the body and getting her hands in the blood, it would be pinned on to her—or he deliberately assumed the crime because he believes she did it. The latter seems likely. It looks like he might have known she killed the man, and deliberately made those footprints to save her."

"Gee! It would take pretty quick thinking, and a lot of nerve, to do that."

"That boy was worn out, emotionally, yesterday, but don't fool yourself he isn't a smart one, or that he hasn't got nerve," said Smith. "I let Clancy bulldoze him a bit to find out. He's got it, all right, and he thinks quick, too."

Ryan looked up with a sudden thought. "It's a cinch he knew that blood was on his heel, because he tried to scuff it off. You saw the marks, didn't you?"

"Sure. Of course, did you stop to think he might have thought it was catsup—from the dummy?"

"Coincidental," said Ryan softly.

"Huh! Rather. Too much so! And that leaves us only one theory. He knew it was there, and he did it deliberately. That means Beaumont killed the man, and her story is straight goods. The scuffing of that blood shows just how quick a thinker that boy is—plus his training! He's been making pictures for years, and he knows, to a finish, all the little touches that build up a drama; the little, what producers call, 'human touches!' Damn it, they all do. That's what makes this case a humdinger!"

"Well, we've disposed of Beaumont and West as well as we can for the present. What about this other bird—Mac-Dougal? You know, that guy looks straight, to me."

"He got that expression being a Redcoat. It may cover up a whole bag of tricks," said Smith shortly. "There's one thing sure, though. Since I talked to him, he's found out something new, something that pins it on him, sure, or on someone close to him. Daughter, of course, or he wouldn't have confessed—not with two other confessions already on the table."

"You know, I think he confessed for the reason he said—he knows those two are innocent. I believe he's straight and—"

"Don't be silly, boy!" said Smith impatiently, "No man is going to confess to murder just to keep an innocent person from hanging."

"Well, that's just a feeling I had. You know you've always been strong on the intuition stuff—"

"Ryan, I've had one about this case, and it won't let me sleep. In the face of all the evidence, I've got a strong hunch that fights with all my reasoning, but I believe—" and he pounded one fist in the other, but left the curious Ryan with an unfinished sentence. In a moment he went on, as if talking to himself:

"There's the finger prints on the chair rocker. Somebody stooped down by that chair and put her fingers—for they are a woman's—on the chair to steady herself. Who? And when? Was it Beaumont, witnessing West kill Hardell, and keeping out of it? Was it MacDougal's daughter, who had sneaked in while her father was at lunch, coming to meet Hardell . . . finding him with another woman . . . goes insane with jealousy, and after she leaves confronts him in anger . . . grabs up the sword, and kills him? Then, terror stricken, she kneels down to see if she has really done it, and with a wild scream of horror runs from the set, leaving the finger prints on the way? Either that, or she goes there to meet Hardell, hears her father coming, who has seen her enter the lot while he is across the street, and hides. Her father either sees her crouching by the chair, or guesses it, and does what he has said he would do—kills Hardell! Then the same action. The girl kneels by the man, screams, flees. Well, we'll have the finger print report complete soon now, and it ought to tell us something. Looking at the possibilities of the various ways that murder could have happened, it tells us exactly . . . nothing!"

"Any one of the ways sounds logical," said Ryan.

"And isn't a damned bit!" said Smith peevishly. Ryan looked up quickly. It must be a pretty tough nut to crack if the Captain was going to get on his ear about it!

"Say, did that fellow at the cigar store tell you what time he saw Hardell and Seibert?" Smith asked.

"Sure. There's nothing off color there. He says it was around 12:30, or nearly that."

"Was his clock, or watch right?'

"He says the men working on that new hotel across from him come in and get their midnight lunch at 12 o'clock. They had all gone, even the stragglers, and they only get a half hour off."

Ryan wondered why his chief's mind went back to what appeared to be a closed question. But all he got to salve his curiosity was, "Well, that makes a sweet dish sweeter! Did you check up whether Beaumont or West wore gloves that night? And MacDougal?"

"Yep. Beaumont wore driving gauntlets. West also. MacDougal has a pair he keeps in his office for odd jobs, or for cold nights. Why?"

"No prints on the rapier," said Smith briefly. Then he ran his hand up through his hair, after throwing his pencil down in disgust. "That's the hell of it! Every time I get an idea that might lead to something, there's more than one answer to it. I'm beginning to think it was a gang-up. It beats anything I ever worked on! Four people on that set, when there should have been but one besides Hardell. Four people with motives for a possible murder, or possible motives for a murder, put either way you want. Three willing to hang on their own testimony that they are guilty. Three people wearing gloves when we find one thing, one place, where there aren't finger prints. Otherwise finger prints, clues, all over the place! Damn it!"

"It's sure a muddle."

"Muddle? It's a farce! It's a tragedy! I might as well go to hoeing potatoes for a living if I don't beat it, because it'll go down in history. Mark my words!"

He stopped, and for a long moment sat staring into space. Then, with a return of his familiar self and his customary confidence, he said:

"Well, my tantrum's over, Ryan. I'm not going to let this thing get me down. Something's got to bust loose pretty soon. There are too many stray ends, too many murderers. If it doesn't, I'm going to forget everything in the shape of a clue, or evidence, that we've gathered, and start following that hunch."

12

And the next morning. . . .

"What the Hell's broke loose in this movie murder?"

"Everything," said Smith laconically, watching with some satisfaction the swelling muscles in the fat jowls of the Chief of Police.

The Chief tilted back in his revolving chair and gazed sternly into the eyes of the Captain of Detectives.

"You remember the Taylor case?" he asked.

Smith grunted expressively.

"My boy, we can't have another murder-mystery left up in the air."

Smith took one of Rosenthal's cigars from his pocket and handed it to the man at the desk.

"Try that," he said enigmatically. For an instant the Chief eyed him impatiently, then did as bidden. The first whiff, and a slow smile of enjoyment spread itself effulgently over his heavy face.

"Ah!"

"Chief, everything about this blasted case is like that cigar," said Smith.

"What'ye mean?"

"De Luxe! It's the prettiest murder I ever saw! Spread with a lavish hand, if you get me. Whoever did it had a sardonic sense of humor, that's certain. In some ways it looks like the work of a silly kid—all messed up with clues that don't join up, that haven't any rhyme or reason. In some ways it looks like the work of a fiend who used to the best advantage all the possibilities of the situation, knowing the tangle it would create. When I went out there day before yesterday I dropped into a nightmare, Chief! Another world! Things are faked so that you can't tell the difference with a spy-glass. I followed up the best I could. I know I was leaving vital things up in the air, but it was a case of grab what I could while the grabbing was good. We won't solve this thing in a week, nor yet a month, nor—"

"We've got to!" snapped the Chief. "I'll throw every member of the force into it, if necessary. Man alive, did you see this?" He held out a paper.

"What Power is Behind This Movie Hoax? Does Arch-fiend Roam At Large While Local Police and Local Picture Magnate Sit Smiling and Inactive?"

"Panning us pretty hard, aren't they?"

"Panning!" snorted the other. "It's outrageous libel! They as much as come right out and state we're in with the picture interests to cover up. What about it?" The Chief's eyes narrowed speculatively upon the Captain. Smith's lips tightened to a thin line of anger as he looked back.

"I've been on this force since I was a kid. What do you think?"

"I think it's easy to go . . . 'the way of all flesh'," replied the other. "You're smoking Rosenthal's cigars, and handing 'em out pretty free."

"If you weren't the man you are, I'd bust you in the nose!" Smith retorted.

The Chief looked with secret satisfaction on Smith's fury-whitened face. "That's fine. He's fighting mad," he told himself. "Now he'll go out and put his mind down to business." Aloud he said:

"All right. We understand each other. Does any one of these three confessions hold water?"

"Every one of them!"

"Eh?"

"You heard me! D'you think I've been losing sleep over this case for nothing?"

For a space the Chief sat in silence. "Have you located that MacDougal girl?" he asked at last.

"Clancy caught MacDougal sneaking to the hospital on the lot, last night. He's following up to-day. Ought to have a report pretty soon."

The Chief grunted.

"I suppose you've tried out the theory that this girl is the meat in the oyster?" he asked.

"Just getting to it," admitted the other.

"Find out if Clancy's in. I'll hear what he has to report."

Ten minutes later. . . .

"You got 'em?" from Smith.

"Didn't you send me after 'em?" from Clancy in an injured tone. "Sure, I got 'em!" He handed his superior an envelope addressed to Miss Beth MacDougal, and marked, "Personal." Smith took the paper carefully by the corner indicated by Clancy.

"Well, Chief, these ought to help a lot," he said.

"Ought to have had 'em twenty-four hours ago," was the reply. "How did you locate the girl, Clancy?"

Clancy stole a quick look at Smith, but finally replied, shame-facedly:

"Oh, the joke's on us, Chief! She was on the lot all the time. Soon's her Dad confessed we got the hunch, and looked at the time sheet of the day Hardell was murdered. She was marked in all right. She never left. MacDougal was in the clear, all right, though—he's only on the gate at night."

"Hm. Well, what did you get out of her?"

"Aw, she ain't in it, Chief! Not the way you two think. She's only a kid . . . a baby! And she's sick."

"Maybe she's got something on her mind to make her sick," snapped the Chief impatiently. "Get into your story Clancy, and cut out the sob stuff."

"Well, I went out there first thing this morning. Say, that nurse is a hard-boiled gal, all right. I had to pull my badge on her and get rough before she'd let me see the kid. Then she keeps glarin' at me like I was a case of smallpox. The kid doesn't know her father's confessed . . . see? First she hauls back in the bed and looks at me like a scared rabbit . . . gets white as the sheet, and starts stuffing her handkerchief down her throat. I goes in and hands her the envelope. She sees her name is on it, and reaches out her little white hand, slow-like, and all the time watchin' me, scared to death, out of her big eyes. Well, she opens it, and . . . you know, there's nothin' in it. She says, 'It's empty,' and looks at me puzzled. Before she gets the idea and spoils the evidence, I take it away from her, like I was goin' to look in the envelope, myself, you understand. Well, then the kid just stares at me, gettin' whiter'n whiter. Finally she says, in a little whisper, 'What did you do that for?'

"I says, off-hand like, 'Oh, that's just to get your finger prints.' And I was goin' to tell her it didn't amount to nothin', when she pulls back on the pillow, and says, 'Finger prints? Oh, my God!'"

Clancy choked, and stopped.

"Go on, man," said the Chief impatiently.

"Well, she just sits there starin' at me, and gettin' whiter'n whiter."

"Impossible! She's done that three times," snapped the Chief.

"Well, she starts cryin', if you like that better," returned Clancy, not without spirit. "She's shakin' all over, so that you'd think she had a chill. I—er—try to make her feel better, see, so's to get her where she can talk. I goes over and—"

"Never mind going into details. I presume you went over and put your arm around her," remarked the Chief sarcastically.

"Well, and so would you have," snapped Clancy. "I tell you the poor kid's scared to death, and sick, and—well, anyway, pretty soon she quiets down, and say! what'd you think she says?"

"That's what we're waiting to hear, Clancy," said Smith, not unkindly.

"She scrouges back into the corner of the bed as far as she can get, and covers her face with her little hands, and cries, 'I wish God had never made men!' Ain't that a hell of a thing to say? And her supposed to be dead in love with that guy Hardell, and me talkin' pretty to her, and makin' it as easy for her as I can? Well, then I springs the dope about her Dad on her. And say, you can put this in your pipe and smoke it: that kid never had a ghost of an idea her Dad was goin' to confess to the murder! No sirree! I watched her careful, and I tell you it knocked her off her pins!"

"I suppose she got whiter'n whiter," said the Chief.

"She sure did," replied Clancy, innocently. "Then she flops over on her pillow and buries her face and—God, how that kid cried! No foolin', I thought she was goin' to bust a G string!" Clancy stopped and gazed into space.

"Did she say anything?"

"The nurse comes in, mad as a hornet, and glares at me. She goes over and feels the kid's pulse, and straightens up and gives me the fishy eye as she yelps, 'It doesn't make any difference to me if the whole police force is back of you, you aren't going to kill this child. Not if I know it!' Can you beat it? She makes me go out of the room and sit in the hall twiddlin' my thumbs for half an hour. She tells me if I've any more damage to do, I'll have to wait until the kid's quieted down. Seems she's got a fever, or somethin', and the nurse says it's as good as curtains if she gets too excited."

"Just what's the matter with this girl?" asked the Chief.

"Gosh, I don't know! She's good and sick, that's certain. Well, while I'm sitting there, I hear her. Gosh, she sounds like a little kid. I seen one once, wandering in the park, rubbin' its eyes and sobbin' and cryin' for its Daddy. Well, that's the way she sounded to me. I heard her sayin', 'They'll hang him! They'll hang my Daddy! Oh, my God! What did I ever do it for!'"

The two other men looked quickly at each other when Clancy's lips pronounced this last. The Chief said:

"Huh! You are certain that's what she said?"

"Sure! But that baby isn't a murderess! She meant somethin' else. I tell you the kid's too little 'n sweet. I tell you—"

"Shut up Clancy," snapped the Chief, "and get out!"

They sat looking at each other, the Chief of Police and the Captain of Detectives. Finally Smith said:

"Well, Chief, shall I go and get a confession out of her?"

The Chief was not in joking mood. He sat silent, looking back into the other's eyes, but milling thoughts of his own. Smith waited patiently. Finally the other slapped his hand down on his desk as he rose to his feet.

"And make it four confessions for the press to chuckle over? Make it a two-reel—four-reel comedy? No. Election's too soon. I'm not going to have people saying I took advantage of a sick girl to force a confession out of her."

"There's this angle, too, Chief. If MacDougal is guilty, her confession isn't going to amount to much. He's already confessed. He'll probably tell the whole story straight when we want it. If the girl's guilty herself, you know what MacDougal will do if we get a confession now? He'll have it thrown out on the grounds that his daughter was sick with fever and out of her head. And that nurse is the sort that will back him up. MacDougal confessed for just two reasons: he did it himself, and the man's got enough conscience left from his Redcoat life to keep someone else from hanging for it; or he did it to save his daughter. If it's the latter he'll save her, confession or no confession from her. He's that sort!"

"Correct. We've got too many confessions on this thing as it is," snapped the Chief. "What we want now is facts. Facts! You go out to that studio, and you work on any tack you want to. I don't care how you do it! I don't care if you throw all precedence to the wind! Professional procedure is out of our line just now. Use your wits—and your hunches. Put a guard on at that hospital. We can't do a thing with that girl until she's pronounced normal by her doctor. We'll sew her up tight. Keep her there, where we can put our finger on her if we want her. In the meantime, I want results and something besides emotional outbursts. Less talk and more action!"

"Right, Chief."

13

Smith knew absolutely that there could not be more action and less talk until he established the matter of Hardell's return to the lot. Giving MacDougal the benefit of the doubt, upon his arrival at Superior Films next morning, he went directly to that portion of the studio grounds known as the "back lot."

Just as motion picture stages are different from anything else under the sun, so is the so-called "back lot" of a motion picture studio. Gaunt buildings, deserted streets, bits of lands reminiscent of all corners of the earth and, unless there is production going on, an eerie silence, broken perhaps by the faint, far distant sound of the city's life, but strangely removed from it. As the Captain of Detectives walked alone through these foreign streets, he seemed to be walking alone in a dream. They gave him that lost and unattached feeling. The thought that came into his mind was, "Quoth the raven, 'Nevermore!'" He could not have told why. Certainly there never could be read into those immortal lines of Poe's, even by the most fantastic stretch of the imagination, any reference to motion picture studio "back lots!" But the haunting suggestion of desolation, the abandoned, decrepit and weird, that lies in them, seemed to fit this place. Walking there alone, his mind toyed with the question of whether it was "Croaked the raven

'Nevermore!'" or, "Quoth the raven, 'Nevermore!'" Then
he dismissed that as immaterial. It was the "Nevermore!"
the hopeless, mourning melancholy of the word, oft repeated, that expressed the feeling in him, the feeling of
desolation that these empty structures threw back to him,
intensified!

Buildings that once were so festive and gay, that had
spilled their lightsome overflow into the starlit nights,
if only for fleeting hours, and now . . . desolate! Smith
felt by this time that if it were not "Croaked", it should
be! "Croaked" went with the tap-tapping of torn shutters
against empty window frames; with the eerie flapping of
once gay and flaunting banners, now grey streaks of rags
against the empty hulls of halls!

He felt these lone buildings grieved together, in a
strange and secret grieving, for habitation within their
walls. They were buildings cheated of their birthrights!
And many of them were but half-buildings, resembling the
street presentations of the "false fronts" of little towns.
He fancied these whispering disconsolately to their neigh-
bors, "Ah, but we are even lonelier than you. We have not
even our own insides to comfort us!"

Queer, this walking alone, through lonely, dead streets
that still held such eloquent small things of human occupancy, even though that occupancy might have been but
for a day. A child's doll, the dress soiled and much-hugged;
a scrap of torn letter; an orange rind; an empty perfume
bottle and an old shoe; and before one little French shop a
flower in pot, just now relinquishing its brave tenacity in
the yellowing of one small green leaf.

For some psychic reason a lump came into Smith's
throat. His common sense told him it was because this
deserted street, echoing vacantly to his passing feet, reminded him of sacked French villages and the horribleness

and unplumbed suffering of War. Some sensitive percep-
tion, not common, made him know it went deeper, back
through the ages, back to century-buried birthplaces of
fallen civilizations. Dead streets, emptied of their human
voices, of laughter, of tears, of the pattering of children's
feet, of the marching of men's feet, always hold a pathos,
inexplicable. He thought it might be because they brought
to mind, in a new, and therefore more effective way, the
inescapable dictum of the three sisters, weaving, measur-
ing, ah, and most tragic, breaking, cutting, ending! For
a moment it was as though he heard the chatter of voices
long since stilled, the appearing, from blackened, sagging
doorways, of figures long since desiccated.

And, even as he turned back along the empty way, he
heard voices. What he saw was a procession of men and
women, laden with many and varied things.

A man, with an apron on which a great pin-cushion
bobbed rhythmically, wearing over his arm a pair of gold
velour draperies. Two more men, with a bedstead swung
between them, and on, and on, to an under gardener,
wheeling a barrow laden with pieces of green, grass-covered
turf. Even as Smith watched, the gardener got down and
began planting them, as tile is laid in squares, about one
of the doorways. The girl in the smock held up a gay little
sign, bearing the legend: "Ye Arts and Crafts Shoppe." A
man, one of those many on a studio lot, known as a "prop"
boy, climbed a ladder and set the sign to swinging gayly
over the entrance. Another sign, "Ye House of Ye Iron Ket-
tle," was hung above the next door. A table, the top made
of bright, imported tiles and set on wrought iron legs, was
put in the little garden at the entrance. Chairs, with flat,
trim cushions of glazed, hand-plaited straw, were put to
the table. A purple umbrella, with gold dragons chasing
themselves around its circular rim, was opened over the

fat little pottery teapot, and the squat, bewitchingly decorated teacups. A sleek, contentedly purring black cat was
made to sit, with upturned rapturous eyes trained upon
a singing canary in a swinging Pagoda cage. The cat sat.
And so he might have sat, occasionally bending to lick his
shining fur affectionately, all the days of his life!

In the space of the short time Smith stood watching,
the raven was ousted and the brilliant plumage of the peacock strutted in its stead.

The whole reminded him of the rose-painting scene in
Alice in Wonderland. He laughed to himself and shrugged.

"Well, that's pictures! It's okay—until you have a murder, a real one, and then what have you? I'm blamed if I
know!"

He started back the way he had come, and now the dead
streets seemed to have been touched by a magic wand, for
another group of workers interested him.

It was the most "ramshackle and foul," as one poet has
it, of the old buildings. And yet it was not ramshackle
enough, nor foul enough, for the purpose to which it was
to be put, for a man with a bucket of slops came and threw
them at its sides. Another carefully laid a dead and bloated
dog in a spot marked in the dirt road. The dog depositor
then turned his attention to a bucket of glue and a couple
of wooden blocks. These he carried with him up a step-
ladder. Smith, standing below, laid his head on the back
of his neck and allowed his mouth to fall frankly open as
he watched him. He realized that what the man was doing
would have made him, Captain of Detectives, swear that
the windows of this rotting building had not been opened
for years, for when the man had finished his work the windows were festooned from sill to pane with a thick curtain
of cobwebs! A blob of glue between the wooden blocks, a
swift grinding and rubbing together of them, a slow pulling
apart and careful swinging toward the glass, and behold, a

perfect cobweb! Then the man got down, seized a new suit of clothes and threw a bucket of rocks and dirt over it. Getting on top of it he began alternating stamping on it with his feet and plumping down on his knees and pounding it with his blocks.

"If you've *got* to beat that suit to a pulp, why pick on a perfectly good one?" Smith asked a bit impatiently.

The man rubbed a shiny patch on the seat of the breeches before he answered. Then he said, not looking up, "Period suit. Matches up with another like it used in the first sequence. Hey Bill, there's supposed to be a dead duck out there, too."

"Oh, Hell! I forgot that blamed duck! What'll I do?"

"You'll go get one!"

"There isn't a duck on the place, dead or alive," protested the other. "But say, there's a couple a chickens in a crate in the 'prop' room. Can't I use one o' them?"

"Von Richten said 'duck', and duck it's got to be," was the firm reply.

"Aw shucks! Well, I'll go get one of those stuffed—"

"No, you won't brother!" snapped the man of the blocks, looking up for the first time. "No stuffed ducks on this set. It's the *insides* he wants!"

"Oh! All right. I guess I can get one down the boulevard a ways."

Laughing a little at the colloquy, Smith, his hands plunged in his pockets, and his head down, started on. Deep in his own thoughts, he did not stop until he was brought up smack against it . . . a waving bit of bright blue satin to which a narrow edge of white lace, torn from a wider flounce, was sewn. For a moment the detective's eyes clung to the fabric. Then he looked about him, half expecting to see a third band of workers busily sticking other "clues" about the landscape. But no one was in sight. No voice came to his ears. A lazy, mid-afternoon wind touched the material with indolent fingers and rippled the high grass growing along the fence. A blackbird came and jeered raucously at him. A ground squirrel scurried out of sight.

"Well, I guess *this* 'set' is the real thing," the detective muttered to himself after a moment. "In that case, I'll manifest a little interest in this all too obvious clue."

Outwardly indifferent, but inwardly excited, he went closer to inspect it. It fell from its place on one of the barbs of the electrically charged fence as his hand reached out for it. Apparently it needed but the suggestion of a touch to dislodge it. Smith whistled softly.

"Thanks. Much obliged," he addressed the fallen clue. "Probably saved me a nice little shock. Now, my fine fellow, we'll see who so obligingly turned off the juice for you on that fateful, foggy night of a week ago!" He placed the scrap of material carefully between the pages of his note book. His exultation over this new evidence had been a bit slow in coming. He was too fresh from scenes of bewilderingly realistic make-believe. But the exultation did come. His step was almost jaunty as he turned back to the "front lot", and he hummed a little tune under his breath.

"But I tell you, Abie, there ain't nobody can get into that svitch box vidout bustin' it!" protested Izzie reproachfully.

Rosenthal swung swiftly around on Smith.

"Vas it busted?" he demanded instantly.

"Nope," replied Smith gravely.

The President of Superior Films threw out his hands in an eloquent gesture of scorn.

"Vell, now you see, busted or not busted, somebody got into it vonce!" he addressed his Production Manager, sarcastically.

Izzie kept a sullen silence. Presently Rosenthal said:

"Vere vas the keys. Think, vonce, now!"

"Ve only got vone key."

"Only vone! Vat if it gets lost? Such a dumb head you haff got, sometimes, Izzie! Don't you know noddings? Only vone key!"

"Vell, ve had three. Hal Gleason, he takes vone vid him by mistake ven he goes to Europe last year. The other vone I don't know vat happens to it. Anyvays, it vas lost a long time ago, long before the vone Hal Gleason takes to Europe."

"Who keeps the key that is left?" asked Smith.

"Our head electrician," Rosenthal answered.

"All right. Let's have him in here," said Smith briskly.

The head electrician was the type that is unmistakably honest. The key had not left his key ring, nor the key ring his possession. Smith was convinced the man told the facts. When he had gone out again, the detective rose to his feet and filled his pocket with Rosenthal's cigars. The President's eyes dwelt upon him with brooding sombreness.

"What's matter? Am I not welcome?" asked Smith cheerfully.

"Sure, sure. Take all you vant. Here, I giff you anodder box!" The President dived down to his bottom desk drawer and came up with a red face and an unopened container of his precious smokes.

"Then what's worrying you?" insisted Smith.

"Efferting iss vorrying me! My business, my vife, my nerffs! Efferyting! I tell you, Smith, dis murder vill be the death off me. Already, Rachel, my vife, she tells me I look crazy around the house! She talks to me. I don't hear her! I don't talk back! Ven you came in vid this evidence to-day, I vas all hopped up! I vas telling myself, 'Ah, now ve vill find out all about it!' But do ve? Do ve find out? No. Ve find out noddings!"

The detective clapped him affectionately on the back.

"Cheer up, old timer," he laughed. "Why should you be downhearted when I'm not?"

Rosenthal looked up, hope dawning in his big brown eyes.

"And you don't feel bad because ve do not find out about that svitch box?"

"Not a bit in the world! That little bit of blue silk told me what I want to know. Of course, I'd have liked to find out who opened the switch box, turned off the juice and then locked it up again; but . . . all in good time, all in good time, my friend."

Rosenthal let out a relieved sigh.

"Vell, I am glad to hear that, certainly."

"Some whiskers, eh, Clancy? How long d'you suppose it took him to grow them?" Smith asked.

Clancy's eyes traveled over the gnarled, bent figure crouched on the stairs to Stage Six. Hands, in which the veins lay corded and blue; eyes, in which the light had long since bleared; an old, old mouth, that trembled constantly.

"God," said Clancy fervently, "I'd hate to be that old!"

"I saw him put on that beard, hair by hair. He takes each one up with a pair of tweezers, and works it into the grease paint on his face. It took him three hours, he told me. Instead of being a hundred and twenty-seven years, as he looks, he's just twenty-seven!"

"You're kiddin', Chief!" exclaimed Clancy, goggle-eyed.

"No I'm not." They stepped aside as a group of people came toward them. When opposite the two members of the police, one of the men let out an oath.

"—! There he goes! Hell bent for election!" he roared, and immediately took up chase. Clancy and Smith ducked as a huge black carpenter bee zoomed straight for their heads.

"Well, keep your shirt on, Don. Let him go. We'll use the 'prop' bee," said a calm, emotionless voice.

"Say, d'you suppose they can *make* a bee to look like that one—and fly?" whispered Clancy, gazing pop-eyed after the party, which had passed on.

"They can make anything in this place. Better keep away from them. I'll bet that 'prop' bee can even sting," returned Smith. Clancy snorted derisively. "I'm telling you, boy!" said Smith with quiet conviction in his voice.

Clancy walked awhile in silence, then he burst out:

"Say, Chief! This is a hell of a place to be working in! How you goin' to believe what y'see? Y'think y'got a clue, and— Gosh, maybe they made it when your back was turned!"

"You said it, boy! That's what makes this case the hardest, and the most fascinating, I ever handled. By the way, I've got a couple of hours on my hands. I'll take this time to talk to that property boy of Seibert's. You said he came back to work to-day."

Clancy nodded.

"You sure that set's been guarded all the time? If anybody has been on there, it won't do any good to talk to him."

"Sure, Chief! Night and day. Two guys with guns."

"All right. I'm going over. Have the man meet me there."

Smith went unchallenged through the little door in the canvas wall. The overhead lights illumined the place dimly. There was still the dark stain on the wood floor. The detective sat down in the director's chair, folded his lean brown hands over his lean stomach, and relaxed. Apparently he went to sleep. But while his body rested, his mind became acutely receptive. Deliberately he threw out

of his conscious knowledge all the things he had previously developed concerning the crime. He sat, tuned in like
a human radio. Once he opened his eyes. They had the
appearance of one drugged. There was no eager seeking in
them. A languid, half-blind gaze. He was not looking for
material evidence, but for those not seen, but felt, impressions that with the truly talented detective are as acute
guides as a blood-stained handkerchief! Several times his
eyes opened slowly and dwelt, without his conscious volition, on different angles of the set. The result was always
the same. Always the camera was the magnet that drew his
gaze, and held it! Smith had often worked on this theory
of his. He would have said, in justification:

"Acts of violence, of any extremely unusual emotional
nature, register what I will call for lack of a proper word,
impressions. I believe it has been found, that, with certain
light and shadow combinations, impressions, discernible
to the eye, have been made. At least there are certain East
Indian wise men who claim so. I am not in a position
to deny it. I know that I have been able to get helpful
impressions by putting myself into a receptive state on the
scene of a crime."

While he distinctly received an impression from the
camera, it did not satisfy him. It was too easily explained
as a natural conclusion.

"The thing is in a pointing position—set to focus on
the floor, from the platform where it stands. It is *pointing!*
The very position draws my attention to it," he decided
finally. He realized, also, that it would be an extremely
difficult thing to set aside one scene from the many that
had been enacted in this place. His mind imagined swiftly
the innumerable things, innumerable as to number and as
to type, that had been done here. How could he hope to
receive a clear impression of this particular murder, when
undoubtedly other murders, staged for the screen but none

the less seemingly violent in action, had been committed upon these very boards!

Clancy entered with Kelsey, Seibert's "prop" boy.

"What's your name?" asked Smith.

"Jack Kelsey."

"I understand that Seibert gave you a dirty deal the other day. Why don't you go after him? He didn't have any right to manhandle you, my boy."

"Aw, what's the use? I want to stay in pictures. I like the game. Anyway, that gink's crazy! He don't know what he does when he goes off his nut."

"Do you really mean crazy?"

"Sure, he's cookoo! Ask anybody! I was mad enough to bust him good when he hit me, but—aw, well, he sent me a fat check and asked me to forget it, and it wouldn't do me no good in the business to go kicking up a smoke about it."

"How long have you been with Seibert?"

"Ever since I come on the lot. Two years, or so."

"Did he ever touch you before . . . or anybody else?"

"Not me, no. The worst I seen him do was to shake a girl most to death because she was one of those Saharas that can't cry and he wanted real tears. Gosh, that girl had a heart of stone! He pictured how she'd feel if she found her mother dying, or her father with his head busted in, and everything he could think of, and she just looked back at him with her eyes so darn dry you'd wonder why her eyelids didn't stick to 'em!"

Smith smiled. "So he shook her?"

"I'll tell the world he did! If she'd had false teeth they'd been all over the place! Was funny, too, 'cause the big boss—Rosenthal, you know—comes puffing along about that time and gives Seibert the devil and says he's going to fire him off the place and blacklist him in all the studios. And just then the girl busts out cryin' and Seibert jumps at the cameraman and yelps, and everybody gets busy and forgets all about the big boss. When it's all over the girl goes up and kisses Seibert's hand and says he's made a real actress out of her. Hell! Can you beat it?"

"I want you to take a look around and tell me if everything is as you left it the day before the murder? I understand that you property boys can tell if a—er—cobweb has been removed or added to a set?"

"Sure we can. That's our business."

"All right. Hop to it, young fellow!"

Kelsey stepped back to the canvas gate.

"I'd better start right here and cover everything, he said. Smith nodded. Kelsey continued, "Of course there's things that happened since that—"

"I understand. What I want to know is how the set looked when you last saw it, before the murder occurred," Smith told him.

The boy gave a swift glance about. "That overstuffed chair was facing the other way," he said instantly.

"Hm. So that if anyone crouched down and put their hand on it, they might, in getting up, swing it just that much out of position?"

"Why—yes," the boy hesitated. "Otherwise, aside from the blood marks, everything looks the same," he added.

"Did you put the 'props' away that evening?"

"Sure. That's my job."

"You didn't leave anything, except what we see now, on the set?"

"No, sir. Serge was all through with the dummy, which was lying right there where you see those chalk marks now, and so I gathered him up, along with the letter, a lace handkerchief, and a box of snuff, all of which was used in the scenes that day."

"How about the rapiers?"

"Seibert's orders to leave 'em out, as he was going to rehearse Hardell that night."

"Hm. Then he would not go to the 'prop' box and get out what he wanted himself?"

"Nope. Anyways, it's always locked, and there's only two keys."

"Doesn't the director have one?"

"What for? He don't mess with the 'props'. I got a key, and there's another on the rack in Cohen's office."

"You just told me the cameraman, Serge, shot the dissolve from Hardell to the dummy, the last thing. Was Seibert here when he did that?"

"Nope. Serge does all that stuff himself. It's all mechanics, you know, after the actor does his business in the scene. Serge is as temperamental as Seibert, and he likes to be alone when he's doing dissolves. Afraid somebody'll upset his counting."

"Counting?"

"Sure. When they make a dissolve they count the revolutions of the camera—like this." He broke off to count in steady rhythm. "One . . . two . . . three . . . four. The length of the dissolve depends on the number of counts. Sometimes in a tricky scene Serge uses a motor to turn the crank. Then he knows he can't miss."

"Hm. Did he use one for this scene?"

"I don't know. He kicked us all off the set. He had one here. He might have used it."

"Is it customary for cameramen to be so temperamental?"

"Some of 'em are, and some of 'em aren't. The guys that make a lot of fuss—always blowing up about something or other and calling a lot of attention to themselves—always seem to get the big salaries, though, and their names in the screen credit list. This here Serge—he's a Russian—is sure stuck on himself! You'd think he was the whole show."

"In short, he thinks the camera end of a picture is the biggest end?"

"You said it! He's always telling somebody that it's the camera, and not the director, that puts over the stuff. He ain't so far off, at that. There's some pictures wrecked because of bad photography, and some rotten stories put over on the screen with good lighting, and all that. But this guy Serge, he's just a nut like a lot of 'em around here."

Smith crossed over and stood under the camera, mounted on its platform. He stared up in silence at the black box-like machine, and Kelsey stared at the detective's back in the same speculative curiosity.

"I'd like to take a look in your 'prop' box," said Smith, turning suddenly. "We'll go right over to the 'prop' rooms now."

"If it's the stuff that came off this set you want to look at, it's all right here. There's a locker on this stage because it's so far from the main 'prop' rooms," said the boy.

At Smith's nod he led the way in the semi-darkness, over and under the underpinning of sets in construction, through the spooky blackness of a pirate's cave, and across the polished floor of a small dance room. Smith by now had become accustomed to feeling his way, and with a little sense of enjoyment he realized his feet had developed that extra sense which made them lift instinctively over unseen barriers, the sense that all actors, and other frequenters of motion picture stages, develop.

"Before you open it, I've a couple of questions. What are those chalk marks on the floor for?"

"Gosh, don't you know? That's what was so dam funny about Hardell's being killed. He was lying right on 'em!" said Kelsey in evident surprise. "They use 'em in a dissolve. The real actor lies there first, and then the dummy is put in the exact position, so that there isn't the fraction of an inch difference."

"Thanks. Now another. That set looks pretty dusty to me, for the short time it's been in disuse."

"Sure. It's supposed to be dusty. We blew it on. It's a room in a deserted house." He waited a moment for Smith to question him further, and then unlocked one of the doors of a wall cabinet at the end of the stage. Before Smith's memory acted he let out an exclamation when the door swung open.

A sprawling figure, one up-turned hand clutching desperately at thin air, the mouth a twisted grimace of horror and the face a bluish white, was crammed into the floor space of the locker. Kelsey grinned.

"Skeleton in the closet's got nothing on this bird," he said, and bent to haul the figure out to get at a black box against which it was leaning. Smith stopped him.

"Hold on!" he cried, and for a long moment he bent down, scrutinizing every detail of the figure, its costume and position. One thing was soon evident. There was no tear in the blue satin. He could find no place where the scrap of material he had found on the back fence would fit. He grunted in satisfaction. He straightened and swung around on Kelsey.

"Part of your job is knowing if anything has been touched—moved—since you saw it last, so that you can be sure things match up in the scenes, isn't it?" he asked.

"Has that dummy been moved since you put it there?"

Kelsey laughed. "'Old Bill' ain't so popular nobody wants to take him out nights," he grinned. "'Old Bill' is what we call him. We usually name 'em before we get through with 'em. We got a regular old standby in the 'prop' room named Betsey Ross. I don't know who done it, but that's what she's been called ever since I've been here. We use her for fire scenes, and comedy stuff."

Smith smiled back at the idea, and then his face sobered as his keen grey eyes fixed sharply on the boy's face.

"I want you to look closely at that dummy, and tell me if it's been moved," he said.

Kelsey bent over 'Old Bill' obediently. After a minute, he said, "Nobody's laid a finger on him. I could swear to it. I had a time getting him in there, and I remember his wig got shoved to one side, like that. It's just the same." He pointed to a couple of the white hairs that had fallen loose and were down over the eyes. "There's your answer! I remember thinkin', when I put him in there, that his wig was gettin' fuzzy and would need dressin'. Them hairs was sticking down like that. It's part of our job to keep the 'props' in condition."

"All right. Now the rest of these things. Are they all just where you put them?"

"Absolutely! Look here," he bent and moved a small box on the floor of the locker, "there's the dust marks! I tell you mister, you're barking up the wrong tree. There ain't nobody touched these things, and what'd they do it for anyway? That's one thing, and another is, nobody can get into here, 'cept Cohen. He's the only one's got a key besides me."

Smith laughed at the boy's earnest face. "All right, Kelsey," he said. "Maybe I am barking up the wrong tree, but a detective has to make a show of asking a lot of questions about something, you know, just to show he's working on the job."

"I guess that's right," agreed the other naively.

14

Clancy hastily put down a copy of the Police Gazette and turned an innocent countenance to his superior. Smith looked from the paper to the red face of his co-worker.

"Is this the way you find out if I can talk to that girl at the hospital?" he asked sharply.

"Aw, Chief, it didn't take me no time. I done it already. So I just come back here to wait for you." Clancy then had an inspiration. "Want to see her? Here she is!" Eagerly he grabbed up the periodical and thrust it out.

"See who?"

"Beth. She's sure one of them regular little pocket Venuses you read about! Ain't she sweet?"

Smith was surprised to find he thought, also, that she was sweet. There was an appealing wistfulness about the little figure, an atmosphere of innocence, despite the deliberate scantiness of her covering.

"What did her nurse say?" he asked.

"That hard-boiled dame gives me a pain! Anyway, she says it's doctor's orders nobody can talk to Beth. She says it might get her excited and send her into brain fever."

"Hm. Well, could you get anything out of the nurse? If you think she'll talk, I'll go out there and see her."

"Her talk? Say, you couldn't pry anything out of her with a can opener! That dame's wise. She ain't no spring chicken, and she's sure a good friend to Beth."

"Well, what did she have to say?" Smith asked impatiently.

"Aw, Chief, that little kid ain't the one—" Clancy started and then shut up instantly at the look in Smith's eyes. "I told you she's a wise bird, that nurse. All I could get out of her was that Beth came on the lot the afternoon of the night of the murder. The kid was sick, and she and the nurse have been friends ever since MacDougal come down here from Canada. They met on the trip, or something. Anyway, she said Beth come in, and she put her to bed, and when she went in to see her the next morning the kid was out of her head . . . fever and delirious. Well, she calls the doctor, and the doctor says the kid has to go to a rest sanitarium and—"

"Why didn't she?"

"'Cause the nurse tells the doctor she's known her for so long, and understands her, and all, and the kid would get well quicker with her. See?"

"Hm. Anything else?"

"Well, that nurse, she gets real uppety with me. Tells me the police don't need to try to pin anything on poor little Beth MacDougal just because she was foolish enough to be infatuated—that's what she said, infatuated—with that bum Hardell! Then she says she knows that's what we're tryin' to do, 'cause Beaumont and West have got money and pull back of 'em. She says the big boss, Rosenthal, don't want either of them to be guilty, 'cause it would be bad for business, but that poor little Beth MacDougal is only a little fool comedy kid, with a pretty face and a swell figure, and the woods are full of 'em in Hollywood! Anyway the nurse says these here Comedy Kids ain't got no morals nor no sense—leastwise that's what folks suppose—so it makes it easy for us to take advantage of Mac-Dougal's daughter."

"Hm. Well, the woman's lying. She knows what the girl did that night, but nothing short of third degree is going to get it out of her."

"Aw, that kid'll come clean when she's well!"

Smith looked at Clancy kindly. "I've got the same hunch myself—"

"Gosh, that sounds good to me!" burst out the sergeant of detectives impulsively.

"Why, Clancy? Have you fallen for that girl?"

"Aw, well—" and Smith knew he had.

The phone rang and Smith answered it. When he had finished his conversation he turned to Clancy.

"Want to go out to the lot and see that stuff Seibert shot of Hardell the day before he was killed?"

"Betcherlife!"

Clancy grabbed up his hat and a florist's box that was parked carefully under the desk. Smith raised his eyebrows but made no comment.

"Don't hurt nothing, does it, to take her flowers?" Clancy said, going red in the face.

"No, of course not, old man!"

They sat in the cool darkness of Rosenthal's private projection room, upstairs in the executive building.

"I am very glad you are going to look at these scenes. Perhaps you help me settle an argument vid Seibert," said the President of Superior Films.

"How's that?"

"I haff been telling him they are all right, and he has been telling me they are all vrong! Now you see them, and I find out vat you think."

"But man alive, I don't know anything about pictures!" Smith protested, laughing.

"Sure you know. You go to see them, don't you? Vell, then you know enough. Sometimes I think ve fellows in the business know too much!"

"I get your point," Smith answered and leaned back in the padded leather chair.

He was aware of somebody joining them. Rosenthal turned on the dim light that stood on a table close to his elbow. It revealed a clerk, with a note book and pencil, sitting there. But this was not the man that drew Smith's interest. It was the short broad figure of Serge, Seibert's cameraman, who had come in quietly and now stood before them. In the dim light he took on the aspect of monstrosity, or abnormality. He had a very large head and a thick, black mane of hair. His face was pale, and to Smith his eyes seemed unusually black and brilliant. Yet this unpleasant impression was dispelled when, at Rosenthal's introduction, he smiled, showing gleaming, perfect teeth.

"Ve think Serge iss the best cameraman in the business, but ve do not tell him very often, for already he has the svell head," said Rosenthal.

"Quit your kidding, boss," said Serge. Smith was entertained immediately by the man's speech. American slang in a precise, and unmistakably foreign, accent.

"All set to go?" he asked next, and Rosenthal grunted. "All right, shoot!" he called back to the man in the projection room, adding, "Stop her right where I hold up my hand."

"Okay. If I don't see you, sing out!"

Smith was surprised to find himself in a slight tremor of anticipation. Rosenthal had turned off the light on the clerk's table, and the room was as dark as a cave. But it was a palpitant blackness, through which only the burning ends of cigarettes were visible, and out of which voices came as though bodiless.

It was quite different from the soft, warm lighted interiors of motion picture theatres. Clancy moved uneasily beside Smith and let out an uncomfortable whisper.

"Gee, Chief! I'm not stuck on this looking at a fellow after he's dead. Gives me the creeps!"

"Rot!" said Smith.

There was a sizzling sound from the projection room and a white beam of light shot towards the screen. A flicker or two, and the picture was on. There was the set on Stage Six—so familiar now to Smith—and Yvonne Beaumont entered the scene. Smith's attention concentrated as Hardell entered. He recognized the man's type. An animal of sex. The sort of man who, when not practicing vice, is planning it. Yvonne, struggling in his embrace, showed plainly her aversion to his physical nearness. Later, using one of the dueling swords, there leaped into her eyes an unmistakable lust for vengeance. Smith found himself unable to decide whether it was acting or realism showing itself.

"I did not know Miss Beaumont wounds Hardell in the picture," he said sharply to Rosenthal.

The President's eyes did not leave the screen. It was a close-up, showing only the two faces, and getting over in this way (a method taught Americans by foreign films) that Hardell received a severe thrust. The action had changed before Rosenthal spoke.

"Sure. Ve put it in because she can really do it. It's good stuff." He stopped to light a cigar, and then added, "I tell you ven I get the idea. It vas because I vent offer to International Artists to a preview, vile ve vere vorking on the continuity for this picture. In that picture I saw offer there, they haff a girl in a dueling scene vid a man. But she iss no good. It iss bum! Right avay I see it. That girl she throws that rapier around like a tennis racket! I tell Yvonne, and she laughs herself sick. Then she says, 'Giff me a scene like that, Rosie, and ve'll show them how it ought to be done. Ve'll knock their eyes out! My fathair, he haff no sons, and so he make me vat you call tomboy!'"

Smith admitted it was pretty work.

A silence fell on them as Hardell's death scene came on. The hero, rushing in and finding his sweetheart at the mercy of a man infuriated by pain and rage, seizes the rapier from Yvonne's hand and thrusts it through Hardell's heart.

And the next thing, startling in its horrible familiarity, was the prone figure of the man, the face twisted in the same frightful grimace and the eyes starting out of the tortured features.

Clancy clutched Smith's arm, and Smith put out his hand and silenced him. There was continued silence on the part of the little audience as the finish slate, held in the hands of the assistant cameraman, came into the scene and obliterated it.

"Seibert Productions. Picture No 186. Serge. Scene 220. Take No 4."

Again the beam of white through the darkness. Smith roused himself from the mental paralysis into which the amazing reality of the thing had thrown him.

"Is that all?"

"No," Serge answered. "There is the dissolve. Would you like to see it?"

"Yes."

Serge stepped back to the projection room and soon Smith was again looking at the sprawled figure of Hardell. A few feet of this unpleasant close-up, and then the enemy of the heavy entered the scene and, standing over him, plunged the rapier again and again into his body.

"God Almighty!" gasped Clancy. "They couldn't do that without killin' the guy!"

Serge laughed.

"Ve can do anything in pictures!" exclaimed Rosenthal proudly. "Just the same, I say it myself, Serge, neffer haff I looked at a better dissolve. Neffer! But don't you go hogging the credit. Vidout Cedric Halland's make-up on the dummy you could not do it!"

Smith said, "It's getting funnier and funnier how much like the dead man the dummy looks—in the picture—and how much like the dummy the dead man looks!"

"Funnier and funnier? Vell, if you vas in my place you vouldn't think so! It's getting fiercer and fiercer! I tell you I don't haff much more patience for you to find out about it, and that's the truth, Mr. Smith! Funny don't express it!" said Rosenthal.

"Meet me on the set in ten minutes. I want to talk to you," Smith told Serge. Then, gripping Clancy's arm, and forcing the sergeant, through sheer force of will power, to keep silence, he propelled him rapidly out of hearing. Clancy broke out volubly the instant the grip relaxed.

"It's a dirty, low-down frame-up!" he panted. "They killed him when they made the picture and the whole gang's sticking together to cover up. Gosh, can you feature it? I'll bet that French broad was tellin' the truth, all right, only she changed the action to get sympathy. Gosh! And that oily Jew, askin' us out here and givin' us the key to the studio, and chucklin' up his sleeve because we're such dumb-bells! What kind of ash cans do they take us for, anyway? The low-down is that Rosenthal is first cousin to every other producer, or darn near all of 'em, and his wife's first cousin to the rest! So he tells 'em that he'll black-list 'em in the studios if they don't stay by him. Nat'ully they don't want to give up their nice cushy jobs, with fat salaries and havin' the rest of the world envyin' 'em on account of bein' in pictures, and so they sit tight! Maybe they figure the guy's dead anyway, and since tellin' the truth ain't goin' to bring him back to life, why let it ruin 'em!"

"That's the way it hits you, Clancy?" said Smith quietly.

"You're darn tootin' that's the way it hits me! I tell you, Cap, that French dame, or the hero, did it! And the big saps that we are, we sit right there lookin' at it and enjoyin' it just because it's a motion picture! Gosh, I don't think much of us!"

"No," said Smith slowly, "it wasn't done then, Clancy, old man," and then he had only time to change his tone to one of sharp command as Serge came up to them. "That's a pretty radical idea, Clancy! Keep it dark—and to yourself! Understand?"

"Sure. I'm wise."

"No. No one has moved the camera since I set it up here," said Serge in answer to Smith's first question.

"Do you usually leave your camera on the set at night?"

"No. But Seibert wanted to re-take the death scene which matched up with the dissolve, and I did not want to chance moving the focus."

"I want to check up, if possible, on the film you shot the day before Hardell was murdered."

"It will take some time, but it can be done. There will be a discrepancy, however. The camera jams sometimes and we waste film in rethreading."

"Did that happen on that day?"

"Yes."

"How many times?"

"I do not remember."

"Then you cannot say how much film was wasted in that way?"

"No."

"Well, find out how much film you loaded and how much you shot—exposed."

Serge showed his white teeth in his sudden, brilliant smile.

"They'll bawl me out good and plenty at the 'lab', but I'll try to get the dope for you."

"I understand that. I'll wait here for you."

"Oh, I'll phone them! They might have an inspiration to throw me in the 'soup' if I went down there in person."

Smith could not detect any double meaning in the man's conversation as he started speaking over the phone.

"Hello. That you Sam? Get me the footage on that stuff we shot the day Hardell was killed. Check up all the NG's and the waste ends, and the raw stock in the magazines. Tally it with the slate and let me have the total. Certainly I am not kidding. Do you want Captain Smith to talk to you?"

Evidently the man did not, for Serge hung up.

Smith was in the chair marked Assistant Director, and apparently dozing, when the cameraman returned to his side. He lay back with his lean brown hands on his lean stomach. Serge smirked at him, and said under his breath:

"If you were fatter, my good detective, you would be very much like a sitting Buddha—in appearance! But I do not think you are as wise. No, not as wise!" and he began walking about the set with quick, elastic steps. Smith opened his eyes in time to see him leap suddenly high in the air, twirl his body in a complete revolution, and land lightly on the balls of his feet. Just then the phone rang and Serge went to answer it. Smith retained an impression of the man's legs, revealed fully as to shape, in the golf stockings frequently worn by cameramen and assistant directors. They were the strangest legs he had ever seen; very short, and huge with bulging muscles. No wonder the man could leap!

"Film issued Seibert Productions March 31 Unexposed straight stock 4800 feet. Panchromatic 400 feet. Exposed total (straight stock) 4200 feet. Panchromatic 132. Not checked in magazine X-124, 400 straight stock. Total print 380 feet. NG's and slated 3520. Shortage 120," read Serge when he returned, looking at the memo in his hand.

"Hm. That means you wasted 120 feet when the camera jammed. Approximately how much waste is there each time it jams?"

"Ten or fifteen feet. It might not all be lost in jamming. There might be a short end left in one of the magazines."

"Why?"

"Well, it usually runs 400 feet to a roll. Suppose we've exposed 380 feet, and Seibert starts a new sequence of scenes which I know will take more than what remains on the roll. We take it out and put in a fresh one."

"How was the camera fixed when you left it? Fresh loaded and ready to shoot?"

"Yes. My assistant had just put on a magazine when Seibert called it a day."

"Then, if no one has touched this camera, why is that magazine not on it now?" Smith asked.

There was a flicker—it might have been surprise—in the man's eyes.

"You have already examined the camera? I have not. I will see if you are right." He went to it with his light bouncing gait.

"You are right," he said, turning back to Smith.

"Can you explain it?"

"I cannot explain it. It is possible I am mistaken. Very often people imagine they have seen the movements of a familiar routine, when they have not. It is a subconscious thought."

"Possible. Can you conveniently get another camera and bring it here?"

"I think so," he answered and left the set.

When he returned, carrying another camera, Smith said, "I want you to show me how a person familiar with a camera would go about taking off the magazine in changing magazines."

Serge's sensitive, steely fingers clasped the camera.

"Here," he said, grasping the back spool, "or here," taking the front one. "With the other hand you unscrew this," he touched the screw that held the camera magazine in place, "and then you throw off the chain from this spool, and lift it off. The new magazine slips into this slot. You tighten the screw again, replace the wire chain on this pulley, and you're ready to shoot."

"Thank you. Will you go through that several times?"

Serge complied.

"Now show me how a person would unthread the film," Smith said.

"Like this." Serge released the catch on the little drop door at one side of the camera and beckoned Smith to come closer to see inside. Then he showed him how the film would be removed from the sprocket.

"Thanks," said Smith again, adding, "I've heard you must clean out these wheels and the interior of the case to prevent static."

"That is so. It must be wiped carefully—brushed out first."

"Did you do that the last time you used your camera?"

"Certainly."

"Thanks. I won't keep you any longer."

"Will you go with me to the commissary and have a drink?" Serge asked, with his flashing smile.

"Thanks again. I will."

"Clancy, go get my car and drive it around to the West side entrance of Stage Six."

"Sure, Cap."

Smith went quickly to the set, whipped a cloth of gold case from a pillow, smothered the camera in it, and, holding the heavy object carefully away from him, his hands where they would be least likely to confuse prints already made, started down the steps of Stage Six. His eyes encountered those of Izzie Cohen, staring with curious resentment at him.

"Hello, Cohen! Will you have a tart?"

"Vat?"

"Will you have a tart? I think I must look very much like the man in Stevenson's suicide club, you know, who went about with a tray of tarts. Only I believe he carried it on his head. I'm not sure."

"Vat iss it you haff?"

"A camera."

"Vere are you taking it, please?"

"Away."

"Vell, you cannot do that, Mr. Smith! Not vidout I giff you a permit!"

"Consider you have given it," said Smith pleasantly, putting the camera down carefully on the seat of the car and getting in himself.

"But it has got to haff a number, and a requisition, and efferyt'ing! I got to keep track off efferyt'ing vat goes off the lot!"

"Go give it a number. Give it anything you want, old chap! Say, how many times do cameras jam in one day?"

"I do not know. It depends."

"Well, see if you can answer this one: What makes that Serge fellow leap up in the air when you're not looking at him?"

"Oh, him? He vas vid the Russian Ballet. He got vat you call muscle bound, so that he iss not good anymore on the stage."

"Know anything more about him?"

"I don't know noddings more, except he iss full off temperament like Seibert. He makes me lot of trouble in the Production Office. I got to charge that camera to somebody. Cameras cost money."

"So do murders."

15

Professor Amely Middleton was just returned from a period of exhaustive research abroad, and he was finding his home shores a trifle unproductive in material for his expert knowledge to feed upon, when Smith walked in and set a motion picture camera down on his desk.

"Ah!" said the Professor with long-drawn, greedy breath. His eyes, fierce black eyes with the predatory gleam of a hunting eagle, fixed on the camera. "Ah! Being the man you are, Smith, I can safely presume you have something here of interest!"

"And being the man you are, Professor, I can safely presume you can make this exceedingly interesting."

Which pleasantries being over Middleton stepped to his door, closed it, came back and seated himself at his desk.

"Commence," he said.

"Hardell murder. You've read of it? All right, then you know what the papers have told. This is new to-day—this camera. Frankly, I'm shooting at the moon. What I want are the finger prints on this portion letting into the sprocket mechanism, or on the door that opens into it."

"How many people, do you think, have had their hands on that part?"

"The camera was wiped out thoroughly before it was used last. Since then I believe—but mind you, I'm not sure—that two people have touched it. I should say, three. I have the prints of two for your identification. Of course, if there should prove to be more prints on the thing, I'm out and injured." He pulled a packet out of his pocket and passed it over. "Here is a section of film with prints of Serge, Seibert's cameraman. This slate has the prints of the assistant cameraman. You will find prints of both these men on the camera, I am sure. What else, I leave to you."

"You're not holding these men under suspicion?"

"Not yet."

"What's developed besides the newspaper stories?"

"Not much. Queer case. I say not much, and yet . . . a lot. Nothing I can actually prove now, but good working material. I expect these prints to put me over the hump."

"I understood there were plenty of prints around that set?"

"Humph! Plenty is correct. Too plenty! That's why I'm looking in another place and passing up the obvious. Of course, if the real criminal wore gloves, then it's useless. It's a long chance anyway, as—"

"Why do you say that?"

"Even the greenest amateur knows enough to conceal his finger prints!"

"But what the greenest amateur does not know, and what even the expert criminal can hardly be acquainted with so soon, is the fact that the gloves do not protect him!"

"Huh?"

"Just that. In wearing gloves the criminal nearly always, because he believes himself safe—he, or she—leaves a very legible palm print. That is, if he has found it necessary to bring his palm in contact with any object during commission of the crime. The lower portion of the palm, that portion lying inside the opening of the ordinary glove, is as absolute an identification print as the finger print."

For a moment Smith looked back into the Professor's bright eyes. Then a great contentment spread over his lean face.

"That's the best news I've had in a month. When did you fellows discover this?"

"My worthy colleague in Science, Dr. Schneichert, of Berlin, made this discovery."

Middleton got up and unlocked one of his filing cabinets. Taking out a sheaf of records, he handed them to Smith.

"These are copies of print records which helped to apprehend three murderers. All three of these criminals wore gloves."

Smith looked at them silently.

"When we have sufficient records established, dactyloscopic science will be as universally applied to these glove cases, as finger print taking is to-day."

Smith looked up. "That's great stuff!"

"It will be a priceless aid to you people."

"Beyond a doubt. It may be the missing link right now. I don't want to rush you, Professor, but when can I get your findings?"

"I'll phone you. It won't be long."

Smith went to his office and locked himself in. He hoped to spend at least a couple of hours working on the murder, but that hope was quashed immediately, and continuously, by the demands of the telephone. First it was a group of persistent reporters. Smith had long ago learned that it is far, far better to talk to reporters than to refuse to see, or hear them. He knew exactly how much insidious meaning could be put into the various ways of expressing that the person interviewed "refuses to talk." So, one and all, he greeted them genially.

"Oh, good morning Crandall! Sorry old man. Nothing new. I'll let you know just as soon—say, I can put you wise to a little news story out there that will keep you going until something breaks."

That was the way he did it. Kept their good humor, talked to them, but told them nothing.

And then the phone calls began getting warmer, warmer, and finally hot. First Rosenthal called.

"Vat a mess!" were his opening words. "I tell you, Mr. Smith, I am being vatched like already I am a criminal! My lot iss full off reporters! Every corner I go around I bump into vone! I cannot eat in the commissary, but I must have meals sent in, and then they send me notes on my tray! Vat shall I do?"

"Talk to 'em," Smith advised.

"But vat shall I say? Already I haff said efferything!"

"Say what I do—that we're doing everything we can to clear up the mystery."

"Mine Gott! Ten million times haff I said it!

They don't belieff me! It gets vorse and vorse! Efferybody commences to look qveer at me—at *me*—just like I had something to do vid it! I tell you it gets on my nerffs! Vy don't you find out some things?"

"I am. You'd be surprised!" returned Smith. "Cheer up, Rosie. Don't let 'em worry you."

"How can I help it? I go to eat, and the place iss full off them! I go to drive home, and the boulevard, it iss full off them, chasing me, I tell you! I get out to go into my house and they follow me. My Rachel she has a nervous breakdown already! My business it iss going to ruin! Effery place are reporters chasing me! Efferytime I stand still for a minute they take a snapshot off me, until I tell you I am on the jump all the time to keep ahead off them! They go all offer my lot—efferyvere!"

"If they try to get on that set they'll get a hole in 'em!" said Smith.

"Sure, and that's only vere they stop. Maybe I should carry a gun. Vat you think?"

"No, no! Don't do that, old man! You just sit tight, and pretty soon we'll have news for them."

"What's that?"

"I said pretty soon we'll have some news."

"At last you haff found out somethings?"

"Uhuh. Say, why don't you go out on a time and try to forget your worries? Do you good. Tomorrow I'll have something to tell you."

"That's vat my Rachel says. She buys already tickets to The Orpheum. Mine Gott! It iss a vaste off money. I do not vant to go."

"Well, cheerio. Maybe I'll take a run out this afternoon."

"I vish you vould, and I vish you vould haff some good excuse for coming, too."

Smith, smiling, hung up his receiver. He liked Rosenthal. He appreciated his position. He felt the sincerity of his protest. The phone rang under his hand. It was Serge.

"Say, just in the case you still want a report on that missing film. I've got it."

"You've accounted for, or located all of it?"

"Yes."

"I would like to see it."

"Sure. Any time you come out. If I am not here, it is at the 'lab'. They will show you."

"Thanks."

A call came from Professor Middleton. Smith listened to it and then said:

"Rather not discuss it on the phone. I've got an errand that will take me a couple of hours. Will you be in your office then? Fine. I'll be over."

From his office he went to the office of a concern that had an agency for the distribution of American camera film.

"What can I do for you, Captain?"

It was the head of the concern himself.

"You can forget this little matter immediately it is finished."

"I have found it wise to have a convenient memory—that has lapse, you know."

"Now we understand each other. You keep a record of all your sales, and the time limit of the usability of film issued?"

"Yes."

"Good. Did you sell any films within the last few months to this party?"

The man took the notation.

"I'll call my stenographer—"

"Don't do that! I'd hate to see a good girl go wrong for the sake of a little bunch of money, and I've a notion she could sell the information that I asked for this data at quite a bit."

"I understand. I'll attend to it myself."

He was gone a little while, and came back to tell Smith they had no record of any such sale.

"You understand Captain," he added, "we are not the only place where such film could be purchased. Just a moment and I'll give you the addresses of other possible sources."

In a moment he was back with a memorandum containing the addresses.

"By the way," he said, "if you don't find what you want at any of those places, I suggest you try the Foreign Agencies."

"That's a good idea. Thanks."

It was at one of these last that Smith found what he sought.

Middleton was plainly gratified. He sat gloating over the prints.

"My first American case," he said.

Smith sat down.

"That means palm prints! In other words, it means that my murderer was a comparatively calm and collected person, who deliberately attempted to conceal his finger prints?"

"It does."

"That means, also, that all of those divergent clues have no direct bearing on the murder."

"Apparently."

"It is not probable that West would protect himself with gloves, and then make those footprints afterwards. There is this, however: He might have had on gloves, which he did not think to remove. But what would he be doing inside the camera?"

"Of course, you understand, I have no palm prints of the cameraman—Serge, you called him—or of the assistant cameraman. This print might belong to either of them."

"That's a fact. I'll remedy that my next trip."

"In the meantime—"

"Keep this under your hat. I'm going to try out a hunch of mine, and if it leaks it's no good."

From Professor Middleton's, Smith went out to the studio and walked into an argument between Izzie and Abie.

"I tell you, Abie, it ain't no use! You should to take a look vonce! Five hundred off t'em, and t'ey just stand and look like noddings! I tell you, ve got to shut it up! Burn it up! Anyvays, ve get the insurance!"

Smith silently leaned over to Rosenthal's cigars. Not for anything would he have interrupted this scene. It afforded him too much entertainment.

"It iss Stage Six ve are talking about," said the President, turning to Smith. "Already ve cut off vone end—the end vere your men vid guns are on guard.

Already ve coffer it vid scenery, so's they shouldn't to see even vone corner of that canvas fence. But Izzie tells me just now they only stand around in bunches and look offer their shoulders like they seen a ghost already! And I should pay five hundred extras for two days ten dollars apiece, to ruin a scene!"

"That's just because the murder is still a mystery. Why don't you wait until we clear it up? They won't act that way about that set then."

"Listen to him!" said Izzie sarcastically, turning to the President. "He says to vait! Vait, ven ve haff got two directors already hollering for de luxe sets, and no place to put t'm! I haff a terrible time vid Giddy, our art director. Already he has made his plans for that ballroom set, and it iss very qviet, very highbrow, you understand? I say to him, 'For Gott sakes, Giddy, put somet'ing on that set to make those people forget there vas a murder on that stage. Put in some naked vomen—vell, you know, not all naked—and do efferyt'ing you can to pep it up!' Giddy has a fit already, but ve do it. But does it—"

"Say, wait a minute!" laughed Smith. "It seems to me you are having all this trouble for nothing. Why don't you put that scene on another stage?"

"Stage Six iss the only vone vid that beautiful marble dance floor," Rosenthal explained. "The other stages they aren't so good. My directors they von't use them for de luxe ballroom stages. Ve got lights, and efferything fixed for the best results on that stage. And then that Hardell should get himself killed on it!"

"Tventy t'ousand dollars, Abie, ve put into that set, into vone set! Think off it!" Izzie complained.

Smith raised his eyebrows.

"That iss so," sighed Rosenthal. "The ballroom scene vas the big scene in that picture. In a veak moment I okayed Giddy's sketches. In a veak moment I did it."

"Yeah, and you know vat happens next? Ve got two directors valking, that's vat!"

Abie and Izzie looked significantly at each other. Smith said:

"You say it like it was the smallpox. What d'you mean?"

"Ven a director 'valks' it means he von't vork. It means he gets temperamental, and he von't do a thing until he feels like it. But all the time ve got to pay him his salary! All the time it costs us two thousand dollars a veek apiece for these two directors. Sure, ve got to pay it. But ve can't make them vork!"

"That's funny—"

"Vonce already I told you this business iss not funny!" said Rosenthal peevishly.

"Yeah, and vile ve pay t'em two t'ousand dollars apiece, ve kiss that other twenty t'ousand good-bye," said Izzie.

"Kiss it good-bye nothings! You go right avay out there and tell those people they get busy and do vat they are told or they get off the lot! You tell them I said so! You tell them neffer again vill they be back on this lot vidout they do it! Then if that boob off a director don't like the stuff he gets, you haff that set coffered all up. Don't let no dust get on it. Kiss it good-bye, I should say ve von't! Ve shut that set up and ve use it in our next picture after this murder business iss settled!"

Izzie went.

"What's Seibert doing these days?" Smith asked, lighting his cigar.

"Cutting his picture. Alvays he shoots ten million more feet than he needs. It iss like cutting off his own arms and hands to take any out."

"If it's good why don't you leave it in?"

"Smith, sometimes you don't use your head about pictures and that's the truth! Leaff it in? And haff a twelff

reel picture vat nobody vants to run in their houses? I
guess not!"

"My mistake," smiled Smith.

"And if you think that bird iss temperamental ven he
iss shooting, mine Gott! you should to see him ven he iss
cutting!"

"Is he working now?"

"Maybe. Maybe not. He comes and goes at all hours.
Sometimes he vorks all night. Sometimes all day. Say, vat
you got to tell me? Vat you find out?"

Smith rolled his cigar a moment thoughtfully. At last
he said, "Trust me, Rosenthal. I've found out something,
but I can't put it into words so soon. It won't be long,
though. Have patience."

"Patience? How can I haff patience ven the papers they
are saying I am coffering up this murder? All the papers
they say it! Mine Gott, Smith, vat haff I done, besides
being a motion picture producer, that they should jump
on me vid both feet? Pretty soon even my friends think I
know something vat I don't know! I try to be patient. I
don't ask you much vat you are doing. I see my business
being ruined—a bad name ve vill get, for that iss the vay
things go in this vorld—and I tell you, more I cannot
stand! Right here I feel it!" He hit his fat chest over the
heart. "Right here it aches me all the time! I cannot forget!
All the time I haff said to myself that I vill keep my studio
clean. I vill not let dirt come on it. No, I vill not! But does
it do any good? I ask you, Mr. Smith, does it do any good
for a business man to haff ideals?"

"You bet your life it does!" Smith saw the puffed green-
white bags out of which the President's brown eyes gazed at
him wistfully. He saw the bilious pallor of his face. He said:

"You're thinking too much about it. Your food isn't
digesting. Take your wife to The Orpheum tonight. You
need a good laugh."

"Laugh! Ven my insides are tvisting vid misery?

"Sure. Laugh anyway."

Rosenthal grunted and picked up his desk phone to answer it.

"Sure. He iss here. You vant to speak to him?" He transferred the instrument to Smith. "For you," he said.

Smith listened a moment. Then, "That's fine. Thanks," he said.

He clapped Rosenthal affectionately on the back.

"Good news, old man! Things are beginning to break. That was Dr. Amden, Beth MacDougal's physician. I am going to talk to her. You go out and forget your worries. We're over the hump!"

16

"You stole out to meet Hardell after you saw the lights go out on the set?" Smith was questioning Beth MacDougal.

"Yes."

She would not look at him, and she gathered her night-gown into a ball in her hand.

"When you got there Hardell was not there. You thought he was in his dressing room. You waited, hoping against hope that he would return to meet you?"

"Yes."

"I found your finger prints on several things. On a book and on a pillow. Very plain prints because the set was so dusty. Then Hardell did come, and before you could speak, somebody else followed him. You hid because you did not want to be found out. You crouched by that big over stuffed chair. I found your prints on the rockers."

"Yes, I hid there."

"And it was then that you saw Hardell murdered!"

Her eyes slid swiftly to him. For a long moment she stared at him, stared as though he were telling her of things she had done but could not remember. Then she shook her head slowly in denial.

"No. I did not see him—killed."

"Those bloody finger prints on the canvas door were yours. They are also on this." He drew a towel from his pocket. "You came back here and washed your hands, but first you tried to wipe it off on the towel. The towel was in the garbage can. Miss Brown should have burned it."

She looked at it, and her blue eyes began to fill with tears, to well over, to deluge her white cheeks. Then she turned her face away from him again and a quivering sigh came piteously into the silence between them. Smith waited. He felt she would talk of her own volition, and presently she did, keeping her face away from him.

"There isn't any use in keeping things back. My father—"

"Did you see him kill Hardell?"

"No. I did not see him. But I know . . . he did it." There was flat despair in her voice.

"How do you know, then?"

"I never heard him tell a lie. He hates a lie."

"And that is the only reason you have?"

"It is enough. That, and because I did not see Yvonne or Billy do it . . . and because—"

"Your father may never have lied before, but he lied the other day at the inquest. He lied . . . to save you!"

And then she turned to look at him.

"To save me?" A tremulous curving of the lips, a smile of hope that would not smile, but hid its pathetic futility behind the sheet that was caught and pressed against it.

"Yes. Your father, I am sure, had some reason to believe you committed the murder. He had some reason that was proof indisputable to him, enough proof to make him confess at a time when two other confessions would have probably cleared him. But he knew. He knew . . . that *you* did it!"

"I want to see my father! I want to see him!" She pulled herself up from the pillows and swung her slender little body to the floor. Smith put out his hand and forced her gently back.

"It is not necessary. Tell me the truth."

"But how can I make you believe me? I did not— Oh, I did not kill him!"

"Tell me all of it!"

Her fingers locked and struggled with each other on the thin material of her gown. Her eyes fixed on some distant point.

"I wanted— I had to talk to Dwight. My father had forbidden me to see him or to speak to him again. It was to be the last time. I did not want to see him. I knew I had never really loved him, but—but—he, that is we—should have been married. I was afraid of having to live with him. I was afraid to be his wife, but it was right to do. I was going to ask him—" She stopped. Smith could find no words.

"You know, even though you don't like to do things, there are some things you have to do," she said at last.

"I understand." Smith's voice was very gentle. She seemed to gather courage from it.

"I went to the stage, and Dwight was not there. I waited. He did not come. He said he would. Then I heard steps, but they did not sound like Dwight's. I hid while Billy West came and stood still a minute, looking about for his script. Then he went straight to his chair and got it, and went out. I waited some more, and I heard someone coming from the direction of the gate. I thought it was my father. I knew if he found me there, waiting for Dwight, he would shoot Dwight when he came. He had said he would. I was so scared. I started to run, to get off the set, and hide on the stage somewhere. I fell, and that's how . . . I found out that he was there all the time, and—and he was dead!"

"You mean Hardell?"

"Dwight, yes. I fell on him. He was—he felt alive. He wasn't all cold. I felt his face, and then I shook him, and called to him, and he didn't answer. And then, when I pushed myself up from the floor, I got blood all over my hands."

"Look at me Beth!"

Slowly she turned to him. Her eyes came up to his.

"You're telling me that Hardell was on that set all the time, and that the only other person who came on the set while you were there was Billy West, and that he did not kill him?"

"No. He did not kill him."

"Beth, did you see anybody kill him?"

"No! No!"

"Beth . . . did you do it?" His eyes held hers.

"No! No!"

"Who was it screamed—the banshee that Lannigan tells about?"

"I did. When Dwight was dead it scared me so. I got up and ran. I screamed. I did not know I was doing it until I heard myself."

"You went straight to that set after the lights were out?"

"In a few minutes, yes. Just as soon as I was sure Mr. Seibert was off the lot, so he wouldn't come back and—"

"And Hardell's body was there when you first went on?"

"Yes. I thought—Billy West thought, too, because he stepped over him—that it was the dummy."

"Lannigan and your father swore that Hardell went out with Seibert. Beth, are you sure he did not come back later, and all this happened later, and you are not telling me the whole of it?" He went close to her and put his hands on her shoulders. He felt her body trembling, like the twanged vibration of a wire. She had been talking through clamped teeth, and her hands were clenched at her sides. He saw that her forehead was wet, as was her upper lip.

"Beth, this is hard to believe. All my evidence is against it."

"I can't help it! It's the truth! He was there—all the time! Oh, I fell right on him! I keep thinking of it. In the night I wake up and think about it." Her teeth chattered.

"Will Miss Brown confirm what you have told me?"

"Yes. She knows. Ask her! Tell her I said to tell you— everything! Mona knows."

He stood over her a moment, holding her cold hands, trying to quiet her shaking body, trying to give her the calm courage of his eyes. She turned her face from him, and after a moment his own eyes misted and he tiptoed away.

"It was a little past twelve when Beth went over," Mona Brown told Smith. "Seibert must have passed her in his car. It wasn't more than fifteen minutes before she was back— white, and scared silly. She ran to the basin, grabbed the towel hanging beside it, and tried to clean off her hands. She wouldn't say anything. I told her to wait, and we'd wash them. Then she keeled over in a dead faint. I cleaned her up and put her to bed. She's been out of her head, off and on, until yesterday. That's all I know—all I can say."

"But you can swear to the time?" Captain Smith demanded sharply.

"Yes."

"How does it happen you were keeping track of the time?"

"We were both watching the clock, wondering how late Seibert was going to work."

"Thanks, Miss Brown. I need not tell you that what you have just told me goes far to corroborate Beth's story."

17

Smith left the Superior Films lot and Beth MacDougal at sundown. He went directly across the street to the lunch room. It was the first time he had honored "Slim's" with his presence. The proprietor was plainly curious.

"Well, Captain, found out anything?" he asked eagerly, putting down Smith's pie.

"We work at it every day."

Slim shook his head. "I sure never thought it was the last time I'd see that poor guy when he went out the gate that night."

"So? You saw him go out?"

"Sure. Sometimes Seibert stops for a 'coke', and I was wonderin' if he was goin' to—"

"Did he?"

"No. But I seen them all right."

"What time was it?"

"Just before Lannigan come over. He usually comes a bit after midnight, between twelve and twelve-thirty. Sometimes a little later."

"Can you remember if he was later—or earlier?"

"Gosh! I never looked at the clock that night, Captain."

"Then you couldn't swear to the time?"

"Hell, no! I couldn't swear to nothin'!" returned the man quickly.

Smith paid for his lunch and went out to his car. He travelled in the direction of Hollywood, and at a certain corner he got out. A moment later the proprietor of the cigar store there was squirming under the sharp gaze of his grey eyes.

"Just how big a lie were you telling about Seibert stopping at this corner the night Hardell was murdered?"

"I wasn't lying!"

"How much is Seibert paying you? How much are you being paid by anyone, to say that?"

"Not a cent, so help me God!"

"You know what it means if you're caught?"

"Say, who gave you the right to come around here and call me a liar? If you don't believe me, take a look at that." He reached over and pulled out an account book, shoving it under Smith's nose. Rapidly he thumbed the pages. "There. That's the box of cigars Hardell told me to charge to him." He called to the back of the store. "Red, come out here and tell this guy what you did with that box of cigars for Hardell, the night he was murdered."

"Went out and pitched 'em in his car, like you said, when they was standin' in the traffic. Hardell, he calls out, 'Charge 'em', so I come back and tells you to charge 'em," said the boy, his frightened eyes leaping all about Smith's tall person.

"Hardell told you to charge them?" snapped Smith.

"Honest to God, sir, he did!"

Smith looked at them both steadily for a moment, and then left. He went straight to the traffic cop on the corner.

"Are you on duty between midnight and one o'clock?"

"Sure. I'm on straight from now on until me relief, which comes later."

"Did you see Seibert and Hardell the night he was murdered? You've followed the case in the papers, of course."

The man grinned. "Sure, I seen 'em, Captain."

"Why the devil didn't you say so?"

"Why the divil didn't you ask me?" retorted the other with a broad Irish grin. "They was the first car in the line, and that Hardell was using his arm to punctuate his talk, and the lace of it was a-flyin' pretty in the breeze."

"Did you see any more?"

"Divil a bit more. They wint on wid the rest," returned the man good-naturedly as he put his whistle to his lips.

Smith turned his steps to the building in progress of construction across the street. He went to the night foreman.

"Have you got the same night crew on you had on the 15th?" he asked.

"Practically. A few men laid off. Two sick."

"I wish you would call them. Is there some place where they can all get together?"

"The first floor's all right," said the foreman, not, however, without the pressure of the law being used upon him.

"All right. Make it snappy."

And a few moments later, standing on a jutting beam and looking down onto a mass of upturned faces, Smith began speaking.

"I haven't time to question all of you in private. Some of you ate at the stand on the corner across from here the night of the 15th. That was the night Dwight Hardell was murdered at Superior Films." A sound came up from the men. They knew that all right! "He was in a car that passed by this corner around 12:25, at the time when you men would be returning from your lunch. Now nobody is going to try to pin anything on you. We know you couldn't have a hand in it, but you can help me catch the person who did if you tell what you know—provided you know anything, of course." He stopped a moment, and then his voice rang out sharply. "Did any one of you see a man in a blue satin costume, lace at the sleeve—which would have showed out of the cuff of his overcoat—in a big purple car, that night, at that time?"

Snickers broke out as he finished. The men turned to look in one direction, and glances were exchanged. But no man spoke.

"Come now!" Smith exclaimed. "The way you are acting shows me you know something. I may have to put one of you in jail to find out—"

"Go on, tell the dick, Johnson!" urged somebody. Smith caught at the name.

"Johnson? Johnson! I understand you've got something to tell me. Come on now, and then the drinks are on me, boys!"

The man named Johnson spoke hesitantly. "Aw, nothin', only I know that director, Seibert. I used to work at Superior Films, but my wife, she didn't like me playin' around where those movie actresses are—" he stopped to turn red as a loud guffaw greeted this part of his narrative.

"That's all right, Johnson," Smith interrupted. "I don't blame her. They're dangerous babies. So you saw Seibert, eh?"

"I was crossin' the street, and I didn't get out of his way quick enough after the traffic whistle blew, and he blamed near cut the pants off me, that's all! Took time to curse at me, too."

"Who? Seibert, or Hardell, the man with him?"

"I don't know. One of 'em. Guess it was Seibert. He was doin' the drivin'."

"But you saw Hardell?"

"The guy had on a lace nightgown under his coat. Sure I saw him all right!"

"Thanks."

Back at his home, Smith went straight to his office and locked the door. The persistent ringing of the telephone finally roused him from an almost feverish assembling and sorting of the notes and objects on his desk before him. He at last lifted the receiver.

"I am offer at my office," came the excited voice of the President of Superior Films. "Can you come right out here? It iss—vell, over the phone I cannot tell you, but it iss very important."

"Has something happened?" Smith's pulses quickened to the beat of excitement in the voice from the other end of the wire.

"Mine Gott, yes! At the show I got it! At The Orpheum! An idea! Please to come right avay!"

"Won't it wait until morning?"

"Right avay I must see you or I vill bust vide open!" was the graphic response.

"Well, if that's the case, I guess I'll have to forego my beauty sleep and toddle out. You are at the studio?"

"Yes. In my office."

"All right. Sit tight. I'll be there."

When he opened the door Rosenthal literally pounced upon him.

"Neffer in my life haff I been so vorked up! I haff it! I tell you I haff it!" he shouted, running forward and pulling the detective into the room.

"Is it contagious?" asked Smith.

"Yes, yes! Oi, vat am I saying? Mine Gott, I hope not, vas vat I mean! You vas only trying to be funny, eh? I tell you this iss no time to be funny! I haff it, I tell you!"

Rosenthal's eyes were fairly leaping out of his head with the excess of his agitation. He made nervous, futile gestures at his hair, his clothing, and pushed the papers wildly about on his desk. All the time his breath came in short, excited gasps.

"Well, all right. You've got it, old man, but calm down long enough to tell me what it is," said Smith, lighting a cigar.

"First I tell you who committed that murder!"

Smith looked up intently.

"Who?"

Rosenthal came over and whispered a name into his ear, and Smith shook his head with a dry smile.

"I got the same idea, but I've just checked over everything. Hardell was seen by at least five people after he left this studio in Seibert's car."

Rosenthal protested vehemently. "No difference does that make! It means nothing! You vait. From the beginning I tell you! I told you my Rachel gets tickets for the Orpheum to-night? Oi, ven I think about it almost I giff them to Izzie Cohen. Vell, first I am bored silly, ven I am not miserable thinking about my vorries. Same old stuff, you know. A bunch off dogs yelping and jumping through hoops, and some acrobats, and a man vat told dirty stories so fast between nice vones you vas laughing at vone ven you meant to be laughing at the other. Vell, anyvay, Rachel iss giffing me dirty looks because I only sit and groan, ven Mine Gott! something comes out on the stage that hits me right between the eyes! Just like that! The minute I see it the idea comes, like a flash. Up I jump and grab Rachel by the arm, and I haff to slap little Izzie because he busts out crying, and Rachel she von't speak to me all the vay out because I made her step on a man's corns and he bawls her out. Vell, it vas fierce, I tell you, but finally I get them out and put them in a taxi and send them home. Then right avay I rush out here. Almost I haff a collision, but I don't care, I am so excited. I tell you I see it all! I know that iss the vay it happened!" Rosenthal drew out his voluminous silk handkerchief and began mopping his brow. Smith saw that his fat, ringed hands were shaking.

"Quite clear," he said dryly. "But you have neglected to tell me who came out and what he did."

"The man—the actor—and right avay I see that iss the vay Hardell vas killed! Listen—" Rosenthal glanced hastily at the door behind Smith, and at the windows. Jumping to his feet he pulled down the blinds, crossed to the door and locked it. Then he drew a chair up close to Smith's, and leaning forward began whispering rapidly into the detective's ear, his eyes darting here and there about the room as though the very walls had ears against which he must disguise his words.

As he talked, Smith's matter-of-fact air dropped from him. He partook of Rosenthal's excitement. When the President of Superior Films finally leaned back and looked at him, the eyes of the two men met in mutual fires of speculation.

"Vell, am I not right?" demanded Rosenthal breathlessly.

"Wild and far-fetched as your theory is, I believe—by Jove, I believe you are!" exclaimed Smith. "But . . . I wonder if the man ever did anything of that sort? Professionally, you know? He'd have to be pretty darn clever."

"You vait! Ve find out!" He picked up a portfolio from his desk. "Vile I vas vaiting for you I got this out of the Publicity Department files. Ve alvays take biographies off our people. Ve use them in writing stories for fan magazines and newspapers, you understand? That iss, off our people under contract. I haff not yet read this, but— Ah, look here!" He ran a pudgy finger down a column marked, "Former Occupations," and then handed the book to Smith, who read aloud.

"Toured Russia, France, America and England, 1907-1912, in Vaudeville. Played also before the crowned heads of Europe. Started Motion Pictures in America in 1914." Smith then continued reading silently until the end of the biography, when suddenly he leaned forward. His quick movement showed plainly that something had struck a vibrant note in his brain. He had come to a page under the heading "Hobbies". He read aloud again:

"Not interested in usual games. Does not make collections. Hobby, if any, an interest in the occult. Thought to have belonged, while in Europe, to leading organizations of this kind, such as scientific research societies, etc., spending many hours in investigations into matters occult and metaphysical.

It is rumored has a rare library, containing ancient and valuable manuscripts on these subjects."

Smith raised his eyes to find Rosenthal's fixed expectantly upon him.

"I haff heard that Black Magic is still practiced—"

Smith put up a deprecating hand. "No, not that, but—" he let out a breath of triumph. "We've got him, Rosie, old fellow! We've got him! That is, he's hooked, but the thing now is to land our fish!"

"I haff thought of that, also," said Rosenthal quietly.

"You have? Shoot!"

"Sure. All the vay out here my mind goes jumping about, trying to find a vay. Then I get it. From a picture ve made last year I get it! In the picture vone of the vitnesses in a murder case turns out to be . . . vell, to be all off on his testimony. How do they prove it? They stage it offer, and show how that vitness has bad ears, and hears wrong. Vell, ve do the same thing. Ve stage it offer again!"

"Huh?" Smith's eyes were fixed quizzically on the other. Never before in the detective's experience had he dealt with a person who had the power to wave a magic wand and duplicate, regardless of the talent or money involved, a complete episode of life. Rosenthal became impatient.

"Sure, sure!" he repeated testily. "Ve do it offer. The whole thing! Vid the same 'props', the same people—efferything!"

"The same people?" questioned Smith stupidly.

"Sure, sure! Mine Gott, Smith, don't I tell you many times ve do anything in pictures?" Rosenthal's mind was already leaping ahead, planning the scene, timing the action, and he did not like being held up to explain. He was accustomed to working with minds that instantly grasped ideas, that knew no limitations to their imagination, that never conceded the impossible in pictures. But here was a man who put up a fence of buts and ifs! He shook his head impatiently and forced himself to tell the detective how, and why, any happening under the sun could be duplicated by the artists of Superior Films.

"You are vondering how ve can bring Hardell back to life, maybe, for vat we vant? How ve can cast the other vone? Easy! I got a make-up man that can make a fence post look like George Vashington! Sure! You don't belieff me? Vait, I show you!" He hurriedly pulled a sheaf of photographs from a cabinet drawer and jammed them into Smith's hands. "Look! Effery vone of those pictures vas the same man! Effery vone!" he exclaimed.

"Impossible," said Smith. It was not an exclamation. It was a statement of fact.

"Ven vill you realize that nothing iss impossible in pictures?" Rosenthal shouted. "I tell you, the man vat posed for all five off those pictures—for Lincoln, Vashington, The Kaiser, The Christ, and that East Indian hunchback— iss right here in my studio. One thousand dollars a veek I pay him, vether he vorks or not. Now do you say I don't know vat I am talking about?" His eyes blazed at Smith.

"Well, I'm not used to such wonders, Rosenthal. Give me time. My only worry is that if we start this thing, you know, we can't afford to have a slip up. I want to be darn sure it's not going to be a flivver. I'd be the laughing stock of the city."

"The fellow vat laughs last, laughs best," said Rosenthal dryly. "But I see I got to convince you. I get Cedric

Hallands himself to come out here to-night—now." He plumped exasperatedly down in his chair and called a number. After a long wait he thrust his fat lips close to the phone.

"Cedric? That you? Rosenthal. I am at my office at the studio. I vant you should come out immediately. Sure, I know you got to dress. Vat? Vell, call a taxi and charge it to me."

He turned to Smith. "His car iss in the shop, but he comes right avay by taxi."

Smith said, "The sooner we do this, the better. But we'll have to do it on a foggy night. The same kind of night. Did you think of that? I suppose you will tell me you can make a foggy night?"

"If it vas for a picture only, ve could make it, sure!" snapped Rosenthal. "But for this, no. Ve got to vait and get a real vone."

"Another thing. That car cost a mint! We'll have to borrow it. There isn't another like it, specially made and all that."

Rosenthal grunted. "And maybe that car iss in Newport Beach, or Palm Springs ven comes a foggy night! No. Ve make vone. Ve copy it!" He saw Smith's dubious look. "Sure. In a closed set ve do it. Nobody knows vat ve do. I got some men who haff been vid me a long time. I talk to them. They keep their mouths shut."

"This is going to cost a pretty penny."

"Money? Say, money means nothing ven my whole business iss at stake! Vat iss a few thousands? I vant to get that murderer off my lot qvick!"

There was a knock at the door and Rosenthal got up to let in a slender, fair, young man. He stood hesitating in the doorway until the President said:

"Cedric, I vant you should meet Mr. Smith, Captain off Detectives."

"Glad to know you, sir," but there was a curious tone in the newcomer's voice.

"I know how you feel!" Smith said. "That sounds as though we got you out here to put handcuffs on you. But, to be frank, it's somebody else we're planning the handcuffs for, and we think you can help."

"Think!" snorted Rosenthal. "Cedric, I vant you to convince him you are the smartest make-up artist in the business—Lon Chaney or anybody else."

Hallands put up a slender hand. "You're too generous, Rosenthal."

"Vill you tell the truth! I spend an hour trying to make Mr. Smith understand ve can copy anything, and then you come out here and—" the President groaned.

"What do you want me to do?" Hallands asked.

"Of course you know about the Hardell case?" said Smith tersely.

"As much as any of us outsiders, yes."

"We want to duplicate a certain scene that took place the night he was murdered. To do it, we have to have a man made up as—" Smith held out the book of biographies, opened at the place where he had read. As Hallands took the book, the detective's eyes fixed hopefully upon him. Rosenthal lay back in his chair and blew contented smoke wreaths.

"It is the ordinary man, without outstanding characteristics, who is the most difficult to portray. Instead of being doubtful, Mr. Smith, I can say that I am sure, absolutely sure, that I can do this. Distinct types are very easy."

"But you are not in the least alike. Your figures, the shape of your heads," said Smith, his eye going rapidly over the other man.

Hallands smiled. "I don't often show the secrets of my make-up case, but I think I can soon convince you."

"All kinds of heads he makes on himself. Vigs vid humps in them he has got!" Rosenthal broke in decisively. "Noses like a pig's snout he can make, if he vants to! I giff you my vord!"

"Hallands, if you can actually do this and do it convincingly—well, I take off my hat to you! That's all I can say," said Smith seriously, looking into the other's eyes.

"Mr. Smith, if my part of it is all that is worrying you, forget it! I've made my living for years doing things like this. It's second nature to me."

"Fine!" Smith rose to shake hands with the man. "Unless Rosenthal wants to keep you longer, I will say good night." He pulled out his watch. "It's late. Perhaps we'd all better turn in, and meet sometime to-morrow."

"I vant to talk some more to you," said Rosenthal to Smith. "But Cedric, you can go. And remember, if vone vord of this leaks out, ve are ruined!"

"I understand," returned the other, and started to the door. Rosenthal sat looking after him with a speculative look in his eye. When Halland's steps were beginning to dim down the corridor, he jumped to his feet.

"Excuse me, but I got to tell him something about—" and he was gone. Smith chewed the end of his cigar thoughtfully until he came back. Then he said:

"We've all been up in the air—talking in the abstract. I want to get down to brass tacks. How long will it take you to make the 'props', as you call them? Can you keep it from the people in the studio here, and just how much of this affair are we going to try to do over?"

"Right now ve write a little scenario, make a list off all the 'props' and the action. That iss the easiest vay," returned Rosenthal, all business. He pulled a sheet of paper to him. "All right. Ve begin. Just like a picture ve do it!"

Then for over an hour the two men sat with chairs close together, listing items, calling upon their memories to go over the scene they wanted, action by action, covering every detail.

At last Smith said, drawing a long breath:

"By Jove, this is great! Great! We can do it!" Enthused out of his customary indolence of body, he began pacing the floor and calling off items and ideas to Rosenthal, who, hunched over his desk, scribbled them furiously. In the midst of this a sharp knock came on the door. Both men looked with quick apprehension at each other. Then with a shrug, and a muttered "Vell, no use to keep still. You vas talking pretty loud," Rosenthal went to the door.

The unmistakable, immaculately dressed figure of Superior Films' most celebrated director stood bowing in the opening. Even at this hour the white gardenia in his buttonhole was without wilt, his white gloves without stain. Smith had an instant of admiration for the man's fastidiousness, before he returned the greeting. Plainly Rosenthal was annoyed.

"Vell?" he asked sharply.

The visitor adjusted his monocle, and stared at them curiously, insolently.

"I thought I was the only one working to-night, but— ah, I find myself intruding?" With another of his quick, stiff bows, he turned on his heel and marched off. Smith looked at Rosenthal, and a soft whistle came from his astonished lips.

"What the devil did he mean by that? And say, d'you suppose he heard us? I'd hate to have anyone get an earful of this right now."

Rosenthal's brown eyes were bent on him with a peculiar, complacent stare. For a moment Smith had a wild idea, a crazy, nightmarish thought, that the President of Superior Films and this erratic, mysterious director were in league together. A quick apprehension that he had been made the butt of some trick, the goat of some carefully schemed plan of the two, swept over him, arousing his instant fury.

As a thousand thoughts can succeed themselves in the human brain in the space of a breath, he remembered Clancy's explanation of the Hardell mystery. Was this, then, another hoax? Another insane, muddled attempt to keep the hand of the law from the real criminal, the real cause of the actor's death? Fire flashed in his eyes and he strode, light and quick as a woods cat, to the desk of the man who had not once modified his almost smiling scrutiny.

"What the devil are you up to?" he demanded, and his customarily indolent syllables slid off his tongue as a razor-edged knife slips through flesh.

Rosenthal imperturbably met the angry outburst. "Efferything I told you ve could do in pictures, and you vould not belieff me. Vell, I show you," he said calmly. "You thought you vas looking at Seibert. Vell, you vere not!"

"Great Jumping Jehosophat!" exclaimed Smith. Excitement, reverence, admiration, exultation, all pulsed in the low amaze of his voice.

18

Night! Outwardly the huge confines of the Superior Films lot seemed deserted. Brooding shadows of dead sets, of huge, silent stages, lay athwart the mist-drenched lawns. These were to be seen only when a late moon, rising over the distant ramparts of San Jacinto, cast its sullen, pale light which was soon swept into obscurity by rolling blankets of fog, billowing inland from the sea. The studio buildings became Gargantuan monsters, clothed in flowing shrouds of grey. The great lights about them dimmed, illumined, and dimmed again. The shrubbery about the grounds became weird, dwarf creatures, shaking gaunt limbs menacingly.

The President of Superior Films peered out from his curtains, then looked at his watch.

"It is here!" he whispered. His hands trembled. "But ten o'clock only! Ve must vait."

Smith looked up from his chair and his cigar.

"Right," he nodded. "Is everything all set?"

"All set. For five nights we haff been ready, vaiting only for this fog."

Rosenthal's hand left the curtain. It moved silently the little distance back to its place, and as silently the two men took up their watch, only the burning ends of their cigars revealing their presence through the darkness of the room.

Nearer midnight the cars out on the boulevard began whisking by, their wheels making a wet, singing hum, their reckless drivers missing death by a skid.

Lannigan, his superstitious soul aquiver, his big coat collar pulled around his ears, clumped out of the murk into the lightened space about the gatehouse. He had no liking for the new gateman, but any other human soul was a comfort on a night like this.

"Hello, Lannigan," said the man at the gate. The little Irishman crossed himself hurriedly. Surprise, not unmixed with terror, froze his tongue.

"Is that the welcome you give me, man?" said MacDougal, a bit sharply.

"God save us! 'Tis yerself, then?"

"No other. Did you think I was a ghost?"

"Naw, I knew ye the minit I set eyes on that big ugly mug of yours!" lied Lannigan, with instant resentment. "Some day, Scot MacDougal, ye'll find out old Lannigan knows a ghost whin it's a ghost, and a man whin it's a man! And the same would have gone a long ways towards saving a life, had ye had the good sense to know it. Now phat do you think o' that?"

MacDougal did not answer. His grim face, and the bleak blue eyes, did not wince.

"Phat the divil are the loikes of ye doin' on the lot this night, anyways, MacDougal? I've a mind to quit me job. I've no agreement wid the Jew to consort wid murderers— self-confessed at that!"

"Ye'll not quit your job, Lannigan."

"And I won't, won't I? And who's to stop me, I ask you? Maybe a few more words from me, and they'll wake up to the nade of a man at the gate that can take a warning and go after a marauder whin one's pointed out to him."

"Are you seeing things in the fog again, Lannigan?"

"Seein' things? And why shouldn't I be seein' things? I remember a night the loikes of this wan, whin if I hadn't listened to the advice of a cold-blooded mackerel like yerself that was born in a fog bank, there'd be a man—now lyin' under the sod— that would be drinking his tea like the rist of us!"

"Aye. I ken what you're driving at, you little scut!" said the Scotchman with a show of temper. "But ye'll get nothing out of me by it! Get out of my office!"

"Sure, an' I'll be gettin' out immedjit! If the life you've been leadin' since you confessed yerself into jail ain't taught you nothin', you are beyont learnin' from yer betters!"

"Be gone the noo!" said MacDougal sharply, dropping into his native dialect. His bleak eyes took fire and blazed down upon the other, and his hand closed on a paper weight.

"I'm goin', you big lummox! If I had me shalailie I could lick ye on a thin dime! Ye—ye demned hot-headed dumbhead!" He started to clump away into the murk. "Bad cess to ye! I hope a gob o' fog chokes ye! Cagin' up some kinds o' animals drives 'em plumb fey!" he sputtered.

And now there were two places on the lot that night to which Lannigan could not bring himself to visit again! Stage Six, from out of which he expected momentarily to see the ghost of Dwight Hardell stalking, and the front gate, where, without explanation, Scot MacDougal had again taken up his post. The night wore on, and the approaching midnight hour, the time when ghosts walk, began to weigh heavily upon him. Need of human companionship drove him back towards the gate, muttering strange Gaelic words to himself.

"Phat wid the curtains on thim dead sets back there a-floppin', and them old scantlin's a-creakin' and a-groanin', and this demned cold fog a-slitherin' down yer spine, 'tis a grand night for a murther."

MacDougal heard him muttering, and called out to him:

"Your boy brought your lunch. Slim's closed up. His wife's sick. Better come up and get it, man.

"'Tis the first night Slim's been closed since I came to the lot," retorted Lannigan suspiciously. "I'll not come near ye, Scot MacDougal! I've a mind what happened the last foggy night, and I'm not ready to go to Hivin!"

"Come and get your lunch, you old fool!" returned the gateman crisply, and the commanding snap in his voice brought Lannigan edging up to him. MacDougal held out the lunch.

"Maybe ye'll act more like a human being with red blood in ye when you get it down ye!" he said.

Lannigan shot him a baleful look, and taking the lunch sat down by the other side of the gate to eat. MacDougal filled his pipe and kept his distance, so that presently the little Irishman's fears abated.

"Will ye have a swallow of good hot coffee, Mac?" he asked.

"I appreciate the peace offering. Thanks. No," returned MacDougal.

"'Tis not a peace offering, ye spalpeen, 'tis the thought of ye not havin' a stomachful the past weeks, was all." He gulped down the remaining hot coffee. "Mac, d'ye remimber that ither night—" he stopped, the thermos bottle gripped in a hand that suddenly shook. "Did ye hear it Mac? And you said awhilst back there was nobody on the lot!" he hissed.

"Not a soul has come through the gate this night!" said MacDougal, peering into the mist. Plain, to both of them, came the purring of a motor from down the murk of the drive—coming their way. Lannigan dropped the thermos and crossed himself, not once, but many times in quick succession.

MacDougal gave a short laugh. "You've got us both acting like a couple of old women! Somebody's worked overtime, and is going home. It's happened before. Stand aside, and don't let them see you crossing yourself like a doddering idiot!" He went briskly to the gates and swung them open for the approaching car.

A purple car, of whose special design and build there was but one known to be in existence, slipped up to the entrance, slowed, and rolled slowly through.

"Good night, men!" called the driver.

"It's a great life if you don't weaken, eh, fellows?" called a bantering voice, and a hand was waved to them as the car turned to the boulevard. The mist swallowed it.

"Holy Mother of God protect us! Holy Mary, Mother of God, have mercy on our souls. Holy Mary, Mother of God!" It was Lannigan, quaking like an aspen against the iron gates, alternately crossing himself and clasping his hands. "Mac, did ye see it? Holy Mary, Mother of God! Good Saint Patrick! He spoke to us, Mac. Did ye hear him? God save us all! And he's dead, Mac. Holy Saint Patrick and all the Saints be wid us this night! 'Twas his ghost—the ghost of Dwight Hardell! Holy Mary, look down on us miserable sinners."

But MacDougal was not listening. Striding like one sleep-walking, he pushed past Lannigan and entered his little office. Amazement had numbed his brain. Habit took hold of his motor centers, and caused him to bend over his time book and make an entry.

"Franz Seibert and Dwight Hardell out at 12:17 a.m." was what he wrote there.

"Holy Mother! What are ye doin' now?" came the whimpering voice of Lannigan. Like a small boy he had pushed after MacDougal, crowding close against him, grateful for the touch of his big body. MacDougal dropped the stub of his pencil and turned a strange face to the Irishman.

"Yon's dead," he said, pointing to the last entry, "dead this long time."

Blue eyes stared into beady black ones.

"But you saw them drive out?" he finished.

Lannigan nodded violently.

"You heard him talk?"

And again Lannigan nodded. "That I did!" He stood a moment staring into the distance. Then he grabbed at his time clock, tearing it off him.

"I'm through! 'Tis bad enough whin a man's murdered and ye have to go walkin' past the spot ivery night, but whin his ghost comes ridin' after ye—ridin' right under yer nose and calls out to ye—I'm through! Not another minnit do I stay in this haunted place. Not another minnit! Phat wid banshees and ghosts, and thim talkin', 'tis more than I can put up wid."

But the big Scotchman caught him as he was sneaking past.

"No you don't, Lannigan! You're going to stay right here until we get this thing settled!" He shook the night watchman savagely. "Why did you come here and tell me there wasn't anybody on the lot the nicht?"

"Let go, ye black murtherin' divil! And don't ye put words in me mouth, ayther! 'Twas yerself as said there was nobody on the lot this night, bad cess to ye!

"Stop evading me! I said nobody came through the gate this night! What were you doing when you were supposed to be making the rounds, that you didn't know what was going on back there? Answer me that."

"And evadin' is it? Let go me arrum and ye'll not think I'm evadin' ye, fer I'll bust ye one on the phyz that'll take ye the rist of yer life in the pinnitintiary to ferget, ye bog trotter!"

MacDougal dropped the squirming Lannigan and fixed him, instead, with his eye.

"Don't lie to me! Why didn't you tell me somebody was on the back lot?" he roared.

"I'm not lyin' to ye! Anyway, how the hell could he be on the back lot, or anywheres else but his grave, will ye tell me that? He's dead, ye great dumbhead!"

"That's right. He's dead," said the Scotchman slowly. "There's something back of this." He picked up the Irishman bodily and set him in the gatehouse, and then closed and locked the door on him. From there he went to the phone booth.

"Get me Mr. Rosenthal's house, Rosenthal of Superior Films," he said. And then memory came to him and he gave the house number.

But Rosenthal was not at home. At the very moment he was filling a pair of glasses from a choice bottle, whose habitual resting place was a wall cabinet back of the large photograph of the smiling face of Yvonne Beaumont.

"Here's to Hallands, the dummy, and the ventriloquist!" he said, raising his glass.

"Here's to Abraham Rosenthal, President of Superior Films, and a second Sherlock Holmes," smiled Smith.

It was a compliment the President never forgot.

19

Rosenthal and Smith were both at the studio early next morning, neither one having slept, but having feverishly waited the dawn and the final act of the drama they had precipitated. When the detective walked into the President's private office, he had a round tin box under his arm. Rosenthal's eyes watched his movements curiously as he laid the box down on the desk, then they raised to Smith's face.

"Tell you later," Smith said, and Rosenthal had to be content with that. Then the detective added, "Have you got all that other stuff ready?"

"Ach, yes!" exclaimed Rosenthal with anxious eagerness. "It iss in the vault, safe under lock and key."

Smith nodded. "Can't take any chances. A slip now, and all would be lost! Now, how soon can I get this . . ." he tapped the tin box with the tips of his long fingers, "developed and a print made?"

"Two—three hours. Vat iss it?"

"Rosey, I wouldn't tell my own grandmother what I firmly believe this to be! I'm not going to trust your 'lab' people, either! This is a job for the superintendent himself—behind locked doors! And I'm going to stay right with him, my pistol cocked for trouble! You phone him

I'm coming over to put this in the soup. I don't want to have to get rough with him if he tries to high-hat me."

"Sure. Sure. I phone him. But really I vould like very much to know vat iss in there! I am all goose pimples vid curiosity already!"

"You just 'goose-pimple' all you want and rest your curiosity. Sorry, but I haven't time to explain. Here's a list of names. I want all these people in your private projection room at four this afternoon. Tell the gateman and office boy to let in Clancy and Ryan with their part—no questions asked. See that the operator who runs the stuff this afternoon keeps his mouth shut. Tell him if I hear a sound out of him, or if he lets anyone in the projection room, I'll half kill him. Then you take Ryan with you when you get that stuff out of the vault, and you get it *yourself*, see? Got all that?"

"Sure, sure," commenced the President amiably, then, realizing Smith was in the way of giving him orders in his own office, he drew himself up stiffly and amended, "Certainly," in his coolest executive tone. Smith leaned down and patted the fat shoulder affectionately.

"No time for ceremony. No offense meant. I'm on my way to the 'lab'. Better phone your man." And he was gone, the tin box clamped firmly against his side under his left arm, his right hand in his pocket. Rosenthal glared after him, lips outthrust.

Then with a shrug and a weary sigh, he pulled the telephone towards him.

"Ach Gott! Vill ve effer get rid of this dirty business, and start making pictures again?" he asked of the galaxy of pictured faces about him. They smiled their famous smiles at him reassuringly, but he was not so easily rid of his resentment against the detective.

"I vould not be so close-mouthed, even vid my Rachel!" he muttered into the receiver. The switch-board girl had to ask him three times for the department he wanted.

In the dim, half-light of Rosenthal's private projection room was gathered the little group made up of those persons having had a part in the Hardell murder case. They did not know why they were there. Minds were nervously speculating, while bodies attempted vainly to compose themselves. Sighs, escaped pent breaths, jerking muscles, the scraping of feet and creaking of chairs, all spoke their unrest. And there was the mental chaos from fear-tensed brains that sent unseen vibrations clashing through the atmosphere.

West, haggard-eyed, his dark hair swept distraughtly across his brow. Yvonne, pale and atremble. But it was not the old joyous, tiptoe verve, in the agitated movements of her slender body. West and Yvonne avoided each other, save when they turned to lock their eyes in an occasional long and questioning agony. MacDougal, grim and silent, and Lannigan darting his bright, beady little eyes furtively upon him. Serge, wrapped in that remoteness which makes Americans hunt for descriptive words, and finally say briefly, "foreign." Beth MacDougal, a pitiful huddled little figure, all the impudent dash of her comedy days gone and an air of apology in her manner.

Apart from the rest, immaculate, sitting in unshakable dignity, was Seibert. He toyed with his monocle, his eyes fixed upon some mind-picture of his own. Apparently he was oblivious to the situation and its significance. He was not enough aware of it, apparently, to be bored!

Clancy slipped into a seat directly behind Beth Mac-Dougal, and Ryan seated himself beside Billy West. Two plain clothes men posted themselves by the door and stepped aside with a brief gesture of respect when Rosenthal and Smith entered.

Rosenthal, not looking to right or left, went directly to the front row, and Captain Smith faced the others in the room from a position beside him. For a few seconds there was silence as he let his gaze encompass them. Then he said:

"I have asked you here, because each one of you has, in some manner, been brought into the murder investigation of Dwight Hardell. Three of you confessed to killing him. I am going to show you now, in the medium familiar to you all—motion pictures—just how he was killed, according to the evidence now in my hands. Mr. Rosenthal and I have endeavored to duplicate, in pictures, what I believe happened the night of Hardell's death. I think the title will be self-explanatory." He stopped to allow for smothered exclamations; for his hearers to accustom themselves to this surprise so that they might get sensibly the full import of his words. Then he continued with slow emphasis:

"Our little scenario begins on the set of Stage Six, where Hardell was found dead. As you all know, Mr. Seibert and Hardell made a final rehearsal there that night. We are starting with that rehearsal. The role of Seibert is played by Hallands, whose wizardry at make-up you all know. Hardell is played by a 'heavy' made up by Mr. Hallands to impersonate the murdered man. I want you all to remain absolutely quiet, no matter what happens. Understand? *You are going to see exactly what happened that night! How Dwight Hardell was murdered!*"

"You mean, Mr. Smith, how you believe he was murdered. Am I not correct?" It was Serge, leaning indolently back in his tilted chair.

Smith ignored him. Raising his voice to the operator, who was peering curiously from his cubbyhole in the rear, he called:

"All set?"

"Yes, sir!"

"Let's go!"

A sizzling hiss, and then the white beam of light illuming the screen; the flickering of the leader and then the title.

MR. SEIBERT REHEARSING HARDELL
FOR THE LAST CLOSE-UP THE NIGHT
THE ACTOR WAS MURDERED

On the screen, following this, came the now familiar set. In this, the actor's last drama, he lay prone in the position of the close-up in which he was to "put over" his last death agony in the story. Above him, leaning close, one hand gripping a dueling rapier, stood Seibert, portrayed by Hallands. Anger and exasperation were expressed in every angle of his body. The watchers did not need the title:

AFTER HOURS OF DRILLING THE DI-
RECTOR STILL FAILS TO GET WHAT HE
WANTS

And now the director cast down his rapier furiously and strode up and down, turning now and again to cast some withering remark at the actor, who stood in sullen immobility. Finally the former turns back, throws himself on the floor in the position desired, himself goes through the tortured writhings of the death scene . . . .

A dry chuckle made tensed nerves jump. It was Serge again.

"Not so bad, Seibert! He has made of himself what Americans call a 'dead ringer' for you!"

"Quiet!" snapped Smith instantly. The film went on. Now a short view of the camera that was supposedly to have photographed the close-up, as well as the two players.

The director, rising from the floor, speaks to the actor, and once more the latter assumes the prostrate position. The director now steps to the camera and carefully removes the magazine, replacing it with another. With white-gloved fingers he slowly threads the film through the sprocket mechanism. Then he turns and speaks to the actor, who nods understandingly. The supposedly dying man assumes an agonized expression. His extended hand tenses, his eyes roll back. The director watches a moment, then steps back to the camera and starts the motor that automatically grinds the film. Now, rapier in hand, he returns to the prone actor, urging him on to intensify his expression. To assist him in putting over a convincing scene, he even leans over, pressing the rapier against his heart and pressing it slowly and unswervingly into the flesh beneath the satin waistcoat. And still the actor looks up, listening to each word from the director, making an earnest effort to give him what he wants.

Serge let his chair to the floor suddenly. Someone smothered a scream.

"Quiet!" Smith again snapped.

Inexorably, like the wheels of time itself, came the steady clicking from the projection room. Hearts thumped in rhythm; pulses raced. The suspense was strained to the bursting pitch when the scene shifted to a close-up, a close-up of Hardell, with the rapier point over his heart. And then a sudden downward plunge of the steel . . . a flash into the scene of a white-gloved hand.

Smith's voice rose above the tumult in the room. "Keep your seats! You are now seeing Hardell in his actual death throes—Hardell, *played by himself!*"

On the screen the grim tragedy went on. Hardell, suddenly betrayed by one he trusted, with his soul shocked out of his body, was gazing piteously, wildly, out at the little handful of watchers who, incapable now of giving aid, must sit helpless and stunned as they watched the actual portrayal of his death. For a moment there seemed to be pleading in Hardell's eyes, a piteous appeal for help, and this was quickly followed by a look of terrible questioning, and of awful fear. Then came the ghastly jerking upward of his body as the rapier was withdrawn and then the body fell back in convulsive writhing.

"Oh, my God! My God! Stop it! Stop it!" Beth Mac-Dougal sobbed. But the scene went on.

Hardell's features were now stiffening, the shoulders sagging, and his head rolled from side to side. Just as the body made its last movement, mercifully the scene was cut by the title:

AND SO HE DIED

The film stopped. In the darkness that followed before the switching on of the lights, no one saw Seibert's swift movement as he slipped a tiny white pellet from beneath an immaculate white glove and lifted it quickly to his lips. Seibert, the master of dramatic episode, director of action, of entrance and of exit, needed no prompter to tell him that his moment of exit had come. But he grimaced, ruefully, as he swallowed. After all, the last exit is not always easy . . .

"Don't move, Seibert!" Smith barked. "You've been covered ever since you stepped in here. Lights! Lights, operator!"

The lights came on immediately, to show Smith standing, revolver in hand, and the white faces of the others with their eyes fixed upon Seibert. Fear of the man was loose in the room. They shrank from him, the while they stared at him, wide-eyed.

Yvonne's voice rose in a little sobbing scream.

"Billee! Billee!"

West gathered her in his arms. They clung together. The grim MacDougal dropped his face upon his cupped hands and the repressed quiver of his stern frame told its own story. Clancy's arm comforted Beth.

During the space of these happenings Seibert and Smith had held their positions, eyes fixed upon each other. Now Seibert arose, a little unsteady on his feet. The lights shone down into the cold depths of his strange blue eyes, revealing at last the fanatical gleam he no longer had need to mask with a stare of cool insolence. He swept them all with that scintillant gaze and started forward.

"Don't move!" Smith warned.

Seibert laughed, mirthlessly. "You will remember, Mr. Smith, that I once said, 'I yield to the inevitable only!' I am no fool. I know when—when I am cornered." He stopped, and plainly labored for breath. Beads of sweat were gathering on his upper lip and brow. "No, I am not the fool! It is you—" he turned and his eyes played like tongues of fire over the little group, "it is you who are the fools—the imbeciles—the cowards! Here, protected by the law, you are afraid of me! I feel your fear. You think I am—insane. You think me a crazy director—capable of doing anything—to amuse, to entertain more fools like yourselves."

He stopped, gasped, and made futile, wild, upflung motion of his gloved hands.

"And yet—fools that you are—you defeated me! What—what matter the price of success? It is the price—of—failure that is—bitter!"

He fumbled for his cane, attempted to bow, punctilious to the last, and failing, sagged back into his chair and slid to the floor.

Smith knelt beside him and felt of his heart, making sure that it had stopped. From that position, he spoke:

"Mr. Seibert has just committed suicide. In so doing he escaped hanging. His last act was an admission of his guilt. You have just been witnesses of the actual picture of his crime. Yet, if there is doubt in any of your minds, I will answer any questions. Are there any?"

"Gott, yes! That close-up. Vere did you get it? Ve did not shoot that!" Rosenthal exclaimed, speaking what was in all of their minds.

"Seibert shot it. Just before committing the murder he started the motor driven camera. Doubtless he told the weary Hardell that they would try the scene once more and that he would make a test shot of it. I suppose he intended to use the actual death of Hardell in the picture instead of the usual substitution."

"You're wrong there, Smith," said Serge, quietly. "He never shot that for the picture that we would release. I thought there was something behind his kick about the stuff we got that afternoon, for I never shot better stuff in my life—and he knew it. Where did you get that film?"

"I started hunting for it immediately after I got his palm prints from the camera. I was convinced then of what he had done. But you have not answered my question. What did he want that picture for?"

"He was a member of a half dozen occult societies. Crazy, every one of them, just as he was crazy. He wanted that film to send to some of his fellow students in one of those secret societies. They study the occult, the question of life after death, and the question of what takes place when a soul leaves the body. They are all nuts, and they even pledge their lives to what they call 'the cause'. When they fail, they do what he did. Huh! And he called us fools." Serge hesitated and gave a dry chuckle. "Well, he was right about me. I'll wager that film was the one I saw in his desk drawer. I even picked it up once and asked him if he didn't want it developed. Can you feature it!"

"Like many criminals, he thought the obvious place the safest," Smith said. "Are there any other questions?"

"Sure, and there is that," spoke up Lannigan. "Maybe you'll be after tellin' me how I saw Hardell ride past me at the gate *after* he was murdered. 'Twas with me own eyes I saw him, and with me own ears I heard him spake."

Smith smiled. "To quote Mr. Rosenthal," he answered, "in pictures we can do anything. We can make a dummy look like a live man and a live man look like a dummy. Seibert took the dummy, made up to look exactly like Hardell, propped it up in the seat of his car and drove out. But the dummy did not speak. It was Seibert, mimicking Hardell's voice, who spoke to you."

"Holy Mary, Mother of—"

Rosenthal lifted himself ponderously from his chair. "Ve vill shut the studio for the day. I must telephone my Rachel. I must telephone—"

Smith slapped him affectionately on the back.

"Don't get nervous now, Rosey. It's all over and—"

"Offer! It's all offer, iss it? And me half crazy, my Rachel half crazy, and half the vorld blaming me for haffing a murder committed on my lot! Gott of Abraham!" he moaned. "Gott of Abraham! Vat a viper that Seibert vas! Vat a viper I took to my bosom!"

THE EDINGTONS
THE HOUSE OF THE
VANISHING
GOBLETS

THE
SLEEPING CAT

Isabel Ostrander

THE SEVEN BLACK
CHESSMEN
John Huntingdon

DEAD
WEIGHT
ADDISON
SIMMONS

Coachwhip Publications

CoachwhipBooks.com

NOVEMBER JOE

DETECTIVE OF THE WOODS

H. HESKETH-PRICHARD

MURDER
IN A WALLED TOWN
KATHERINE WOODS

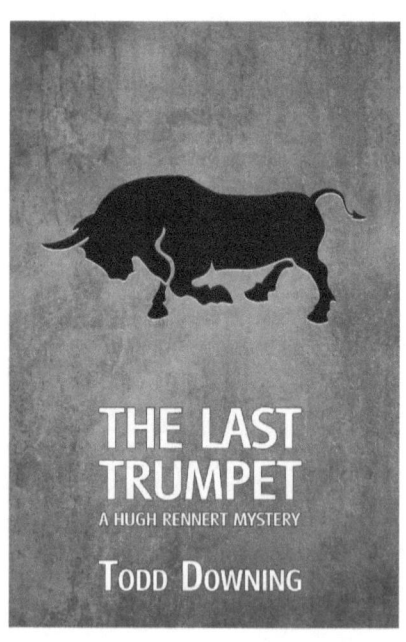

THE LAST TRUMPET
A HUGH RENNERT MYSTERY

TODD DOWNING

DEATH SAILS THE NILE
F. BURKS McKINLEY

Coachwhip Publications
CoachwhipBooks.com

FEAR OF FEAR

FLORENCE RYERSON
COLIN CLEMENTS

MURDER IN THE FAMILY

NICE PEOPLE MURDER

Mary Hastings Bradley

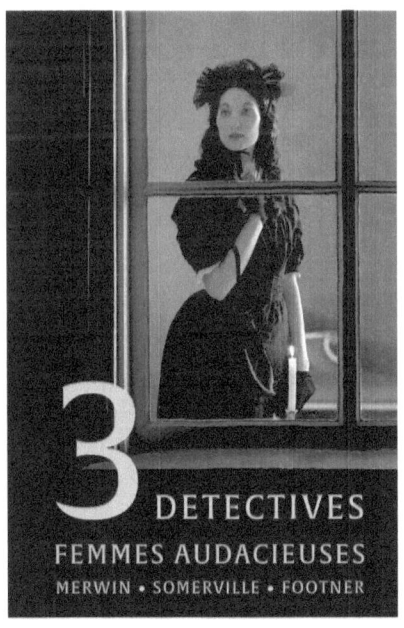

3 DETECTIVES
FEMMES AUDACIEUSES
MERWIN · SOMERVILLE · FOOTNER

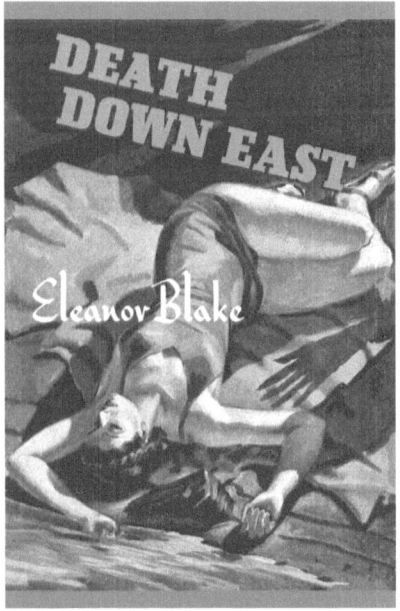

DEATH DOWN EAST

Eleanor Blake

Coachwhip Publications
CoachwhipBooks.com

THE
MYSTERY
OF THE
FOLDED
PAPER

HULBERT
FOOTNER

The
Hollow Tree
Mystery

MADELON ST. DENIS

VIRGINIA RATH

FERRYMAN,
TAKE HIM ACROSS!

No Face to
Murder
EDITH HOWIE

Coachwhip Publications

CoachwhipBooks.com

THE QUINNY HITE
MYSTERIES
CHINESE RED · HERE LIES THE BODY

RICHARD BURKE

I'll Hate Myself in the Morning

Murder on the Left Bank

Elliot Paul

MURDER'S COMING

GRAVE WITHOUT GRASS

BY
DONALD CLOUGH CAMERON

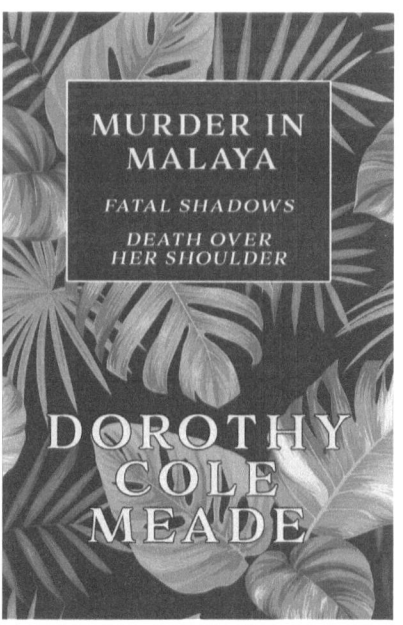

MURDER IN
MALAYA
FATAL SHADOWS
DEATH OVER
HER SHOULDER

DOROTHY
COLE
MEADE

Coachwhip Publications

CoachwhipBooks.com

Coachwhip Publications

CoachwhipBooks.com

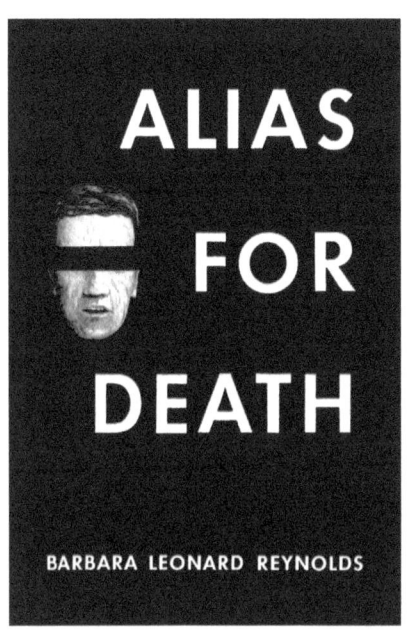

ALIAS FOR DEATH

BARBARA LEONARD REYNOLDS

THERE IS NO RETURN

THE ADELAIDE ADAMS MYSTERIES

ANITA BLACKMON

Jack Dolph

MURDER MAKES THE MARE GO

FEAR CAME FIRST

VERA KELSEY

Coachwhip Publications

CoachwhipBooks.com

MURDER AT DRAKE'S ANCHORAGE

E. LEE WADDELL

MURDER AT THE KENTUCKY DERBY

CHARLES PARMER

MURDER ENDS THE SONG

ALFRED MEYERS

3 DETECTIVES
MURDER ON THE RAILS
WHITECHURCH • THORNE • TORGERSON

Coachwhip Publications

CoachwhipBooks.com

THE FIRES AT FITCH'S FOLLY

KENNETH WHIPPLE

DRESSED TO KILL

Emma Lou Fetta

GRIMM DEATH

THE GROUSE MOOR MURDER

JOHN FERGUSON

Coachwhip Publications
CoachwhipBooks.com